ESTABLISHED
1986

A SOUTHERN ORIGINAL

CANNIBAL

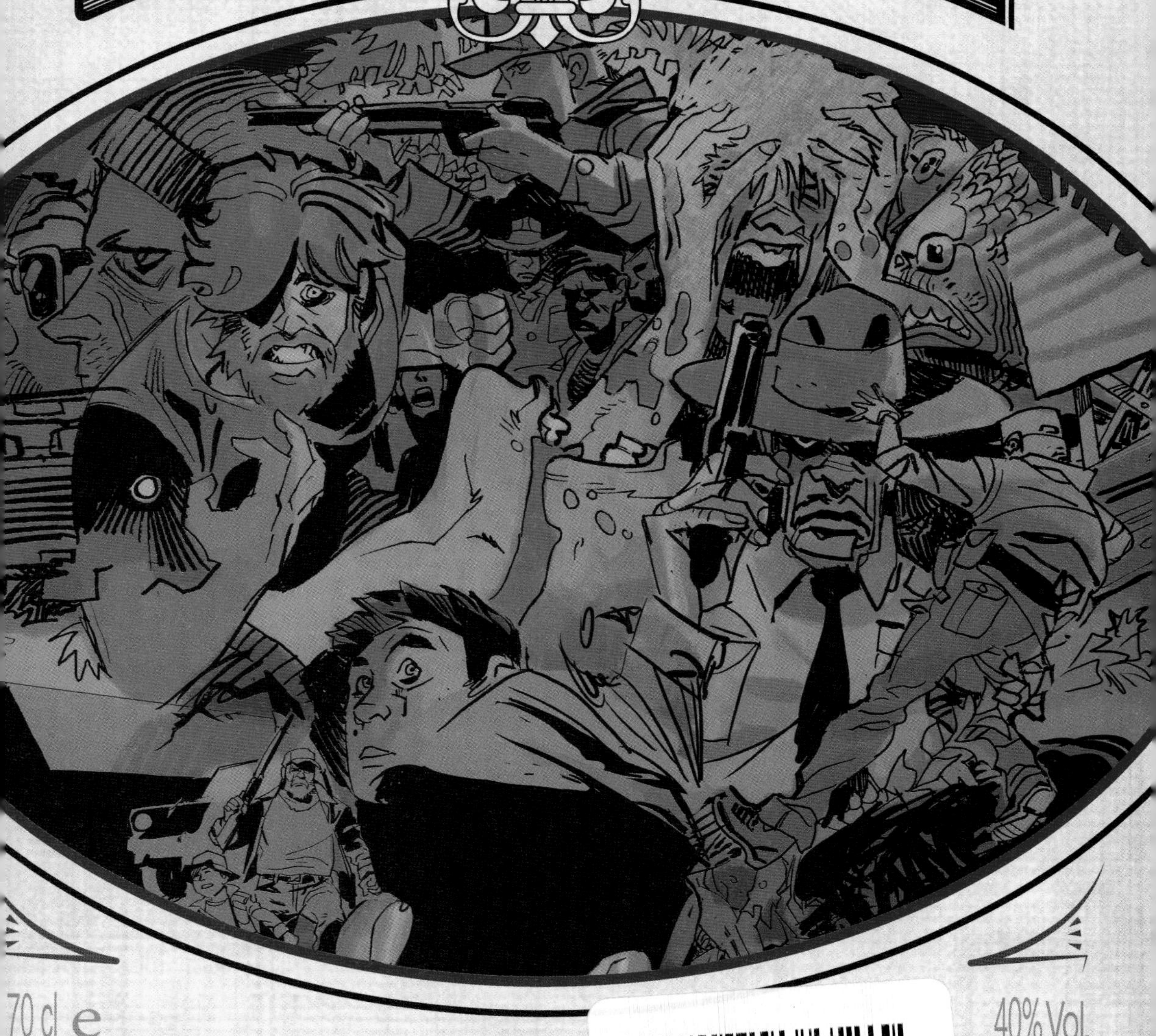

70 cl e

40% Vol.

VOLUME T

GOVERNMENT WARNING:(1) ACCORDING TO THE SURGEON GENERAL, WOMEN SHOULD NOT DRINK ALCOHOLIC BEVERAGES DURING PREGNANCY BECAUSE OF THE RISK OF BIRTH DEFECTS.
(2) CONSUMPTION OF ALCOHOLIC BEVERAGES IMPAIRS YOUR ABILITY TO DRIVE A CAR OR OPERATE MACHINERY, AND MAY CAUSE HEALTH PROBLEMS.

IMAGE COMICS, INC
.
Robert Kirkman — Chief Operating Officer
Erik Larsen — Chief Financial Officer
Todd McFarlane — President
Marc Silvestri — Chief Executive Officer
Jim Valentino — Vice President
Eric Stephenson — Publisher
Corey Murphy — Director of Sales
Jeff Boison — Director of Publishing Planning & Book Trade Sales
Chris Ross — Director of Digital Sales
Jeff Stang — Director of Specialty Sales
Kat Salazar — Director of PR & Marketing
Branwyn Bigglestone — Controller
Kali Dugan — Senior Accounting Manager
Sue Korpela — Accounting & HR Manager
Drew Gill — Art Director
Heather Doornink — Production Director
Leigh Thomas — Print Manager
Tricia Ramos — Traffic Manager
Briah Skelly — Publicist
Aly Hoffman — Conventions & Events Coordinator
Sasha Head — Sales & Marketing Production Designer
David Brothers — Branding Manager
Melissa Gifford — Content Manager
Drew Fitzgerald — Publicity Assistant
Vincent Kukua — Production Artist
Erika Schnatz — Production Artist
Ryan Brewer — Production Artist
Shanna Matuszak — Production Artist
Carey Hall — Production Artist
Esther Kim — Direct Market Sales Representative
Emilio Bautista — Digital Sales Representative
Leanna Caunter — Accounting Analyst
Chloe Ramos-Peterson — Library Market Sales Representative
Marla Eizik — Administrative Assistant

IMAGECOMICS.COM

PRODUCT OF USA
HAND MADE
PROUDLY DISTILLED
IN EVERGLADES, FLA

...NIBAL, VOL. 2. First printing. November 2017. Published by Image Comics, Inc. Office of publication: 2701 NW Vaughn St., Suite 780, Portland, OR 97210.
...pyright © 2017 Brian Buccellato & Jennifer Young. All rights reserved. Contains material originally published in single magazine form as CANNIBAL #5-8.
..."Cannibal," its logos, and the likenesses of all characters herein are trademarks of Brian Buccellato & Jennifer Young, unless otherwise noted. "Image"
...nd the Image Comics logos are registered trademarks of Image Comics, Inc. No part of this publication may be reproduced or transmitted, in any form
...y any means (except for short excerpts for journalistic or review purposes), without the express written permission of John Layman or Image Comics, Inc.
...l names, characters, events, and locales in this publication are entirely fictional. Any resemblance to actual persons (living or dead), events, or places,
...without satiric intent, is coincidental. Printed in the USA. For information regarding the CPSIA on this printed material call: 203-595-3636 and provide
reference #RICH–769876. For international rights, contact: foreignlicensing@imagecomics.com. ISBN: 978-1-5343-0375-1.

ESTABLISHED
1986

A SOUTHERN ORIGINAL

**BRIAN
BUCCELLATO**

&

**JENNIFER
YOUNG**
STORY

**MATIAS
BERGARA**
ART

BRIAN BUCCELLATO
COLORS

TROY PETERI
LETTERS

VOLUME TWO

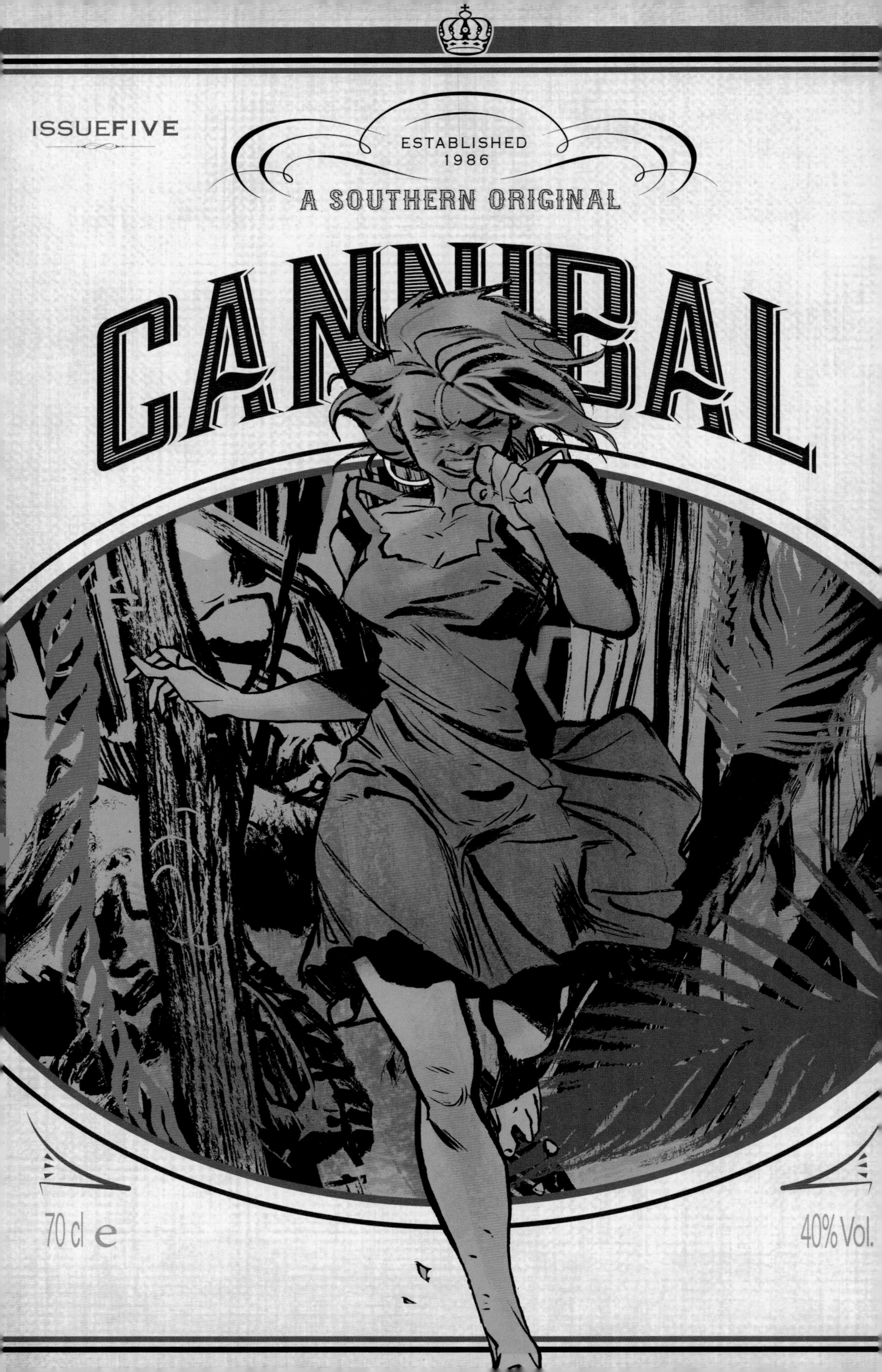
ISSUEFIVE
ESTABLISHED 1986
A SOUTHERN ORIGINAL
CANNIBAL
70 cl e
40% Vol.

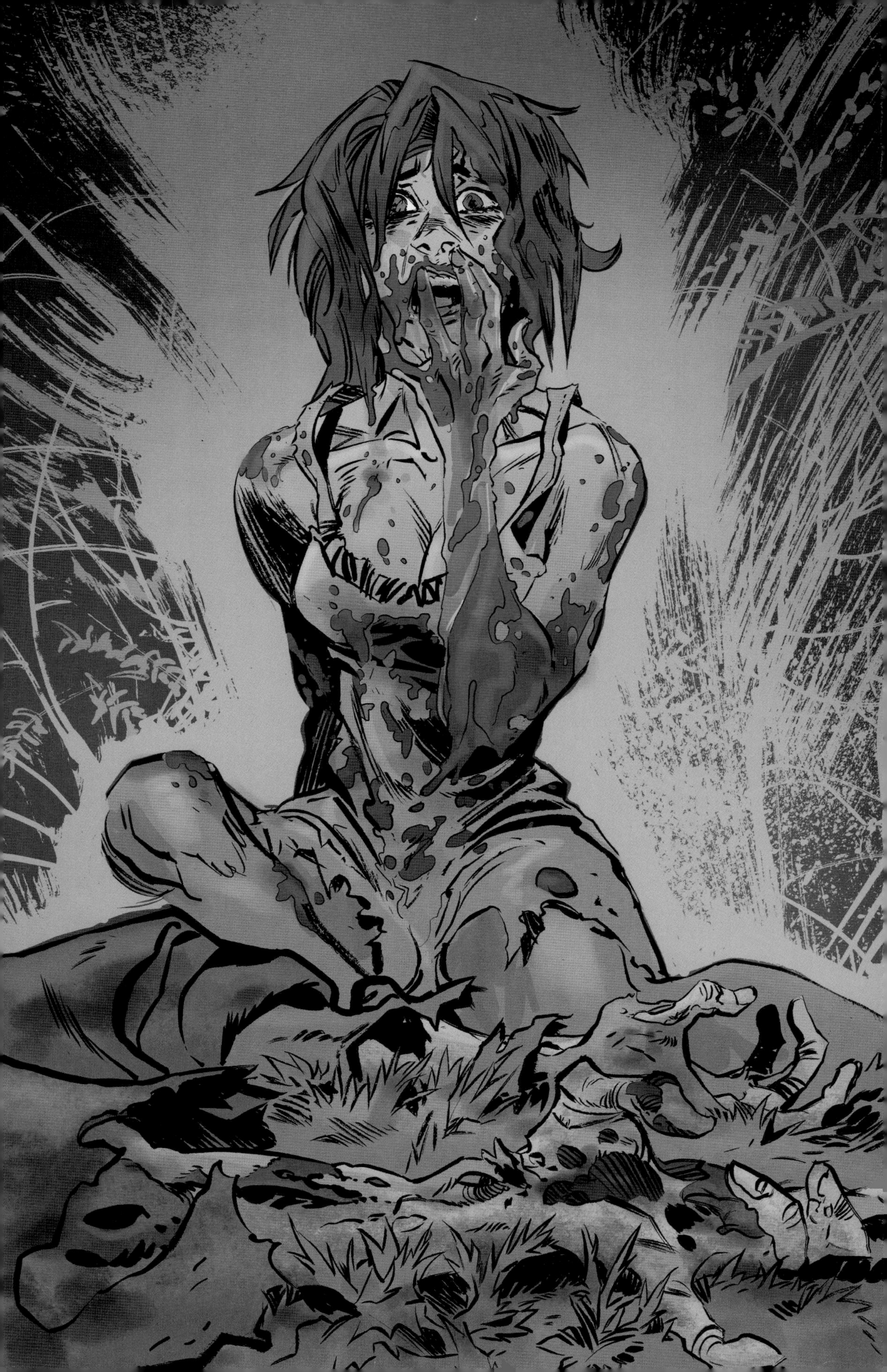

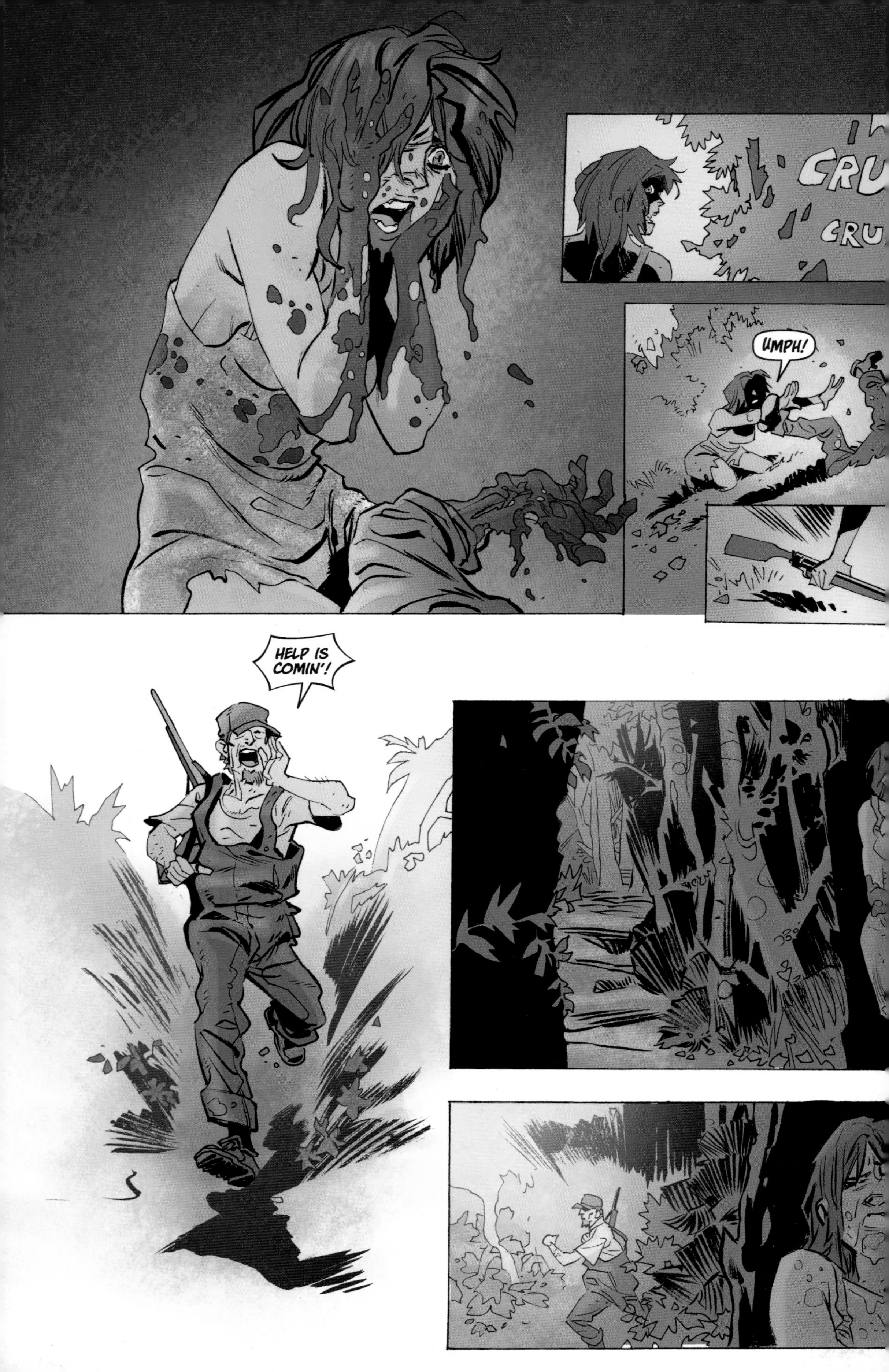
CRU
CRU
UMPH!
HELP IS COMIN'!

POWWW

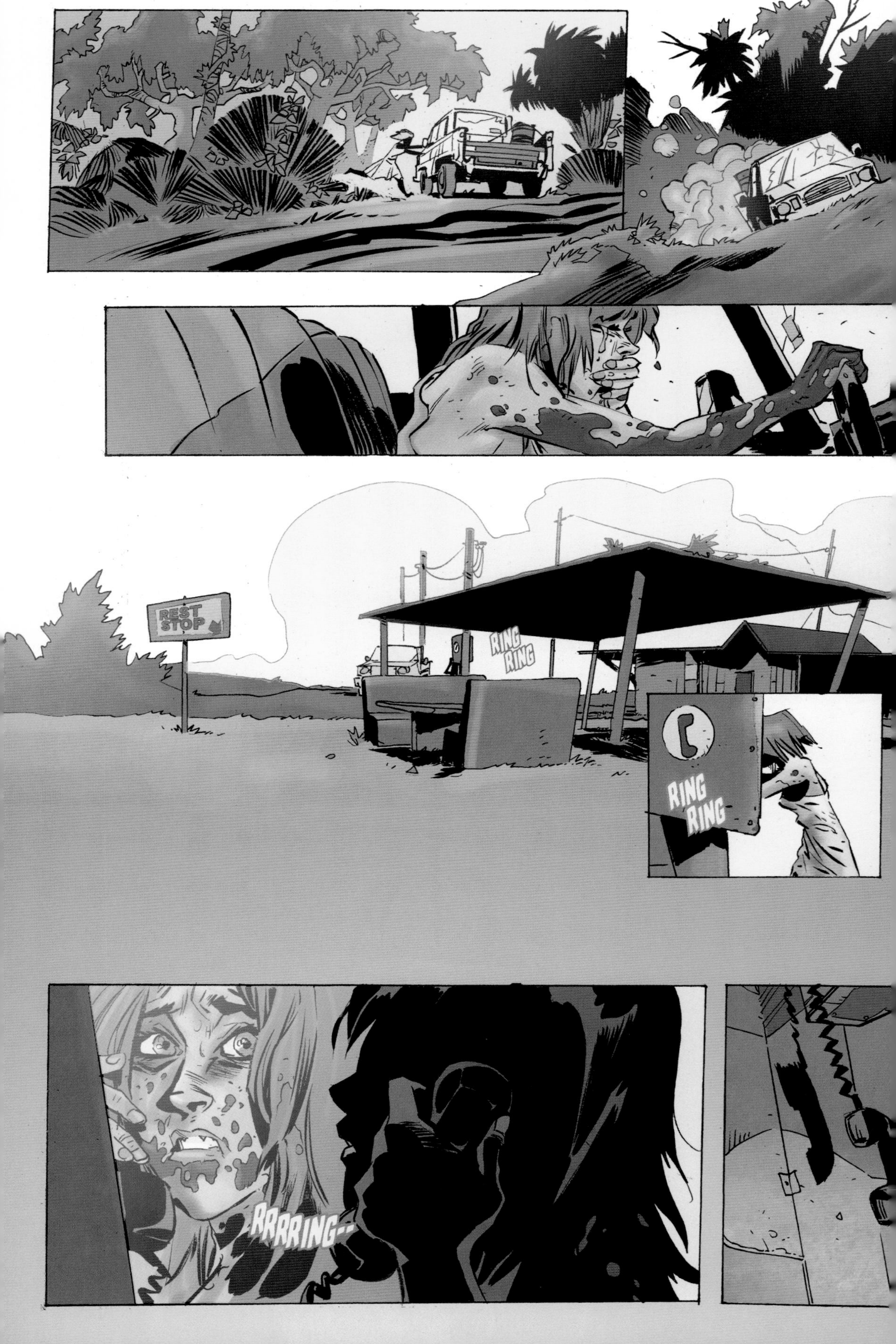
REST STOP
RING RING
RING RING
RRRRING--

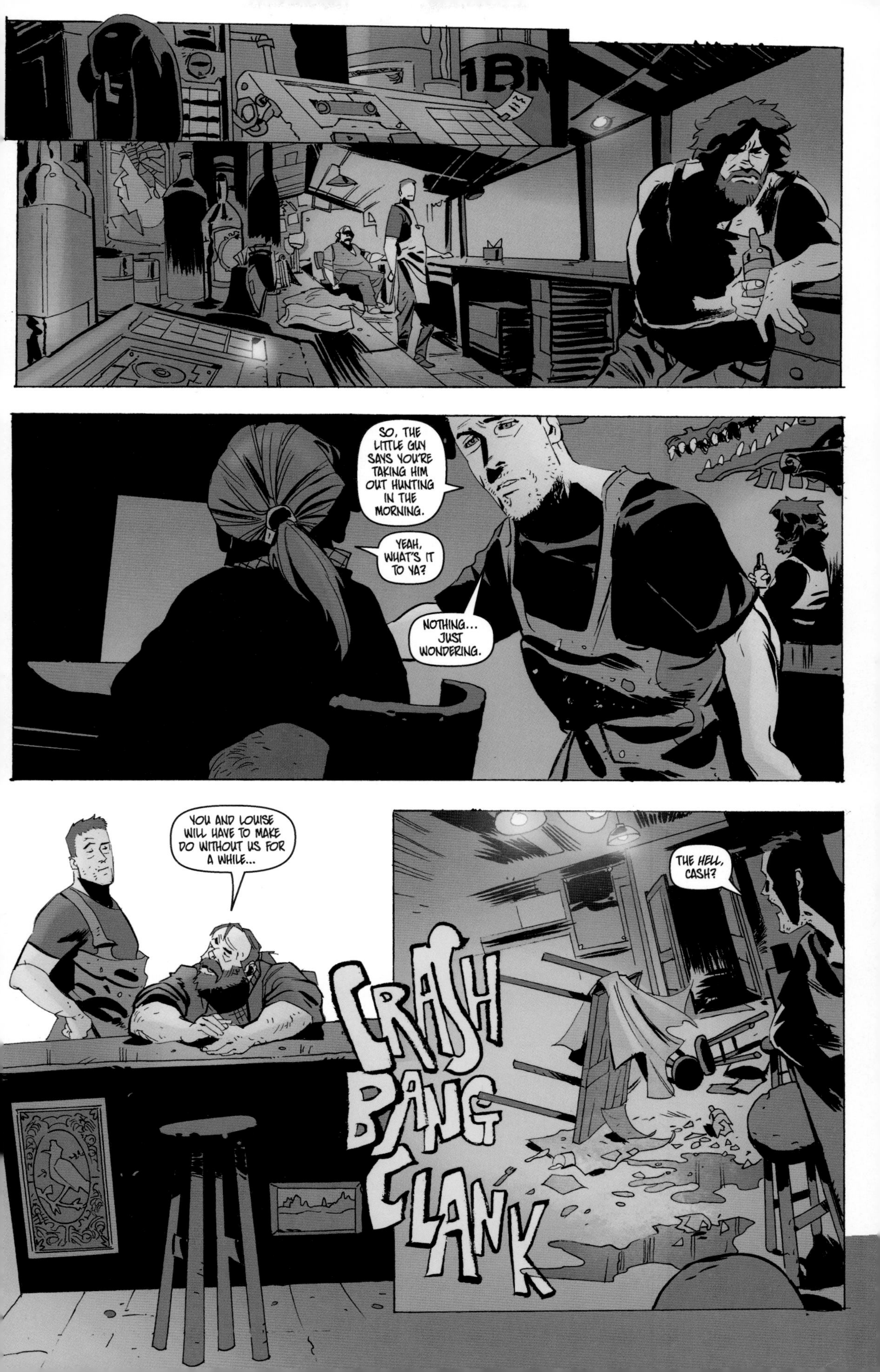

SO, THE LITTLE GUY SAYS YOU'RE TAKING HIM OUT HUNTING IN THE MORNING.
YEAH, WHAT'S IT TO YA?
NOTHING... JUST WONDERING.
YOU AND LOUISE WILL HAVE TO MAKE DO WITHOUT US FOR A WHILE...
CRASH
BANG
CLANK
THE HELL, CASH?

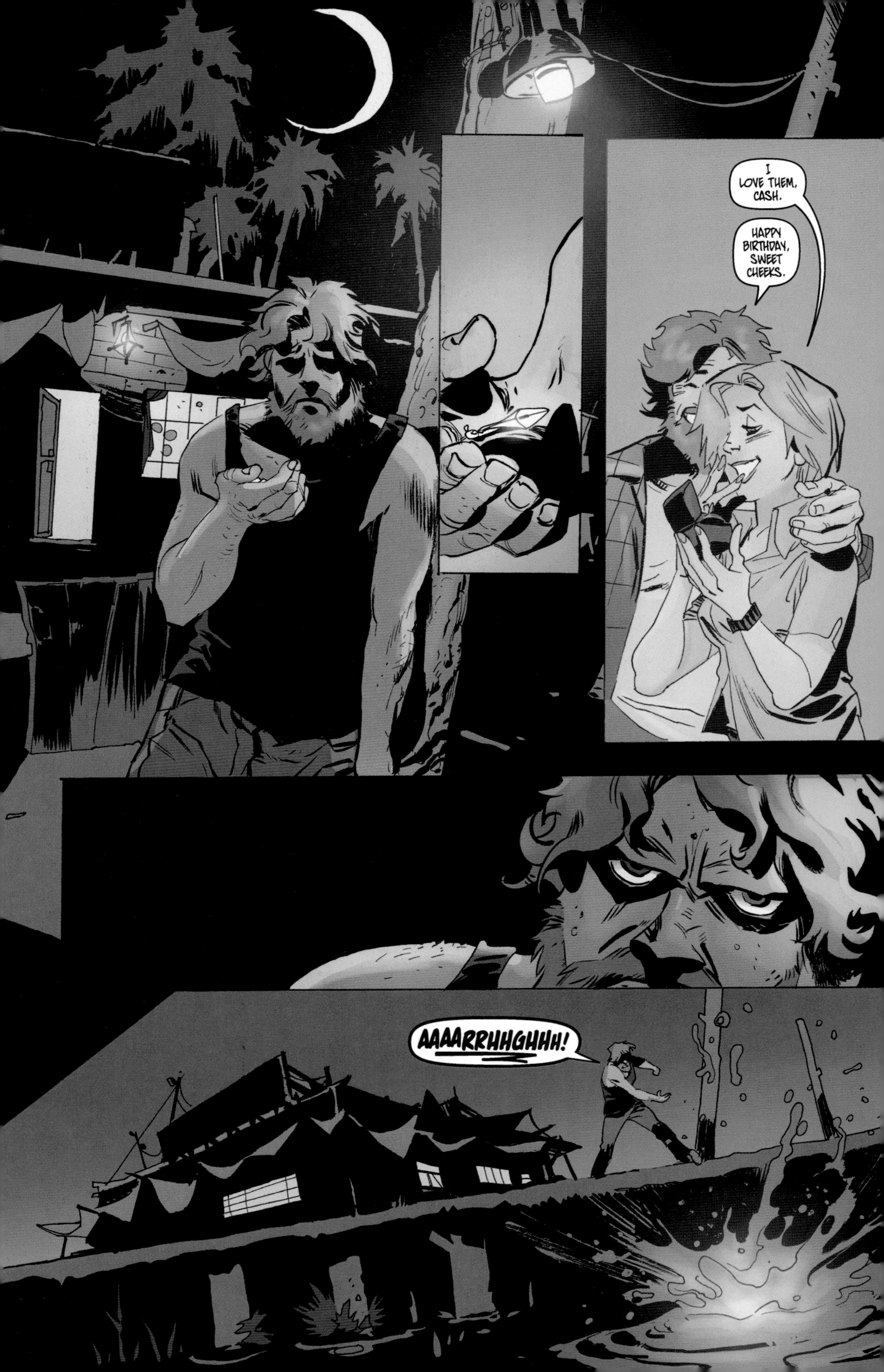
I LOVE THEM, CASH.
HAPPY BIRTHDAY, SWEET CHEEKS.
AAAARRHHGHHH!

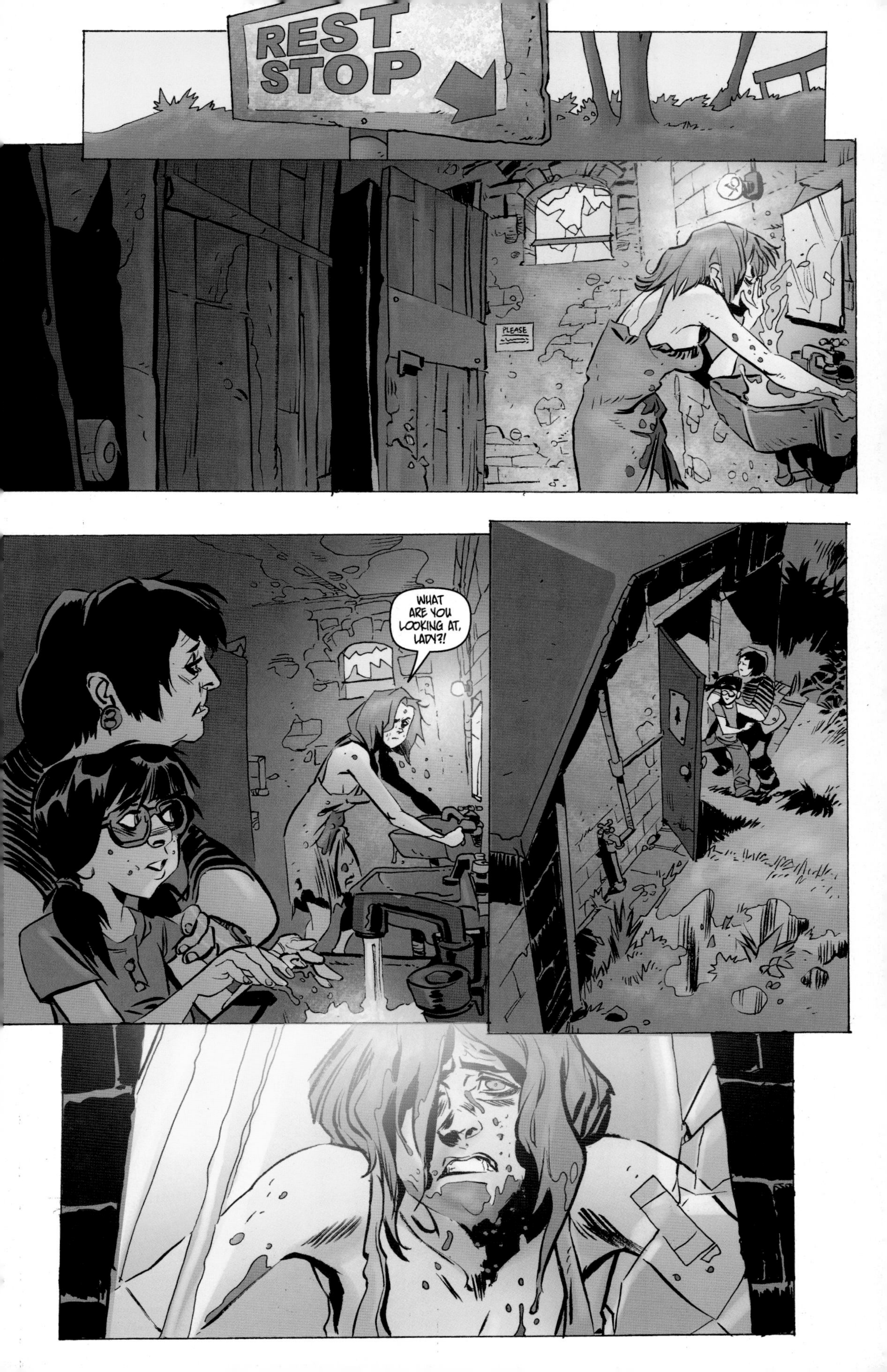
REST STOP
PLEASE
WHAT ARE YOU LOOKING AT, LADY?!

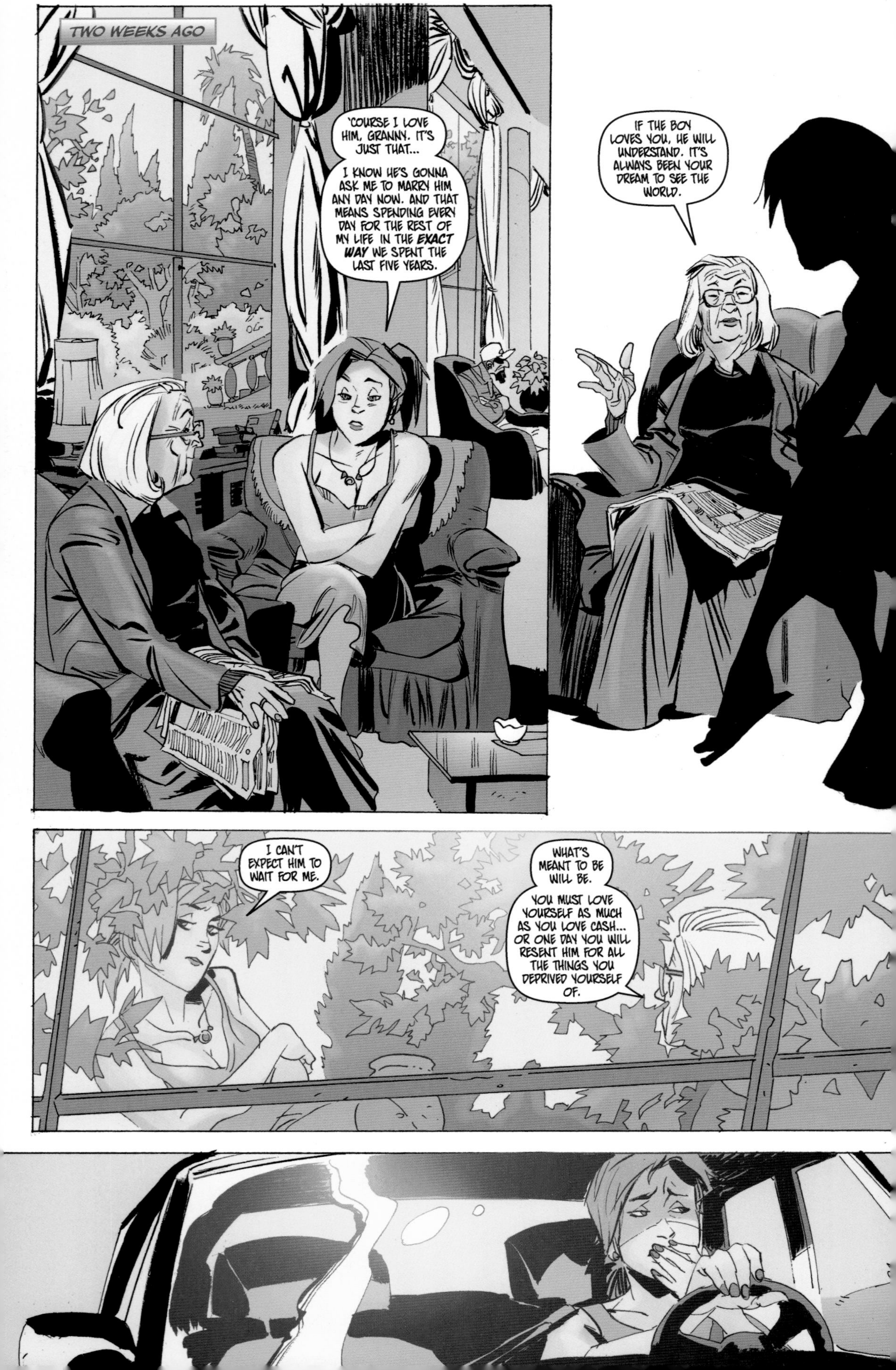
TWO WEEKS AGO
'COURSE I LOVE HIM, GRANNY. IT'S JUST THAT...
I KNOW HE'S GONNA ASK ME TO MARRY HIM ANY DAY NOW. AND THAT MEANS SPENDING EVERY DAY FOR THE REST OF MY LIFE IN THE EXACT WAY WE SPENT THE LAST FIVE YEARS.
IF THE BOY LOVES YOU, HE WILL UNDERSTAND. IT'S ALWAYS BEEN YOUR DREAM TO SEE THE WORLD.
I CAN'T EXPECT HIM TO WAIT FOR ME.
WHAT'S MEANT TO BE WILL BE.
YOU MUST LOVE YOURSELF AS MUCH AS YOU LOVE CASH... OR ONE DAY YOU WILL RESENT HIM FOR ALL THE THINGS YOU DEPRIVED YOURSELF OF.

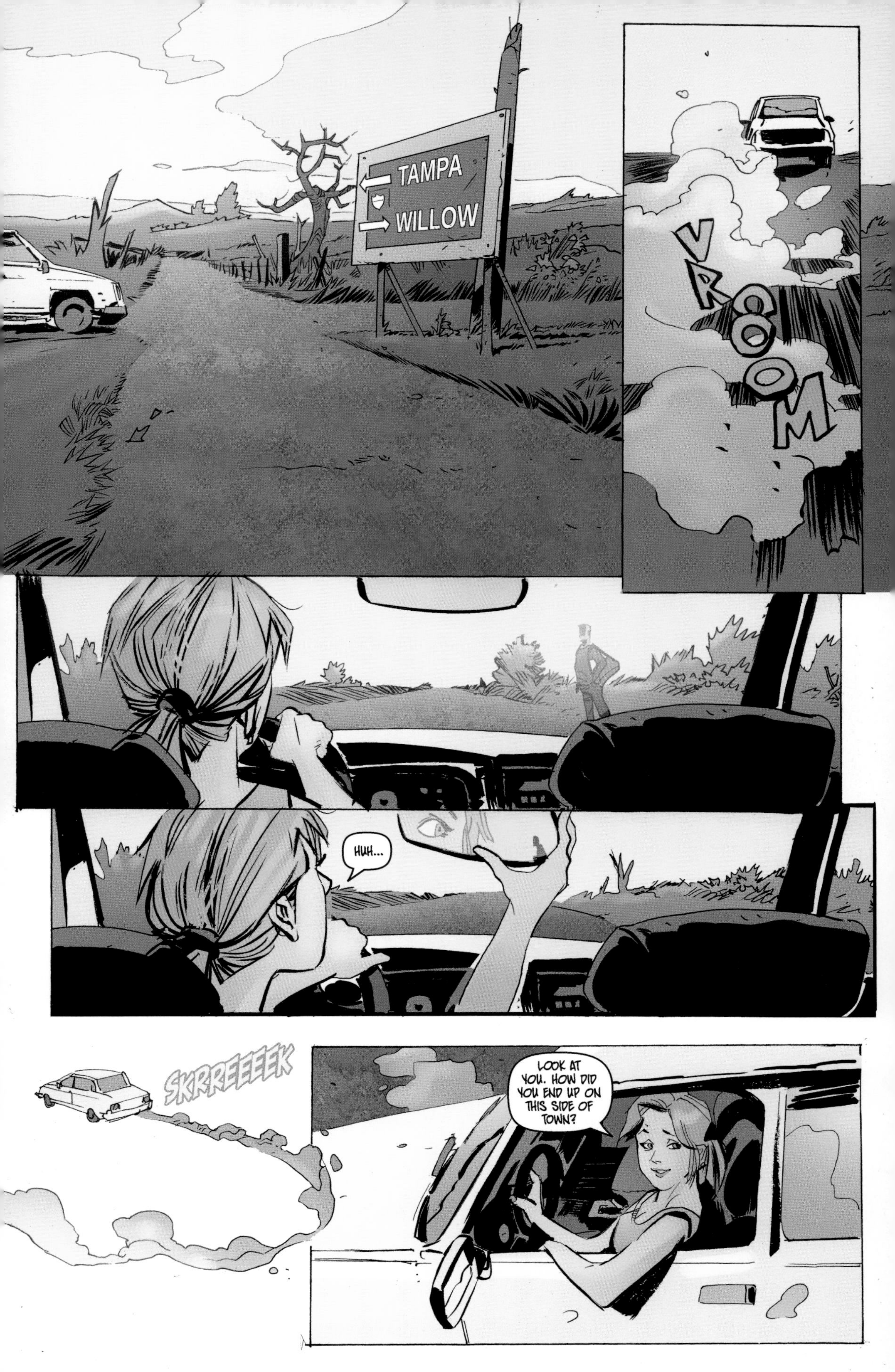
TAMPA
WILLOW
VROOM
HUH...
SKRREEEEK
LOOK AT YOU. HOW DID YOU END UP ON THIS SIDE OF TOWN?

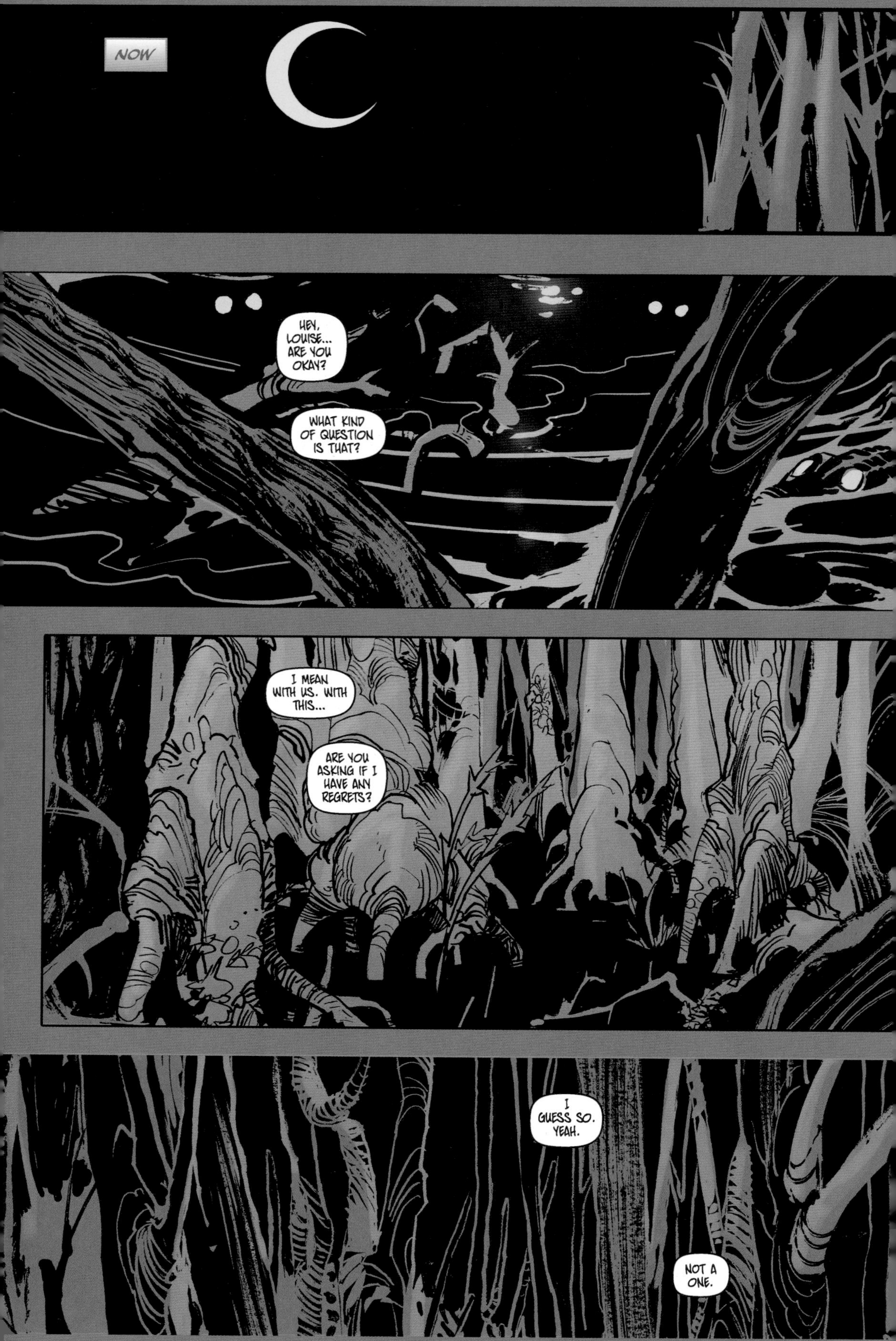
NOW
HEY, LOUISE... ARE YOU OKAY?
WHAT KIND OF QUESTION IS THAT?
I MEAN WITH US. WITH THIS...
ARE YOU ASKING IF I HAVE ANY REGRETS?
I GUESS SO. YEAH.
NOT A ONE.

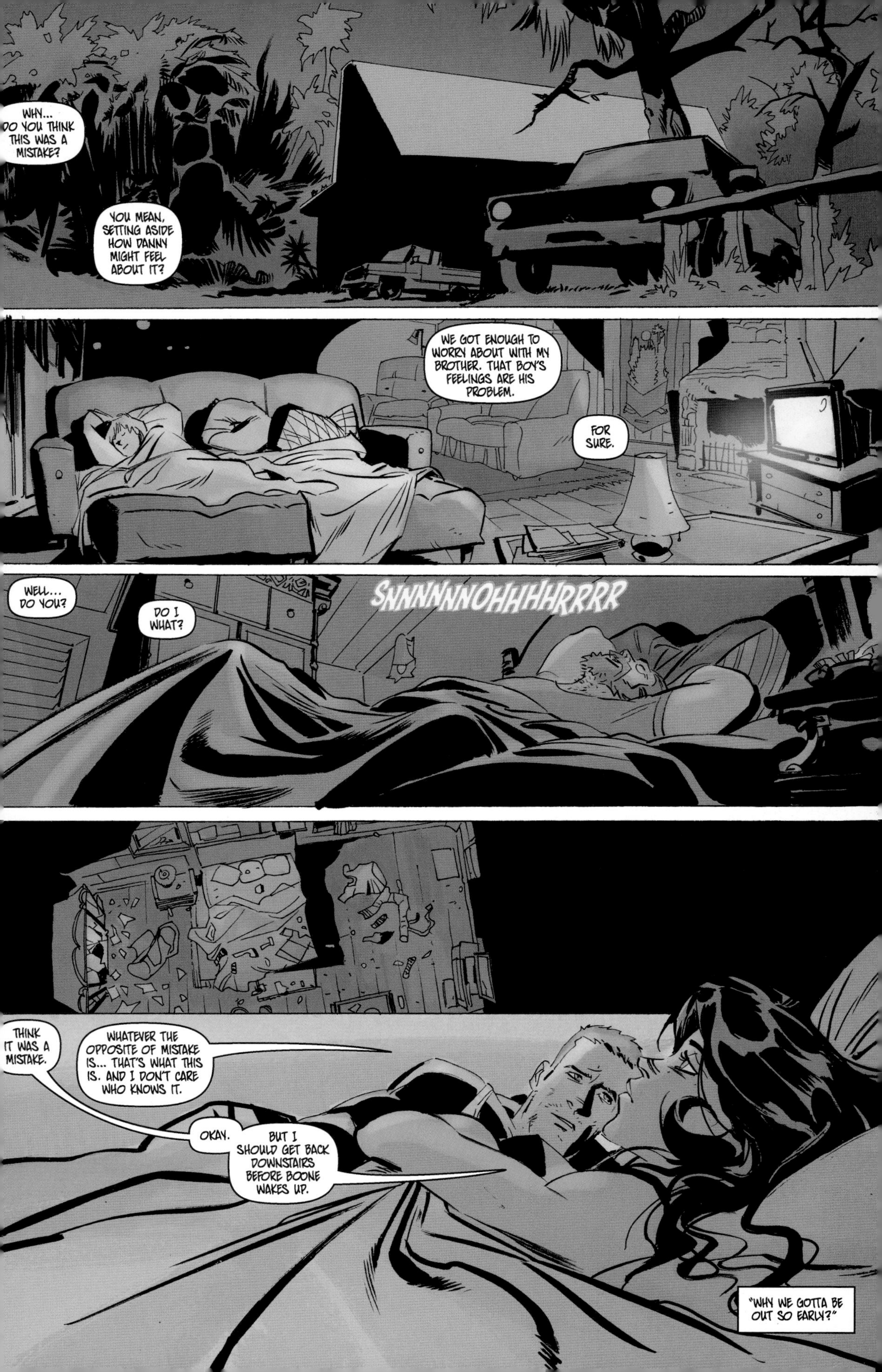
WHY... DO YOU THINK THIS WAS A MISTAKE?
YOU MEAN, SETTING ASIDE HOW DANNY MIGHT FEEL ABOUT IT?
WE GOT ENOUGH TO WORRY ABOUT WITH MY BROTHER. THAT BOY'S FEELINGS ARE HIS PROBLEM.
FOR SURE.
WELL... DO YOU?
DO I WHAT?
SNNNNNOHHHHRRRR
THINK IT WAS A MISTAKE.
WHATEVER THE OPPOSITE OF MISTAKE IS... THAT'S WHAT THIS IS. AND I DON'T CARE WHO KNOWS IT.
OKAY.
BUT I SHOULD GET BACK DOWNSTAIRS BEFORE BOONE WAKES UP.
"WHY WE GOTTA BE OUT SO EARLY?"

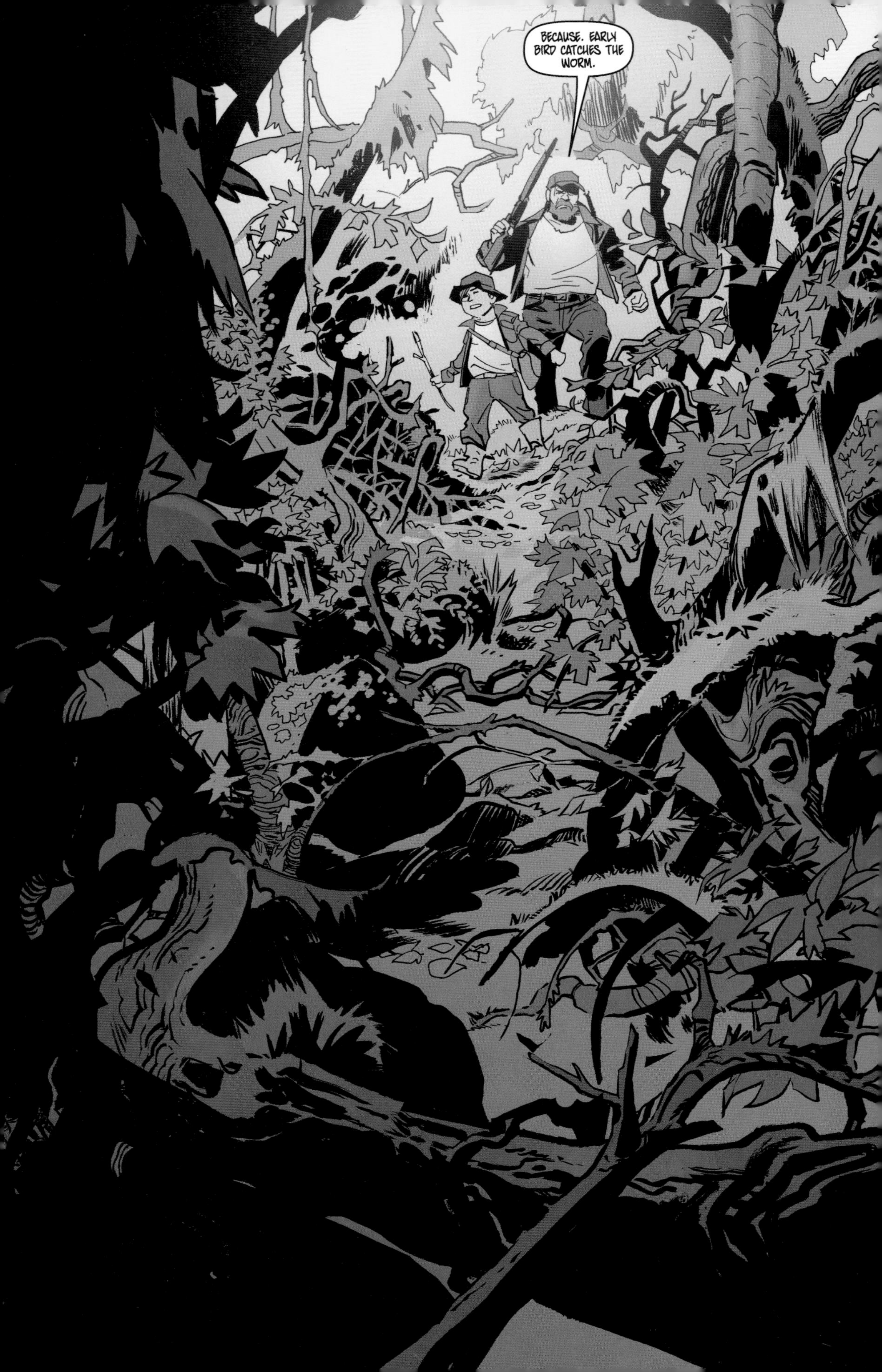
BECAUSE. EARLY BIRD CATCHES THE WORM.

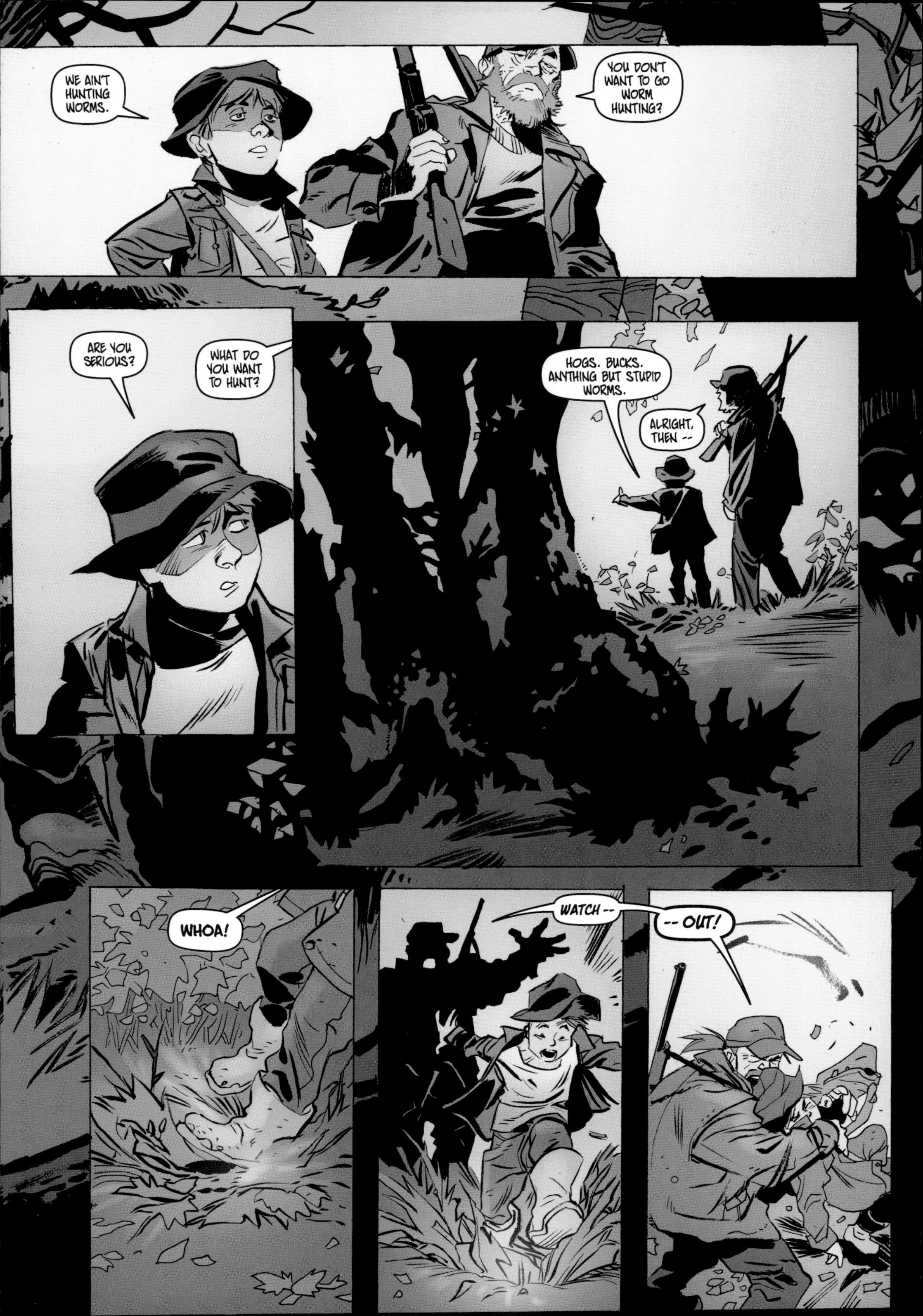
WE AIN'T HUNTING WORMS.
YOU DON'T WANT TO GO WORM HUNTING?
ARE YOU SERIOUS?
WHAT DO YOU WANT TO HUNT?
HOGS. BUCKS. ANYTHING BUT STUPID WORMS.
ALRIGHT, THEN --
WHOA!
WATCH --
-- OUT!

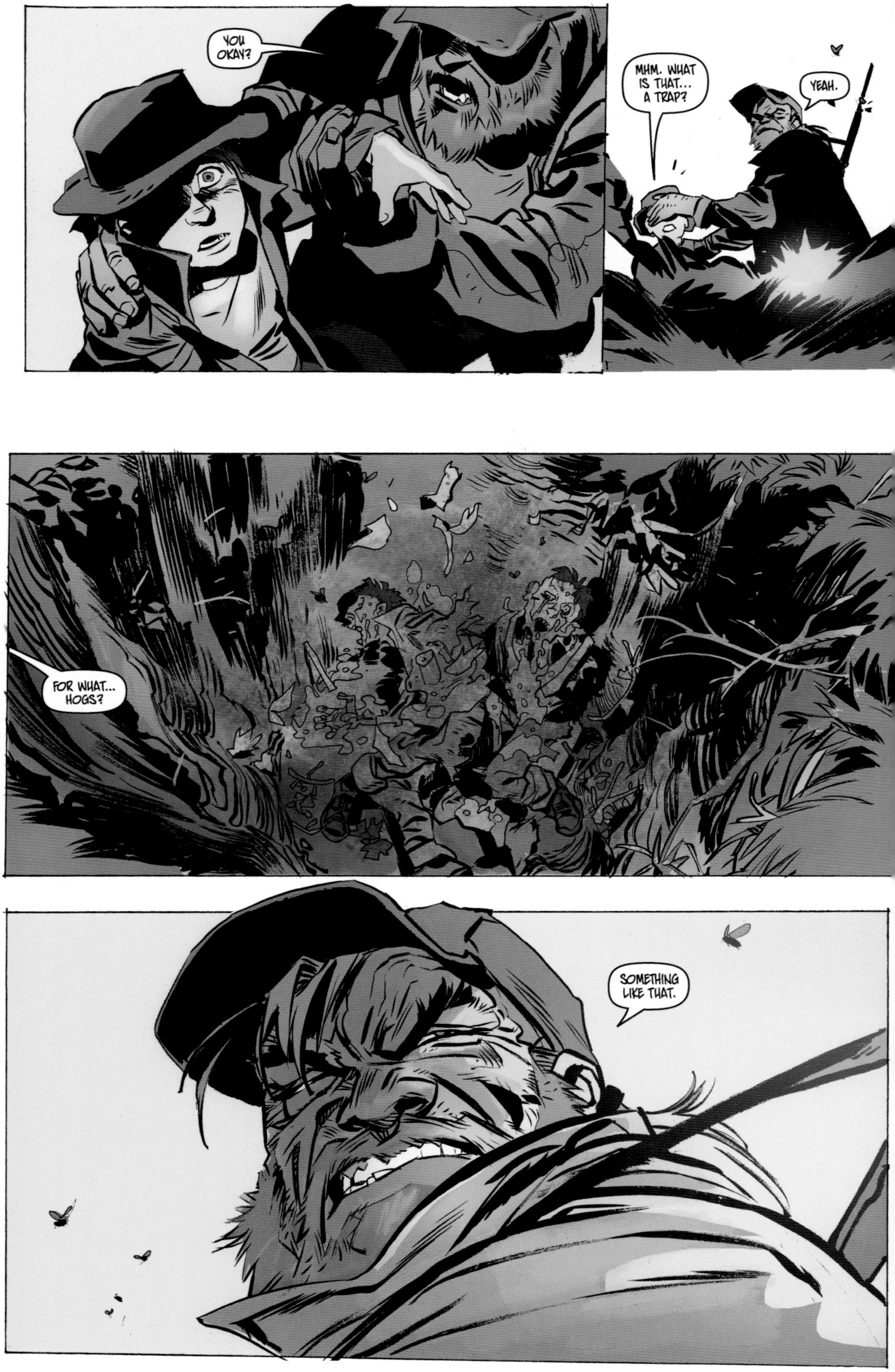
YOU OKAY?
MHM. WHAT IS THAT... A TRAP?
YEAH.
FOR WHAT... HOGS?
SOMETHING LIKE THAT.

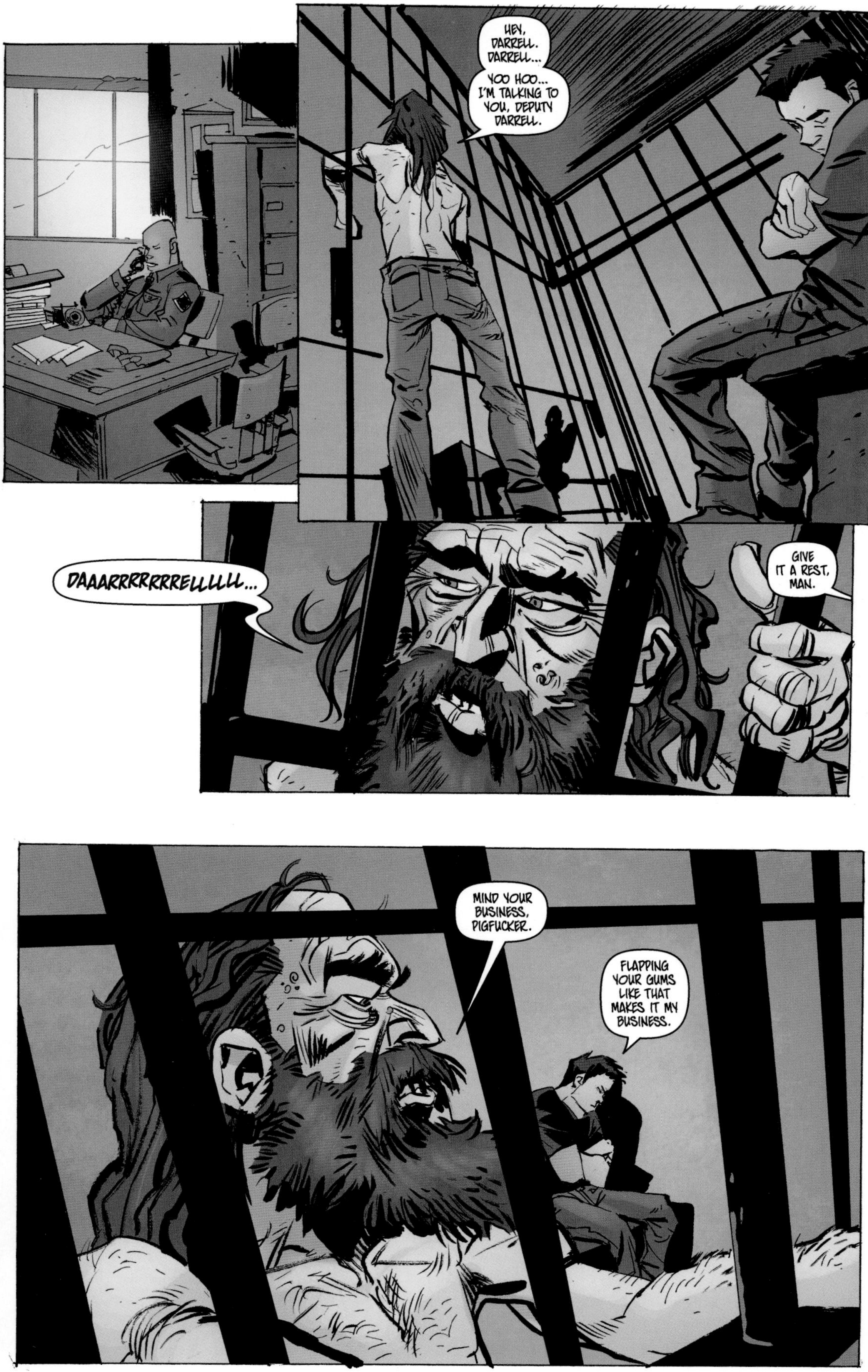
HEY, DARRELL. DARRELL...
YOO HOO... I'M TALKING TO YOU, DEPUTY DARRELL.
DAAARRRRRRRELLLLLL...
GIVE IT A REST, MAN.
MIND YOUR BUSINESS, PIGFUCKER.
FLAPPING YOUR GUMS LIKE THAT MAKES IT MY BUSINESS.

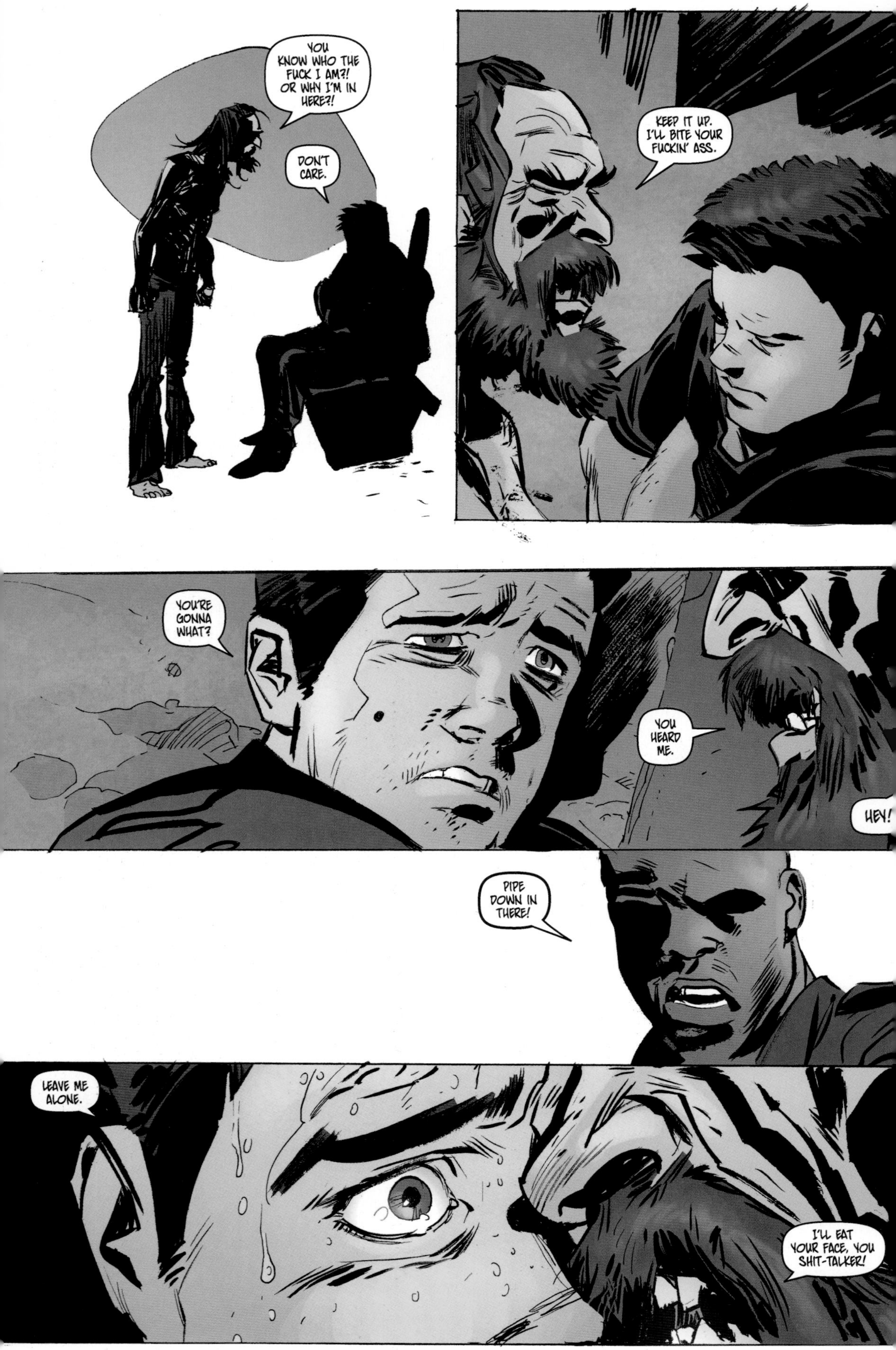
YOU KNOW WHO THE FUCK I AM?! OR WHY I'M IN HERE?!
DON'T CARE.
KEEP IT UP. I'LL BITE YOUR FUCKIN' ASS.
YOU'RE GONNA WHAT?
YOU HEARD ME.
HEY!
PIPE DOWN IN THERE!
LEAVE ME ALONE.
I'LL EAT YOUR FACE, YOU SHIT-TALKER!

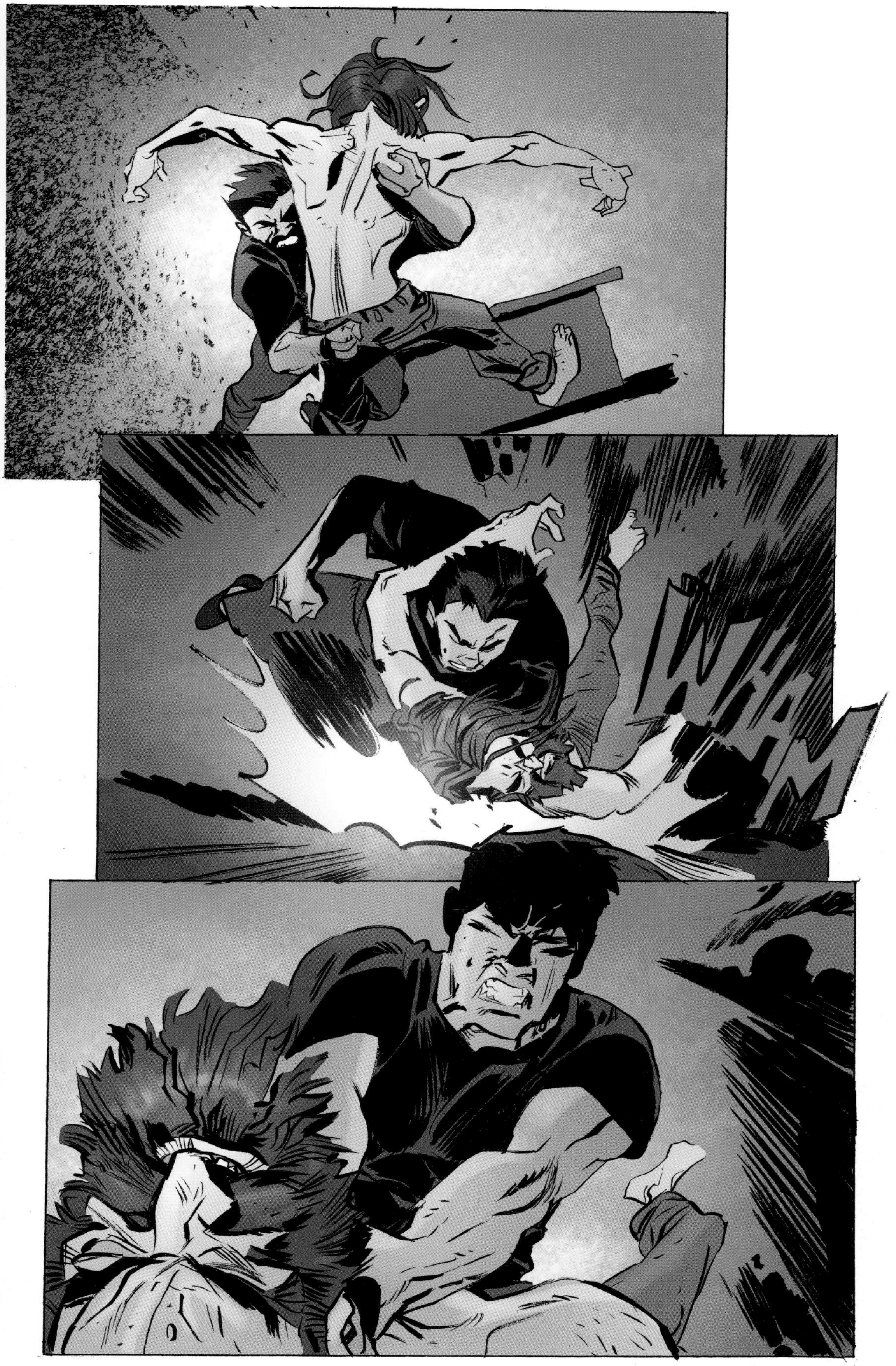
WHAM

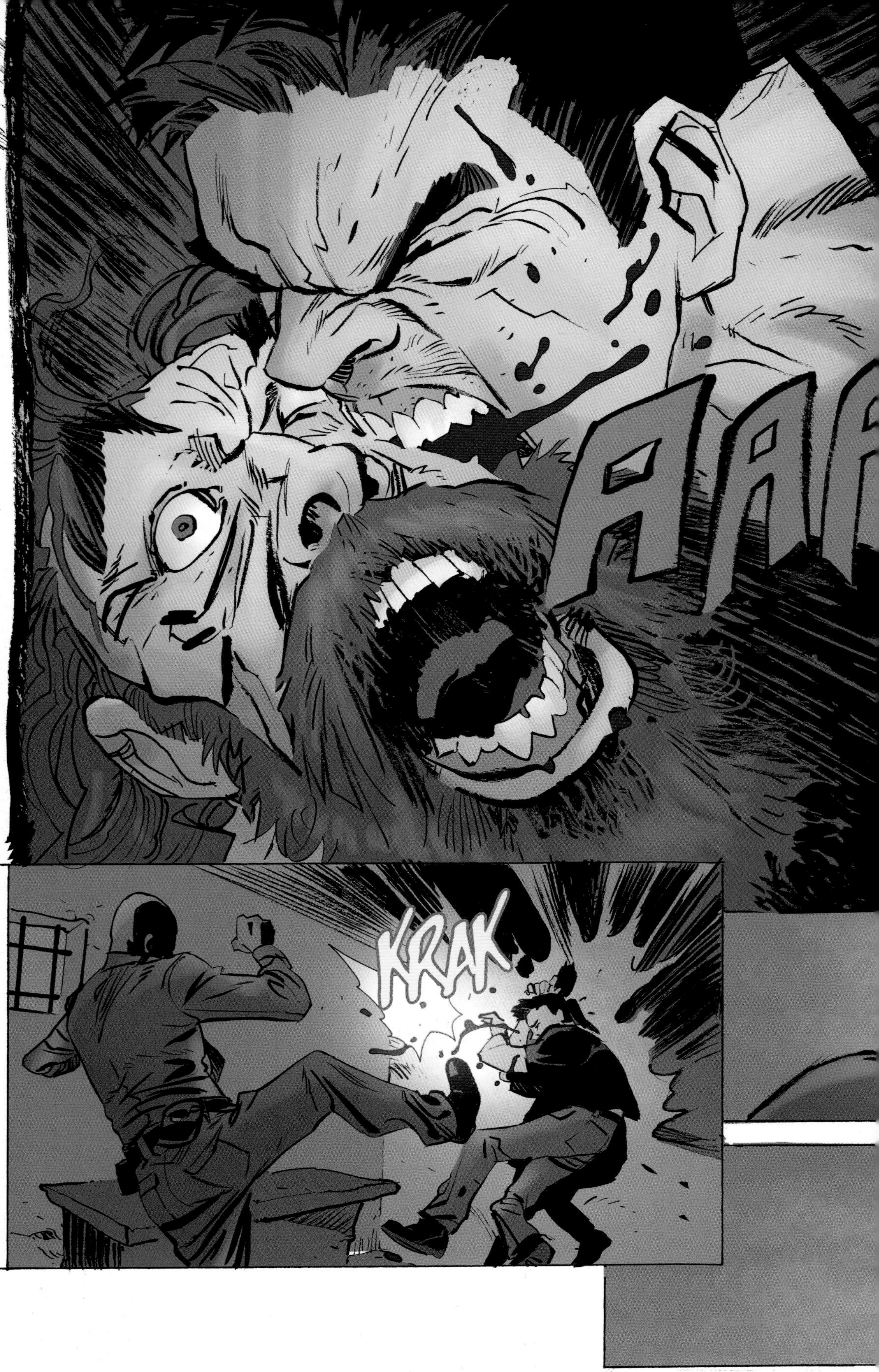

AAA
KRAK

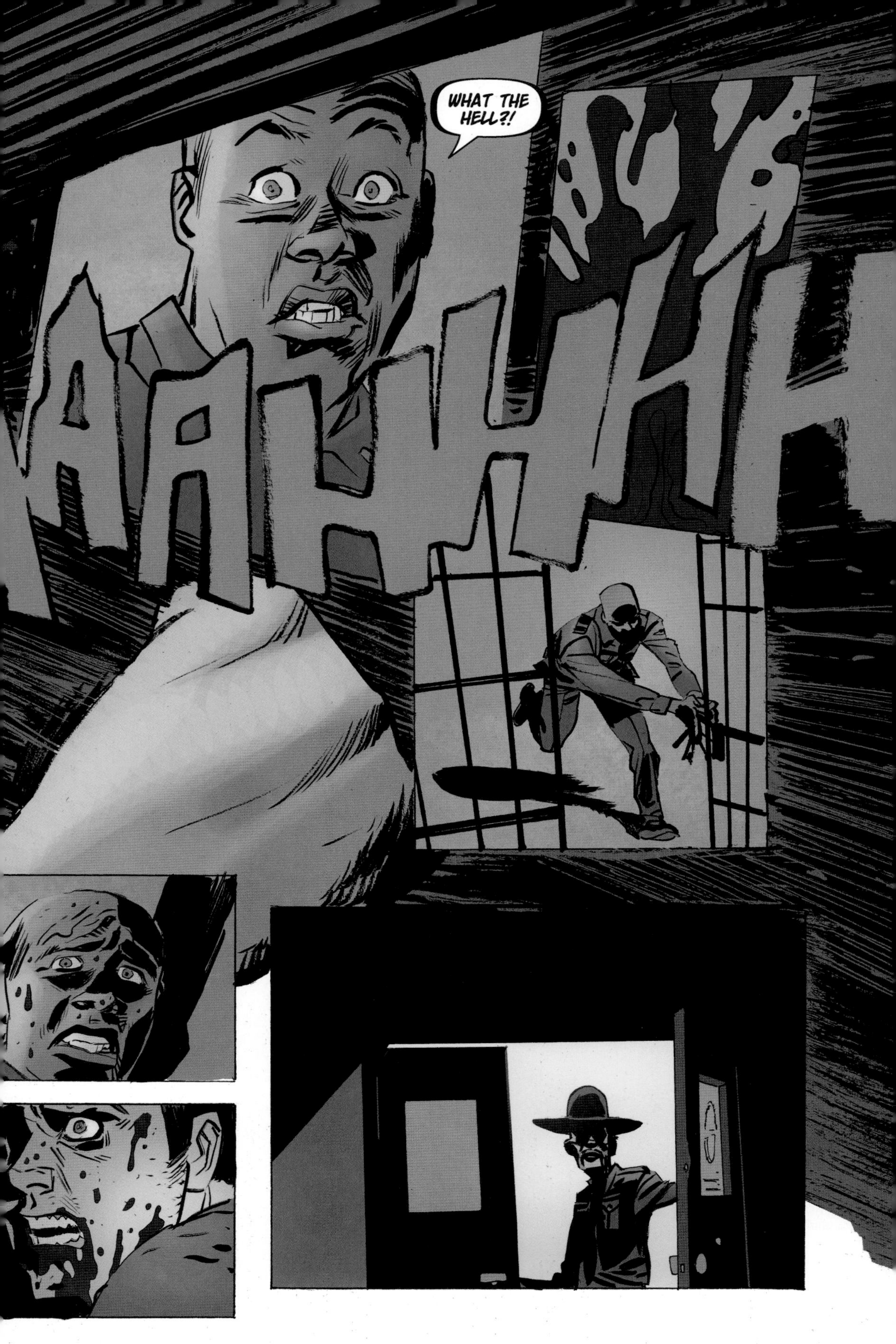
WHAT THE HELL?!

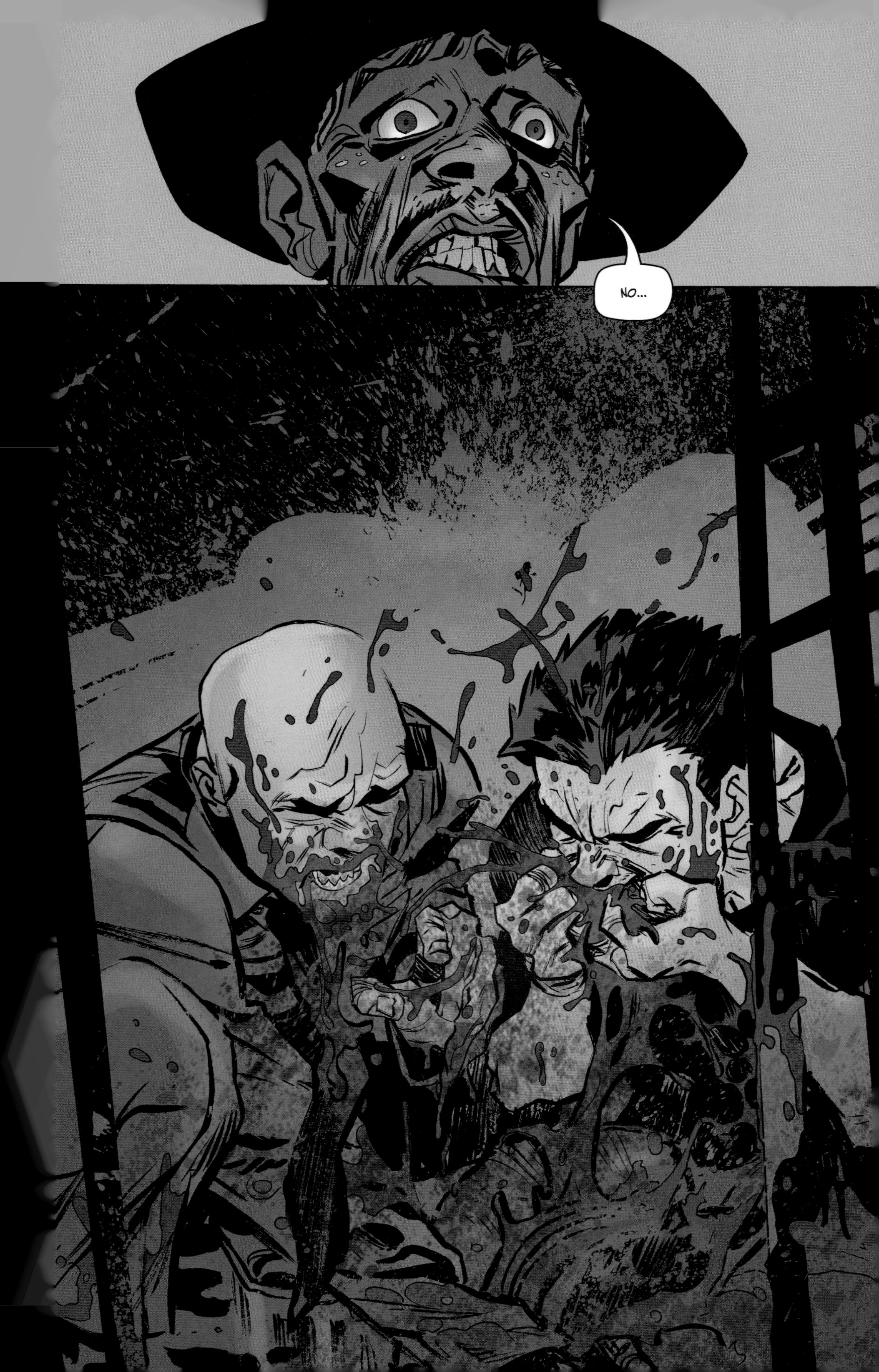
NO...

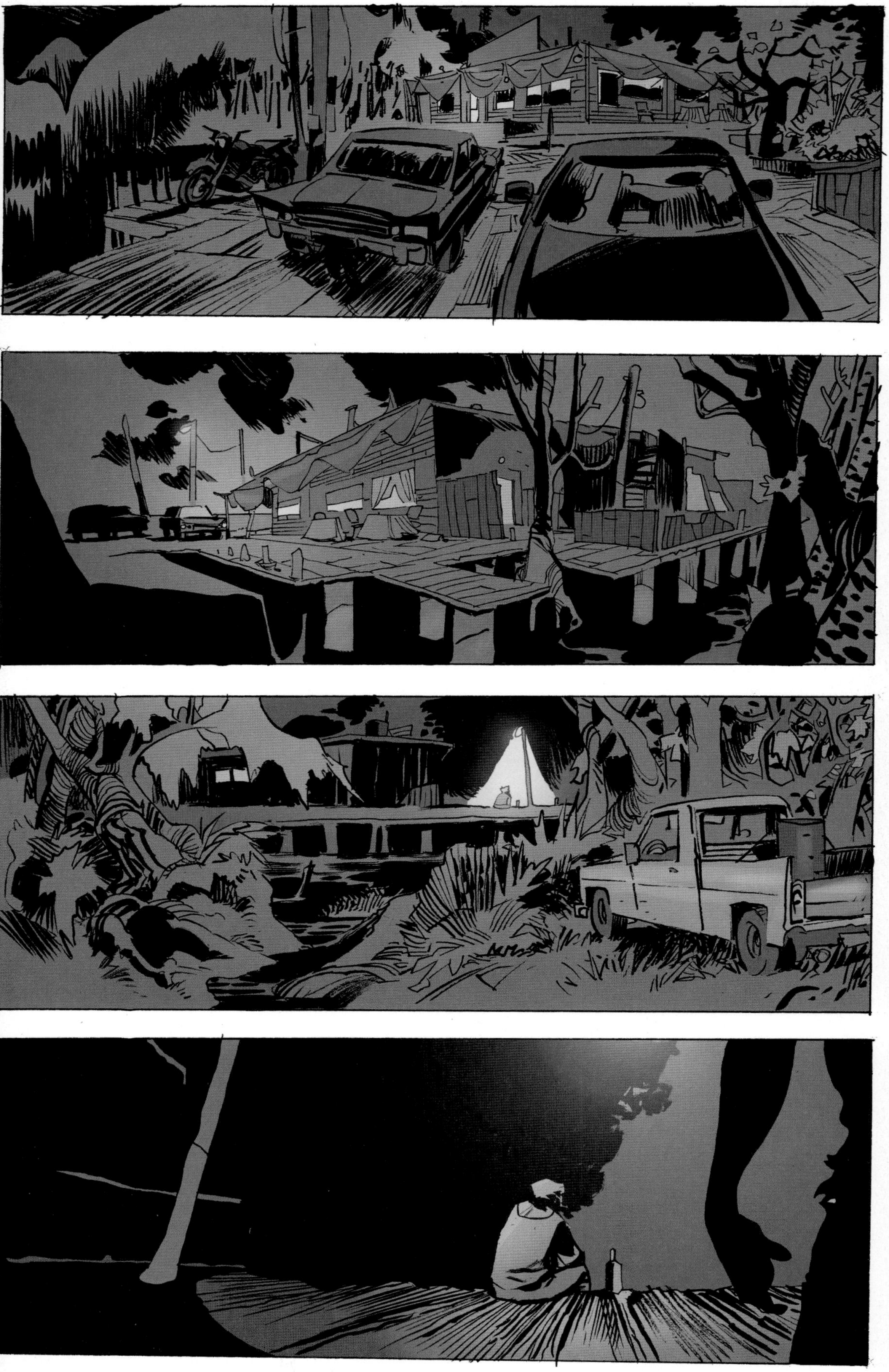

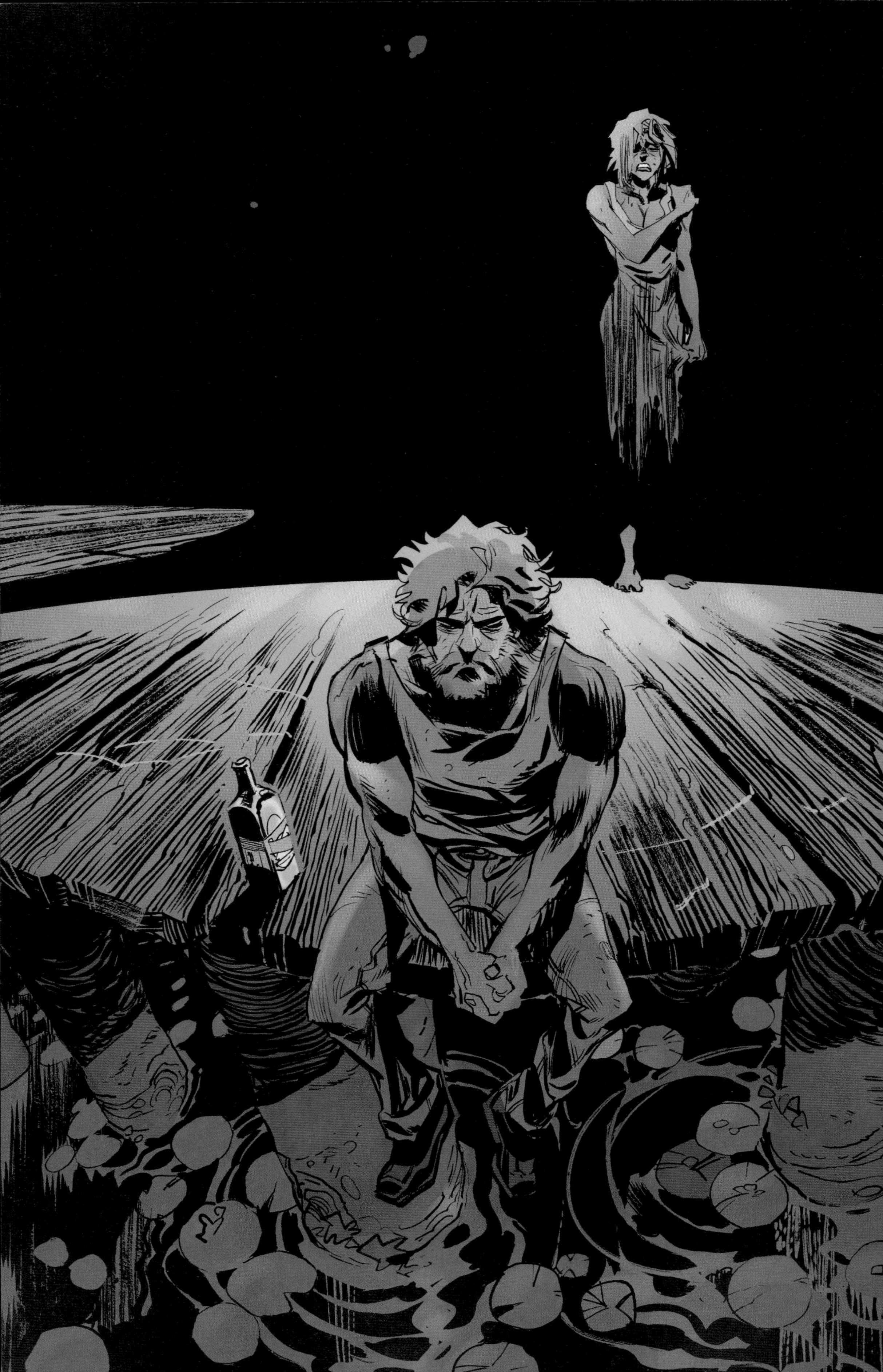

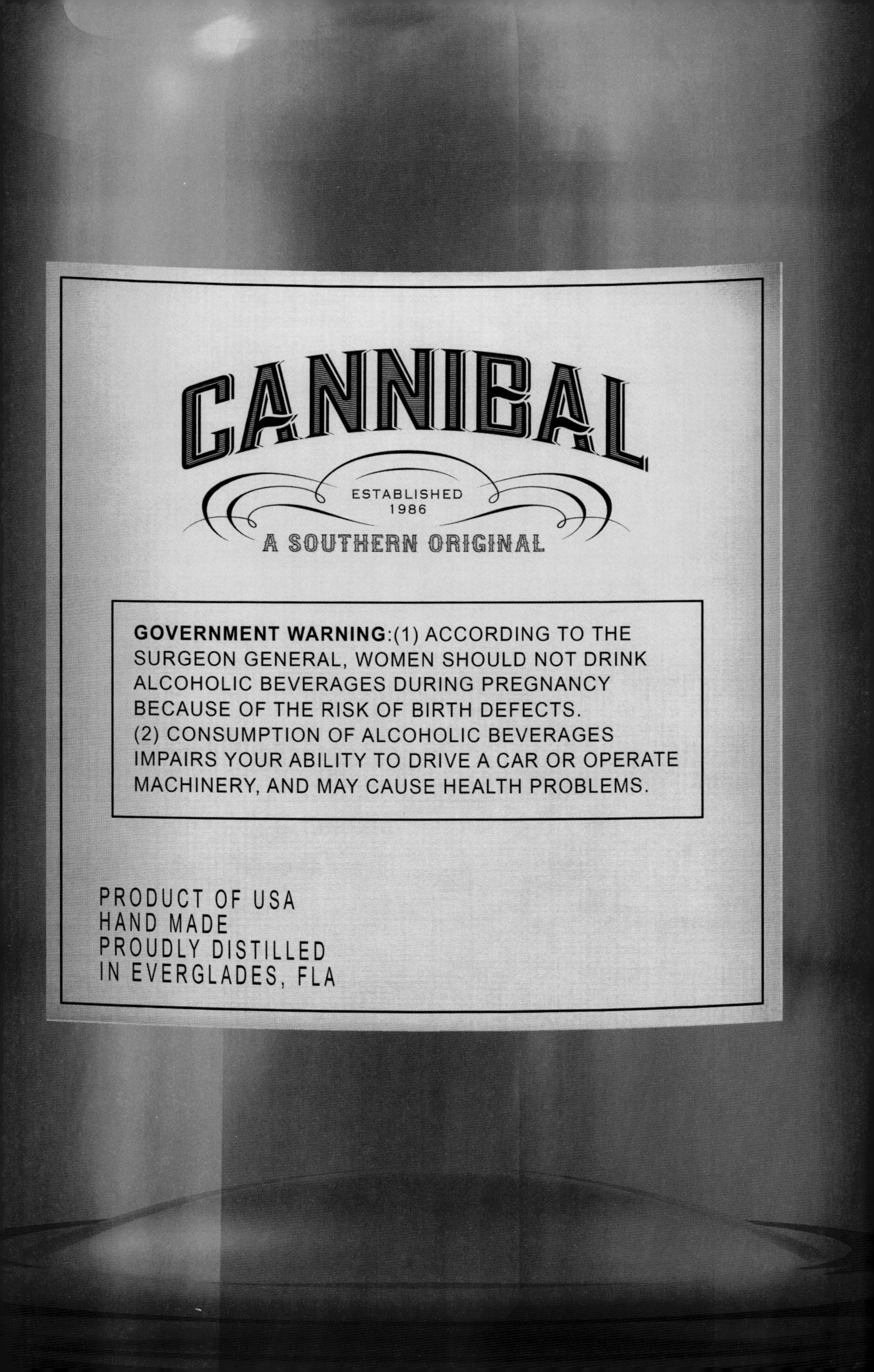
CANNIBAL
ESTABLISHED
1986
A SOUTHERN ORIGINAL
GOVERNMENT WARNING:(1) ACCORDING TO THE SURGEON GENERAL, WOMEN SHOULD NOT DRINK ALCOHOLIC BEVERAGES DURING PREGNANCY BECAUSE OF THE RISK OF BIRTH DEFECTS. (2) CONSUMPTION OF ALCOHOLIC BEVERAGES IMPAIRS YOUR ABILITY TO DRIVE A CAR OR OPERATE MACHINERY, AND MAY CAUSE HEALTH PROBLEMS.
PRODUCT OF USA
HAND MADE
PROUDLY DISTILLED
IN EVERGLADES, FLA

ISSUE SIX

ESTABLISHED
1986

A SOUTHERN ORIGINAL

CANNIBAL

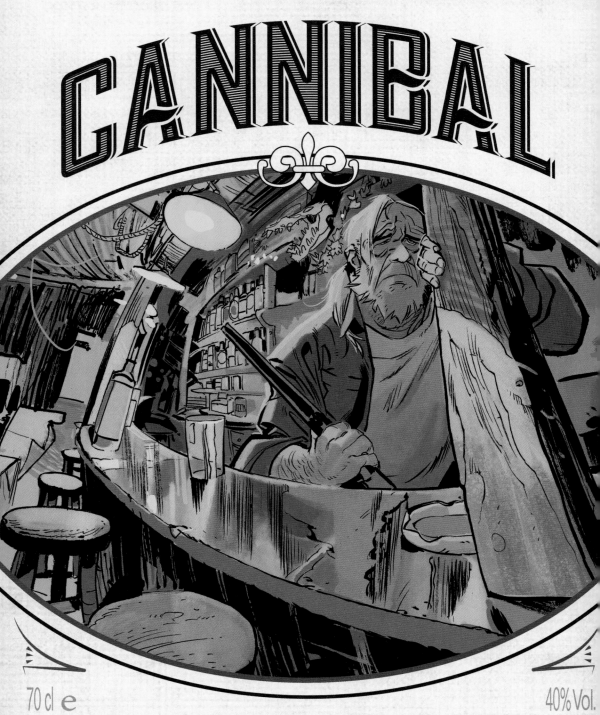

70 cl e

40% Vol.

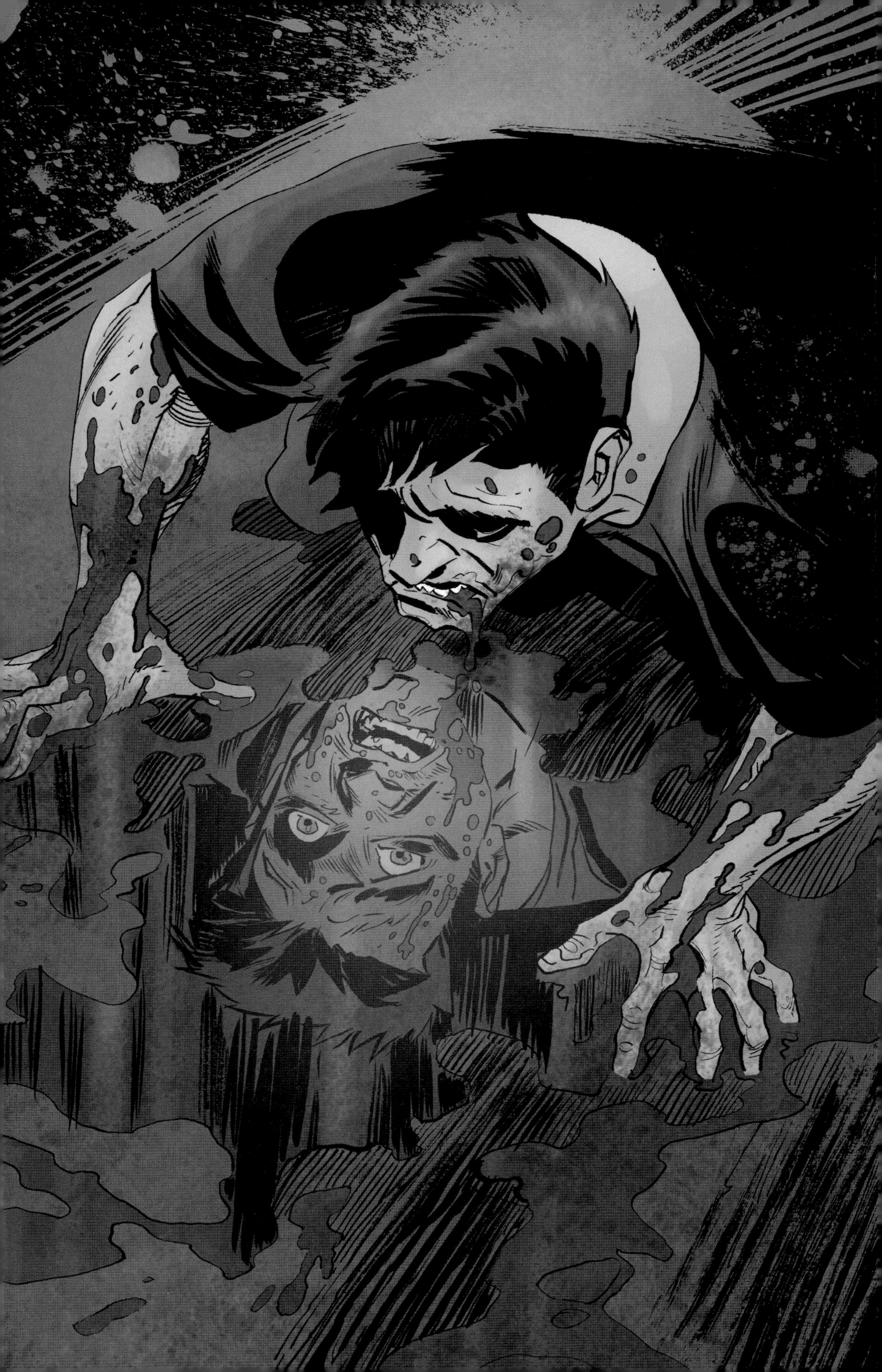

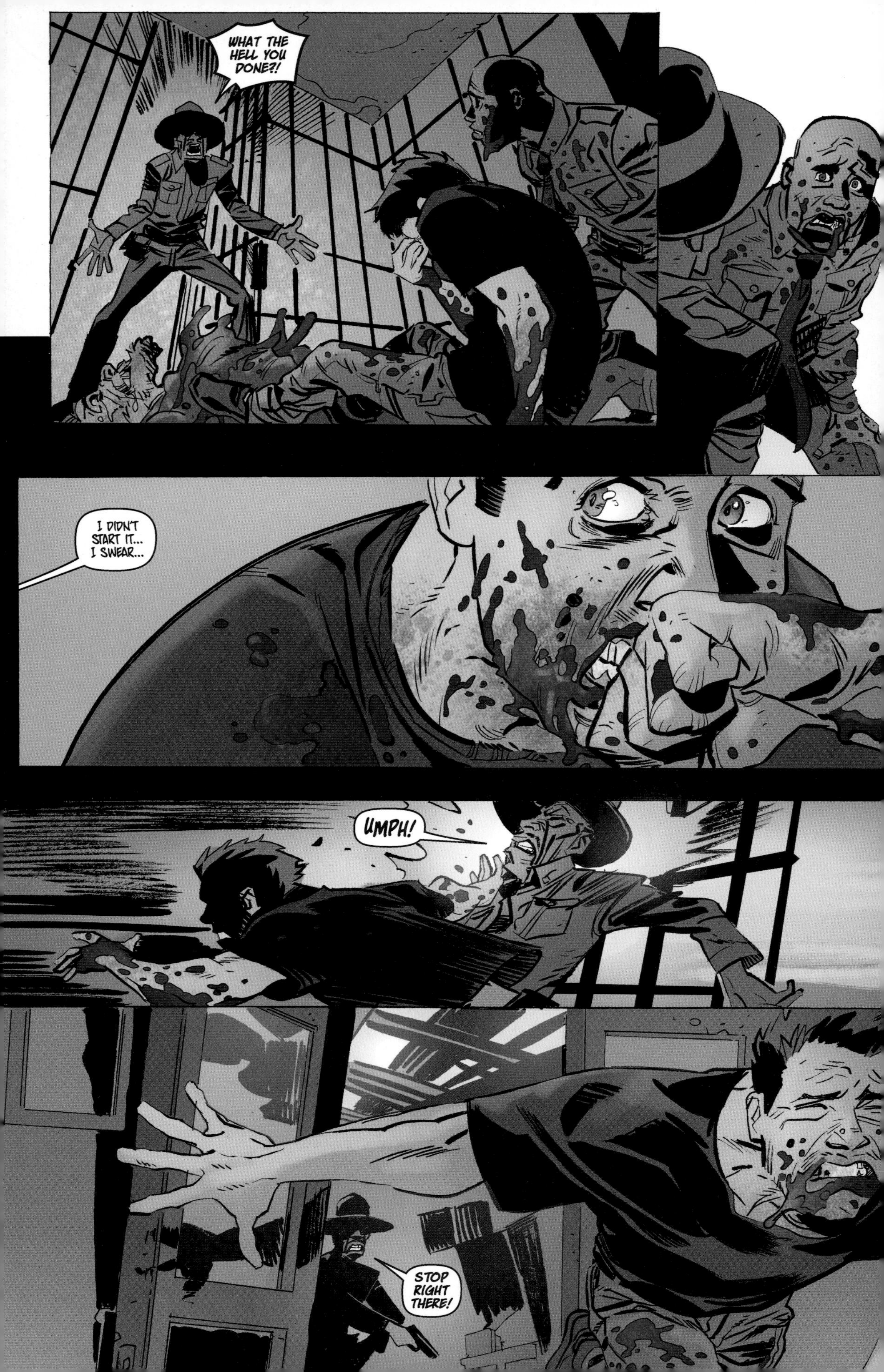
WHAT THE HELL YOU DONE?!
I DIDN'T START IT... I SWEAR...
UMPH!
STOP RIGHT THERE!

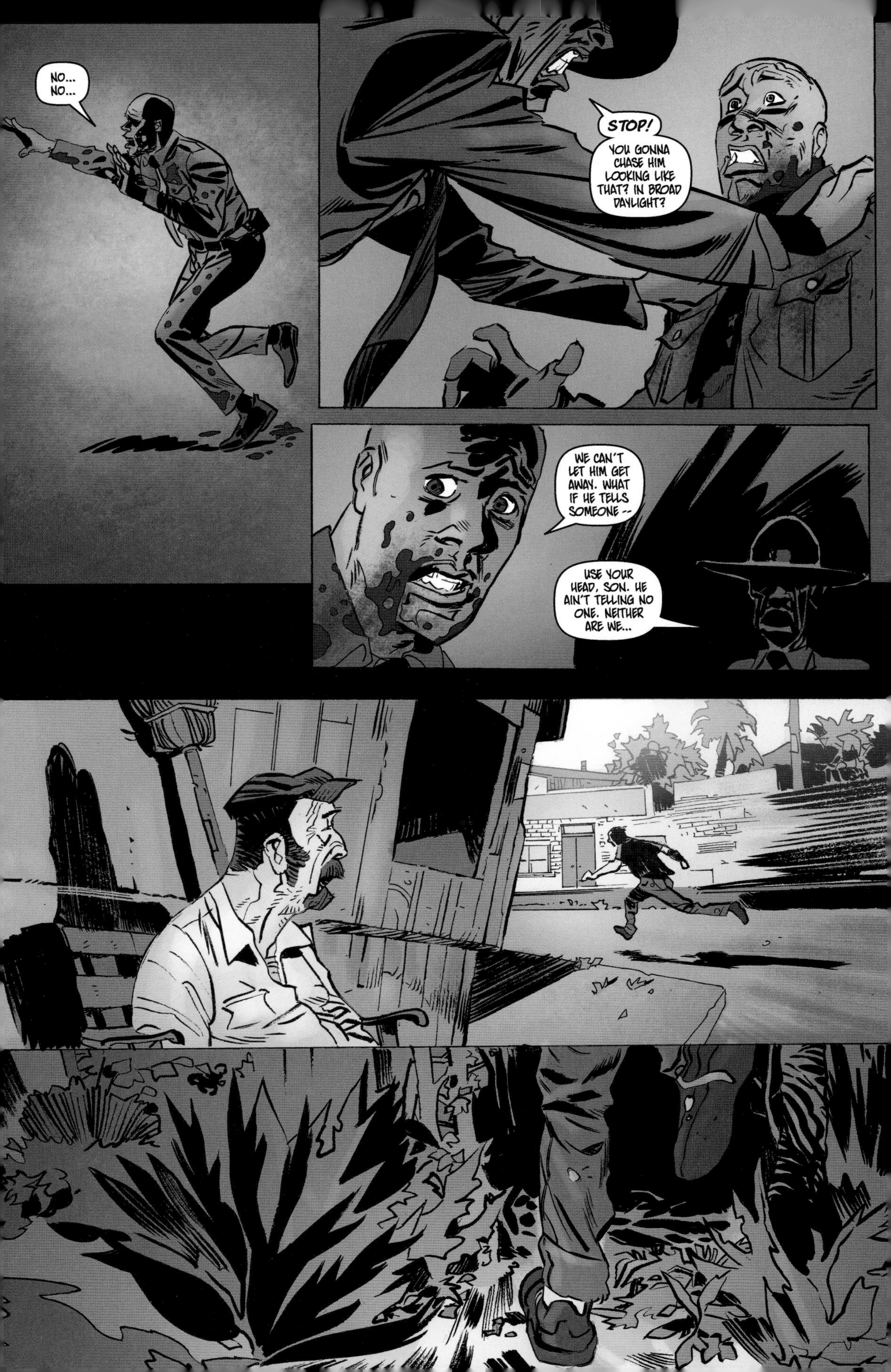
NO... NO...
STOP!
YOU GONNA CHASE HIM LOOKING LIKE THAT? IN BROAD DAYLIGHT?
WE CAN'T LET HIM GET AWAY. WHAT IF HE TELLS SOMEONE --
USE YOUR HEAD, SON. HE AIN'T TELLING NO ONE. NEITHER ARE WE...

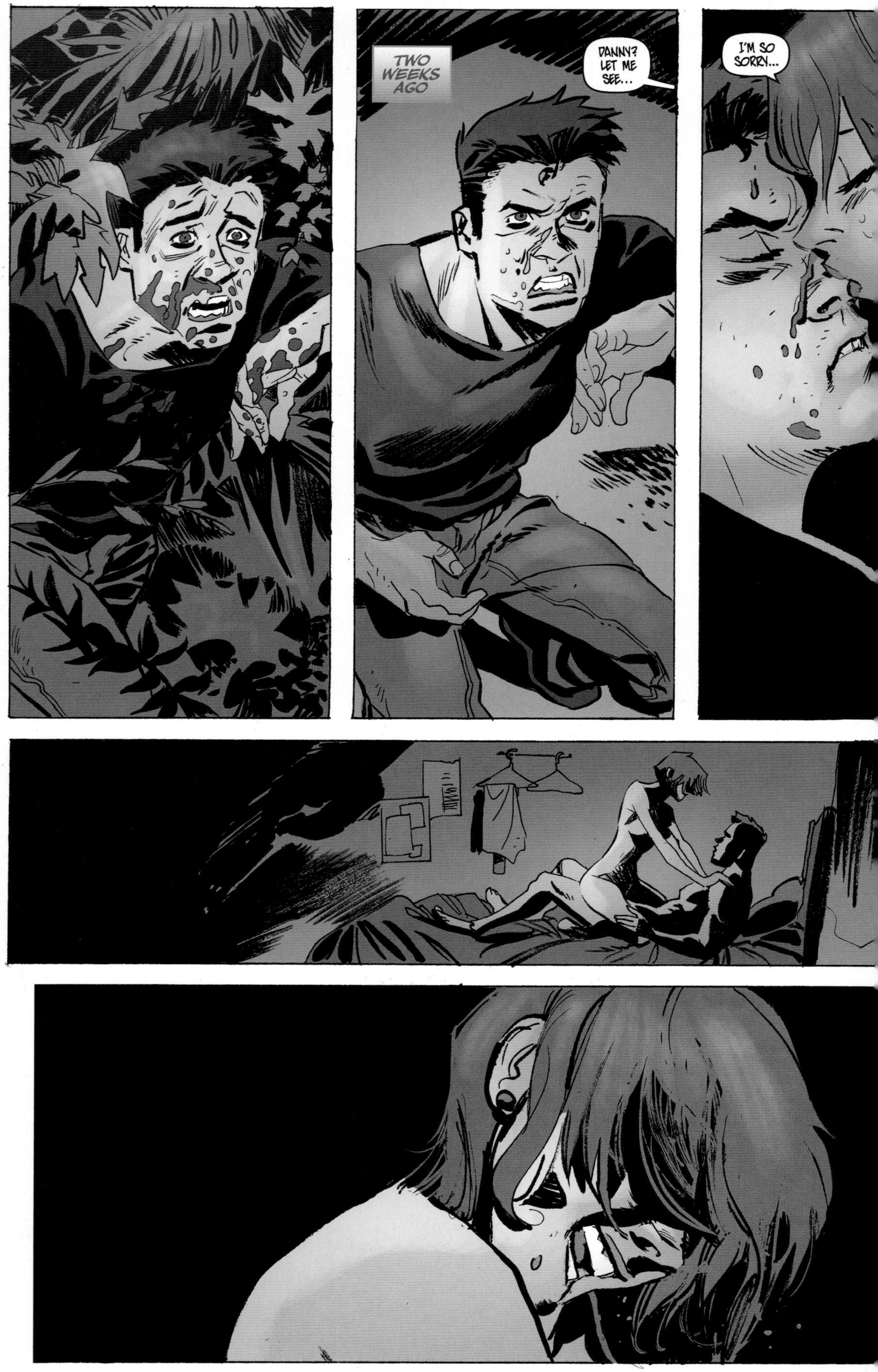
TWO WEEKS AGO
DANNY? LET ME SEE...
I'M SO SORRY...

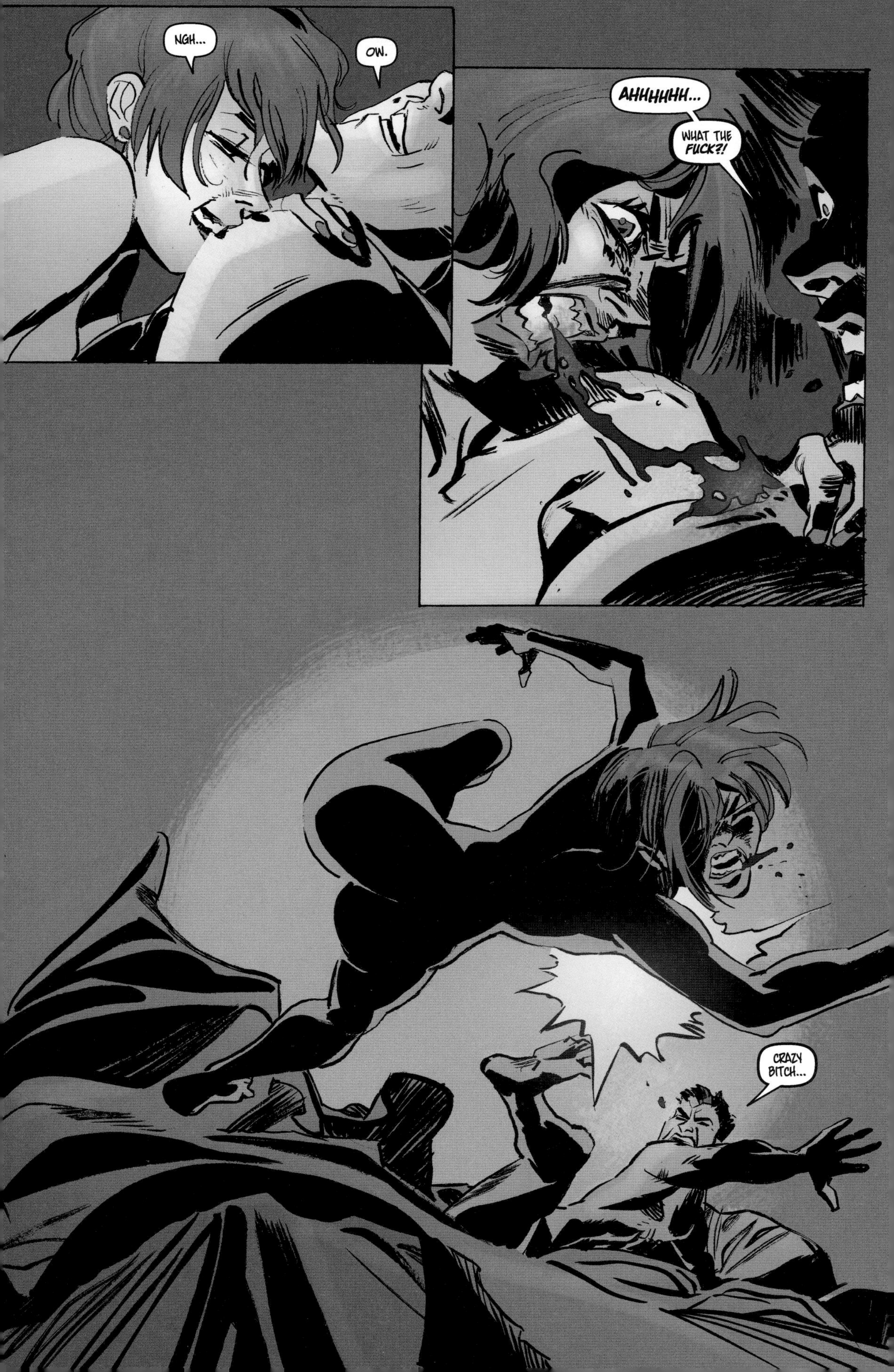
NGH...
OW.
AHHHHHH...
WHAT THE FUCK?!
CRAZY BITCH...

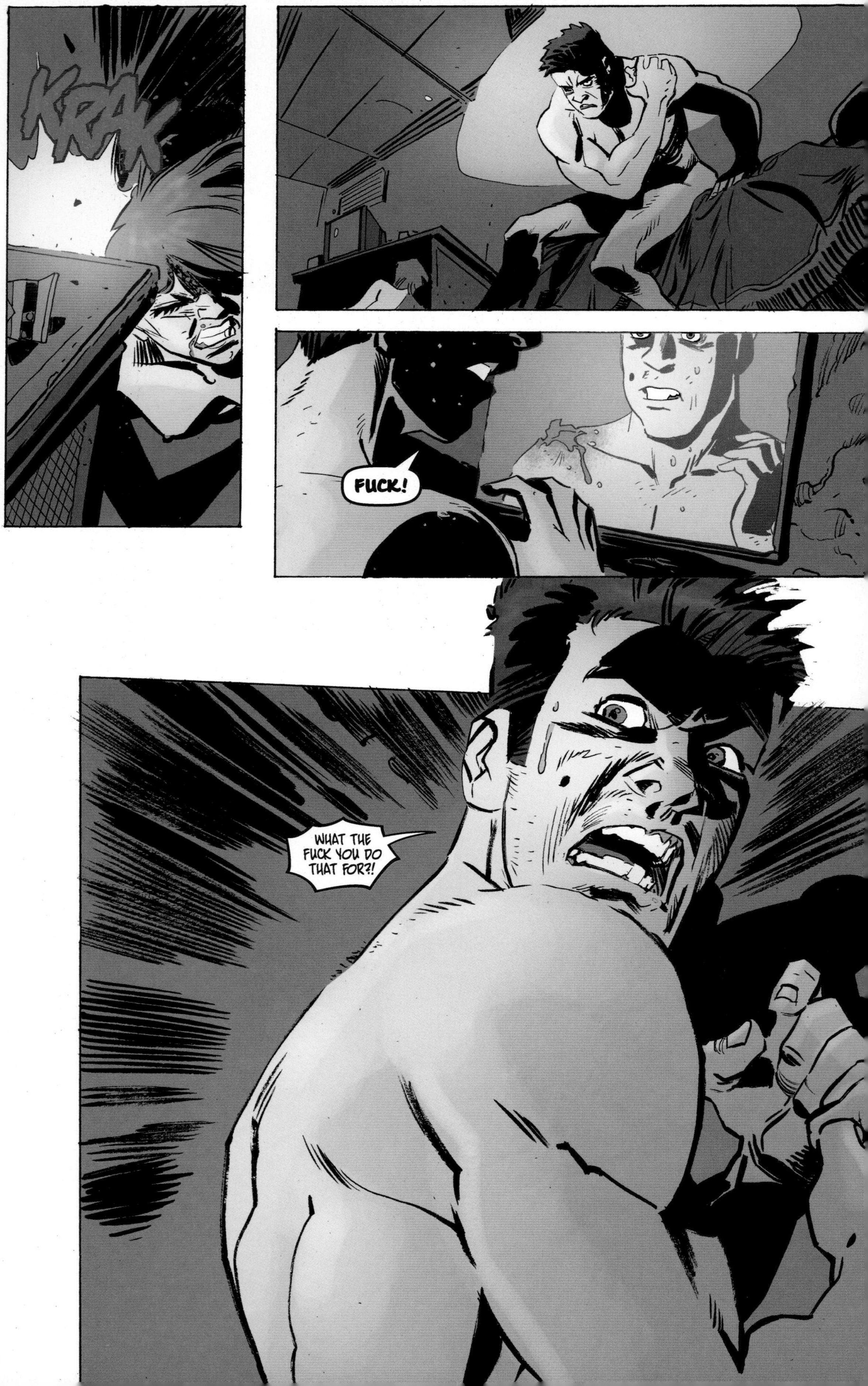
KRAK
FUCK!
WHAT THE FUCK YOU DO THAT FOR?!

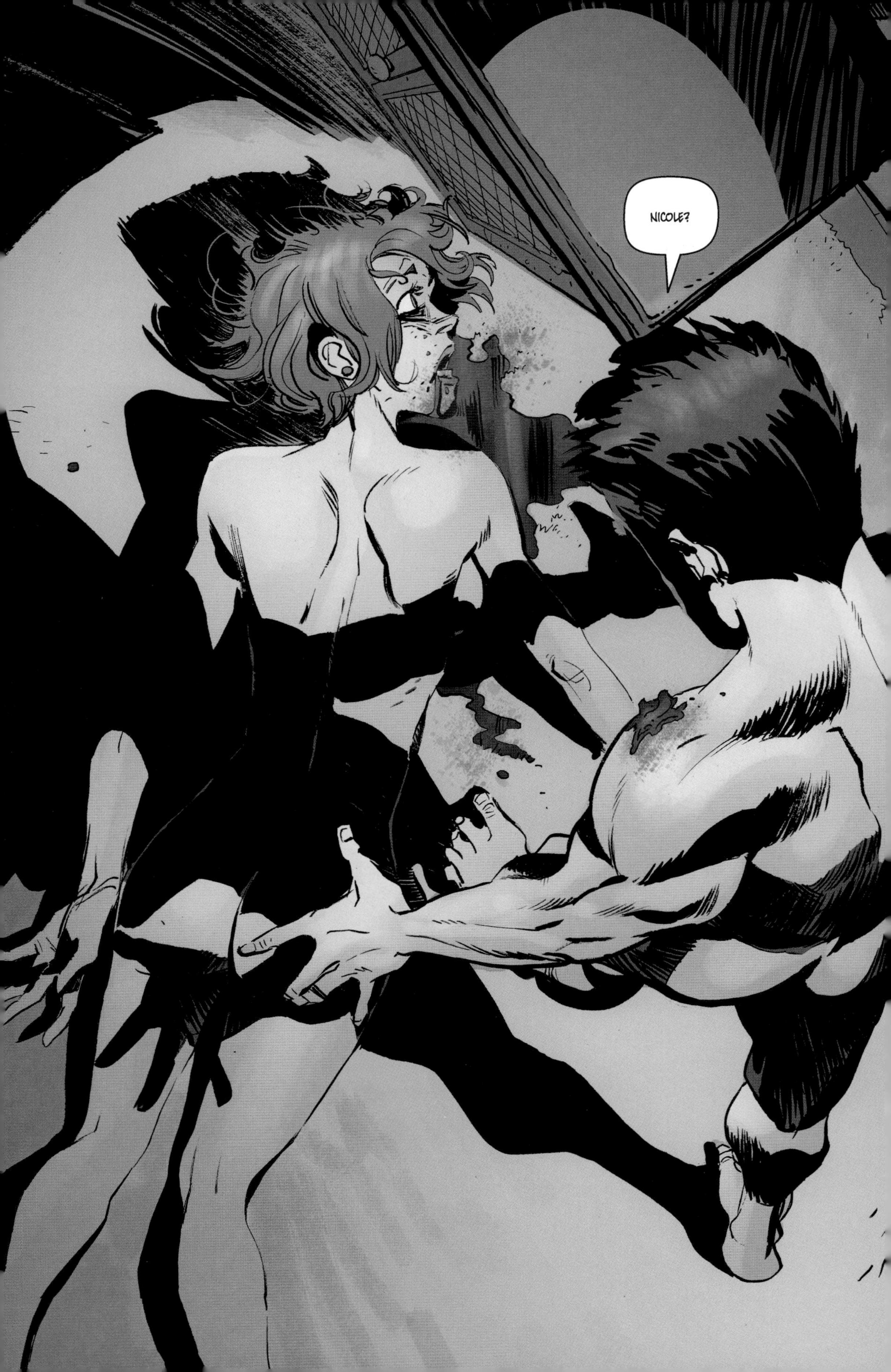
NICOLE?

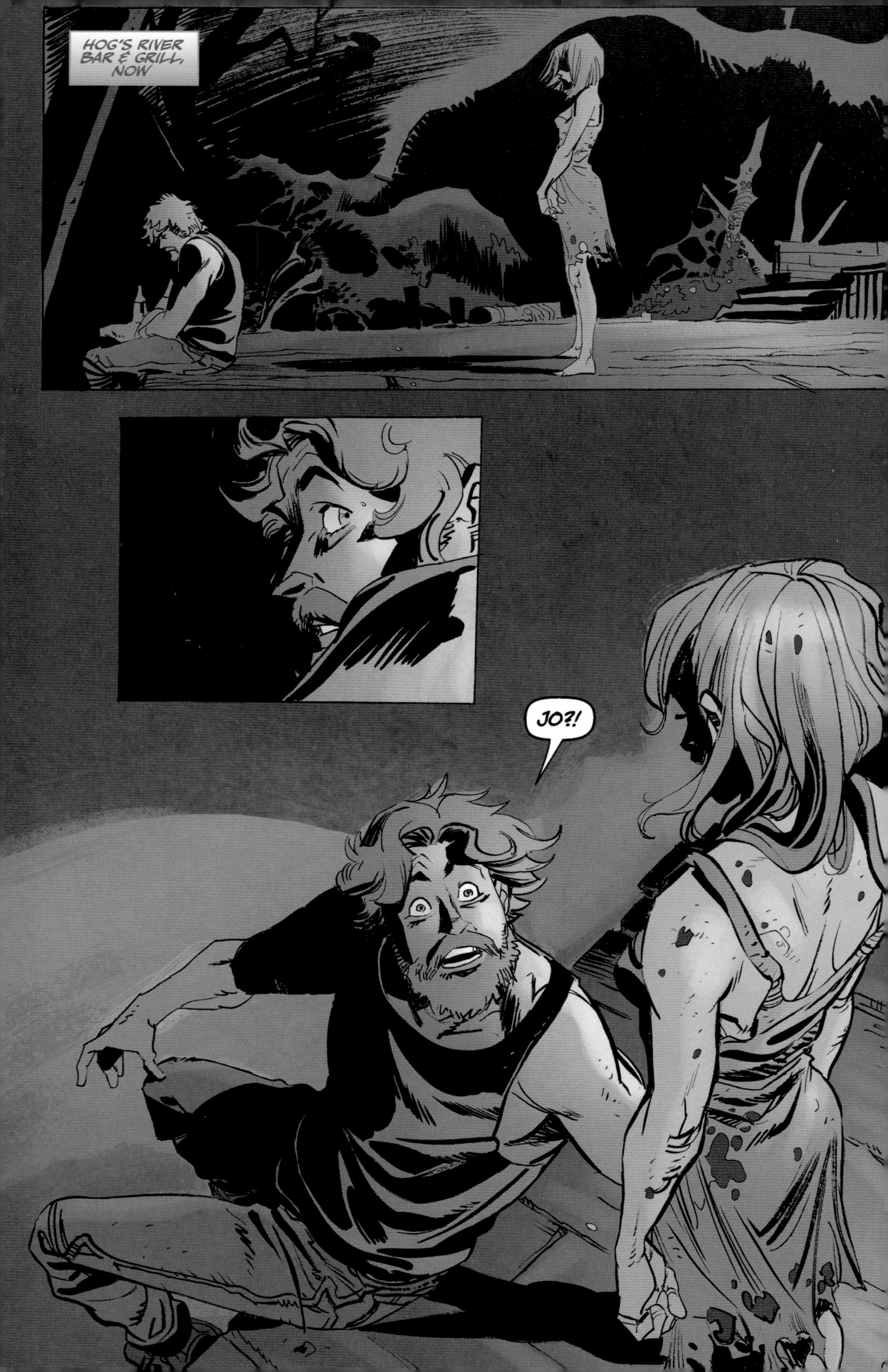
HOG'S RIVER BAR & GRILL, NOW
JO?!

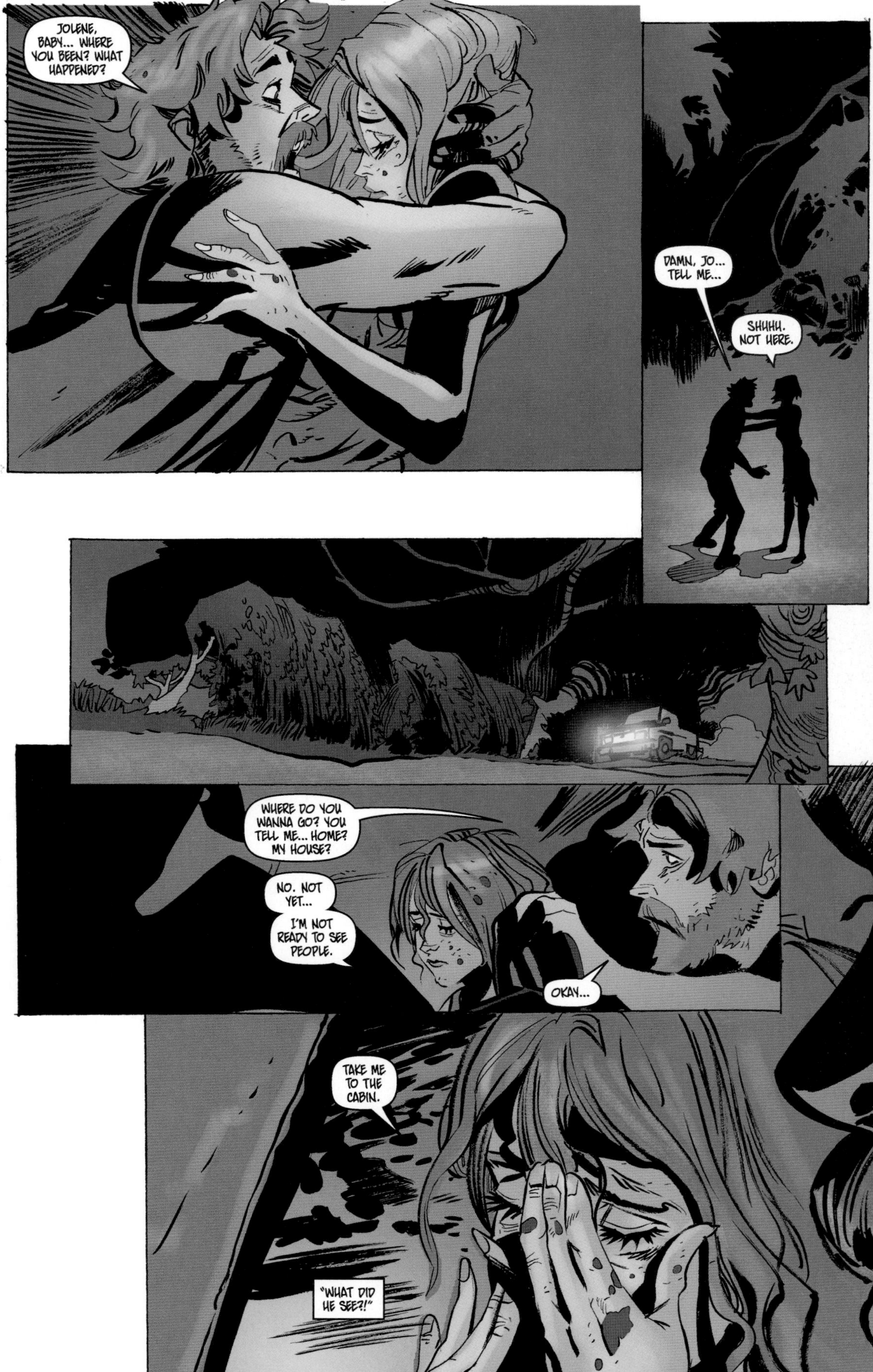
JOLENE, BABY... WHERE YOU BEEN? WHAT HAPPENED?
DAMN, JO... TELL ME...
SHHHH. NOT HERE.
WHERE DO YOU WANNA GO? YOU TELL ME... HOME? MY HOUSE?
NO. NOT YET...
I'M NOT READY TO SEE PEOPLE.
OKAY...
TAKE ME TO THE CABIN.
"WHAT DID HE SEE?!"

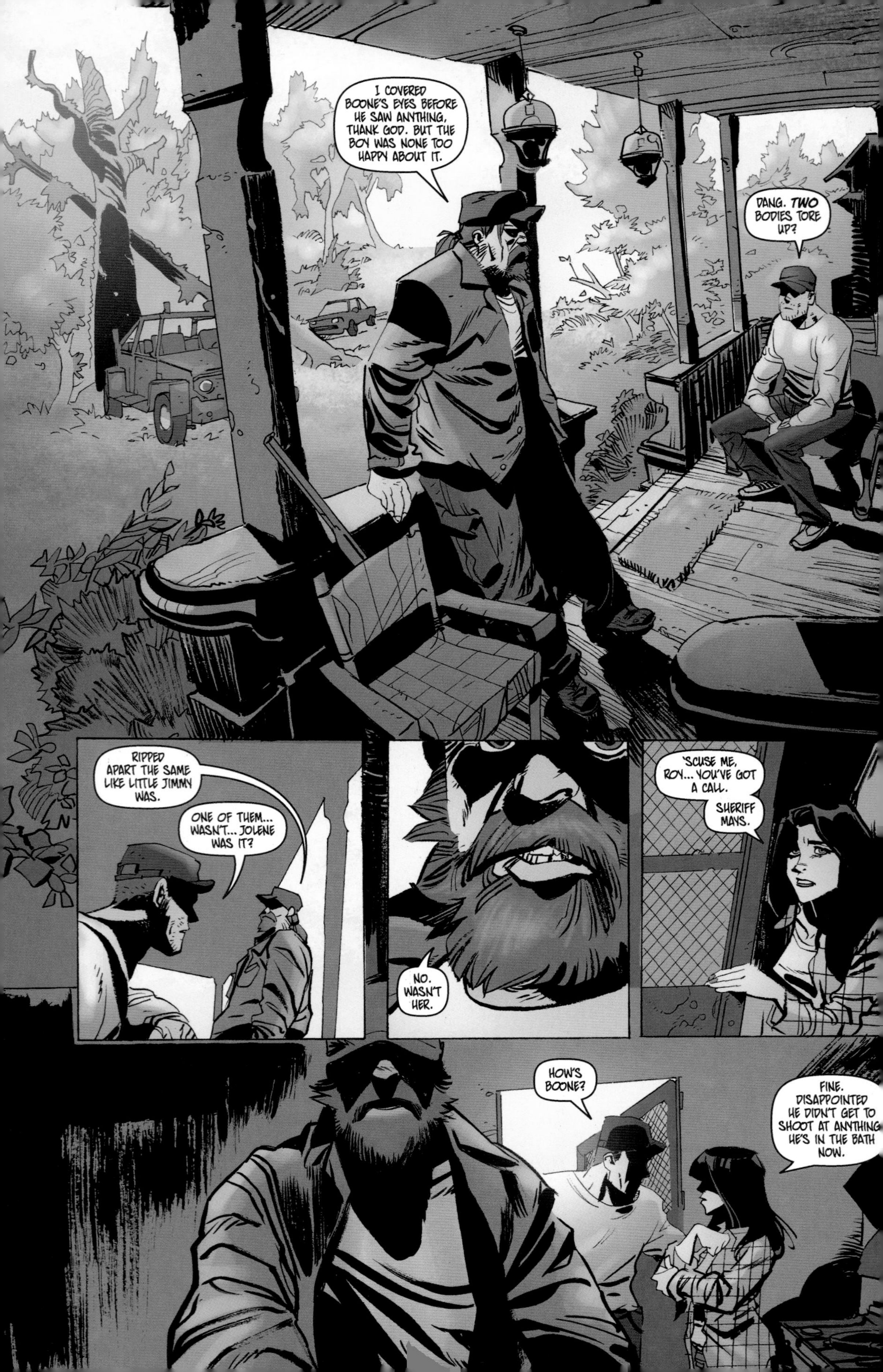
I COVERED BOONE'S EYES BEFORE HE SAW ANYTHING, THANK GOD. BUT THE BOY WAS NONE TOO HAPPY ABOUT IT.
DANG. TWO BODIES TORE UP?
RIPPED APART THE SAME LIKE LITTLE JIMMY WAS.
ONE OF THEM... WASN'T... JOLENE WAS IT?
NO. WASN'T HER.
'SCUSE ME, ROY... YOU'VE GOT A CALL.
SHERIFF MAYS.
HOW'S BOONE?
FINE. DISAPPOINTED HE DIDN'T GET TO SHOOT AT ANYTHING. HE'S IN THE BATH NOW.

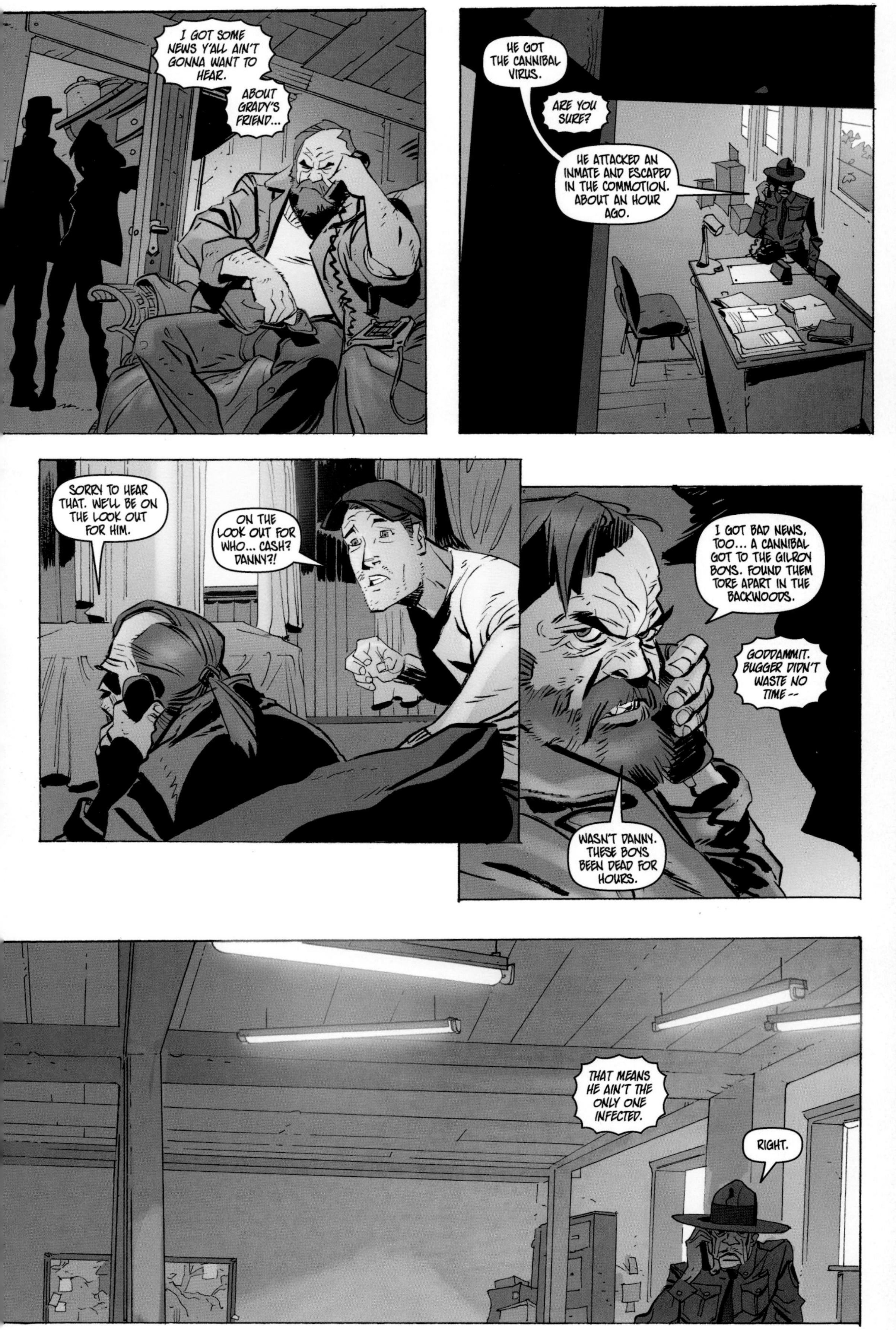
I GOT SOME NEWS Y'ALL AIN'T GONNA WANT TO HEAR.
ABOUT GRADY'S FRIEND...
HE GOT THE CANNIBAL VIRUS.
ARE YOU SURE?
HE ATTACKED AN INMATE AND ESCAPED IN THE COMMOTION. ABOUT AN HOUR AGO.
SORRY TO HEAR THAT. WE'LL BE ON THE LOOK OUT FOR HIM.
ON THE LOOK OUT FOR WHO... CASH? DANNY?!
I GOT BAD NEWS, TOO... A CANNIBAL GOT TO THE GILROY BOYS. FOUND THEM TORE APART IN THE BACKWOODS.
GODDAMMIT. BUGGER DIDN'T WASTE NO TIME --
WASN'T DANNY. THESE BOYS BEEN DEAD FOR HOURS.
THAT MEANS HE AIN'T THE ONLY ONE INFECTED.
RIGHT.

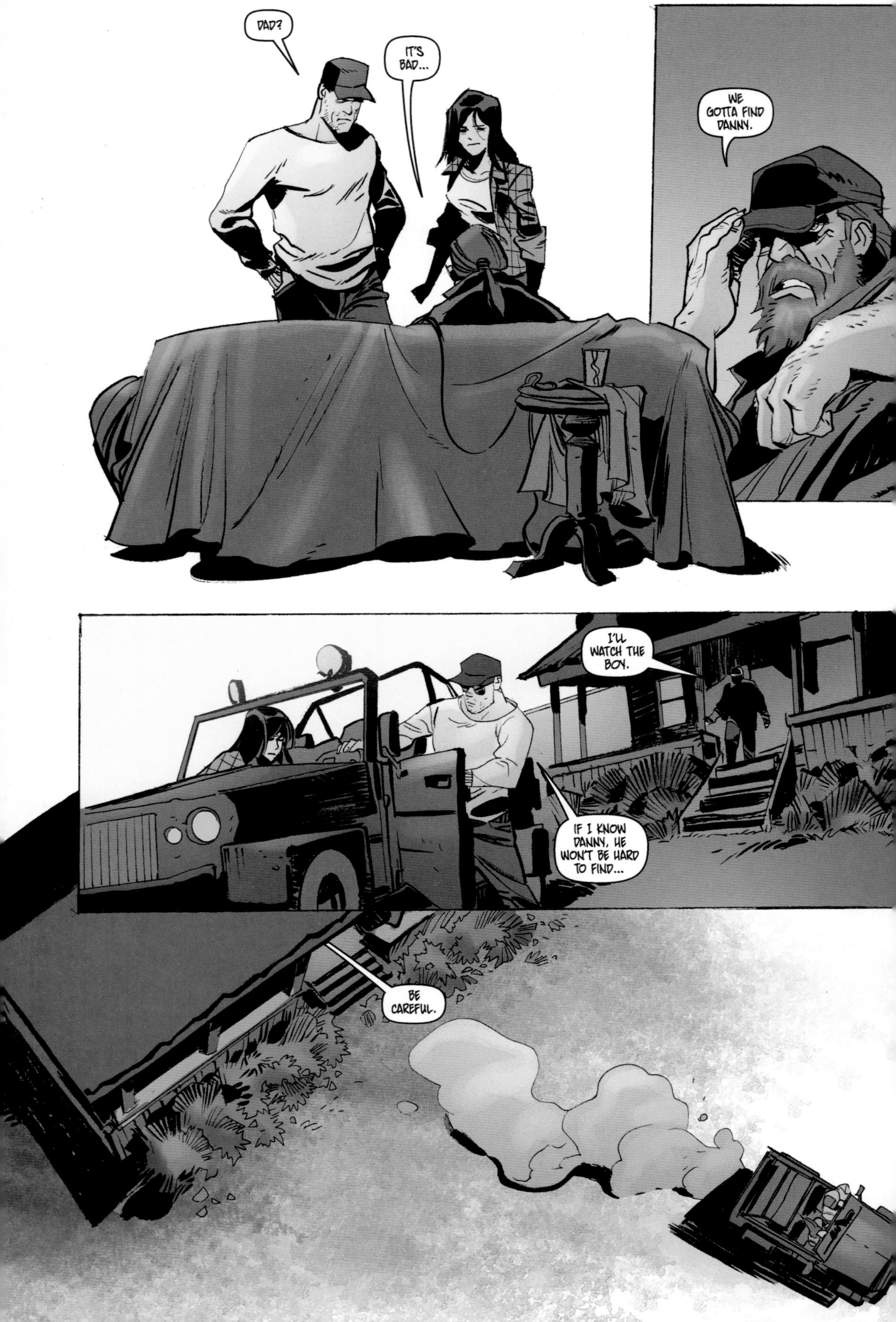
DAD?
IT'S BAD...
WE GOTTA FIND DANNY.
I'LL WATCH THE BOY.
IF I KNOW DANNY, HE WON'T BE HARD TO FIND...
BE CAREFUL.

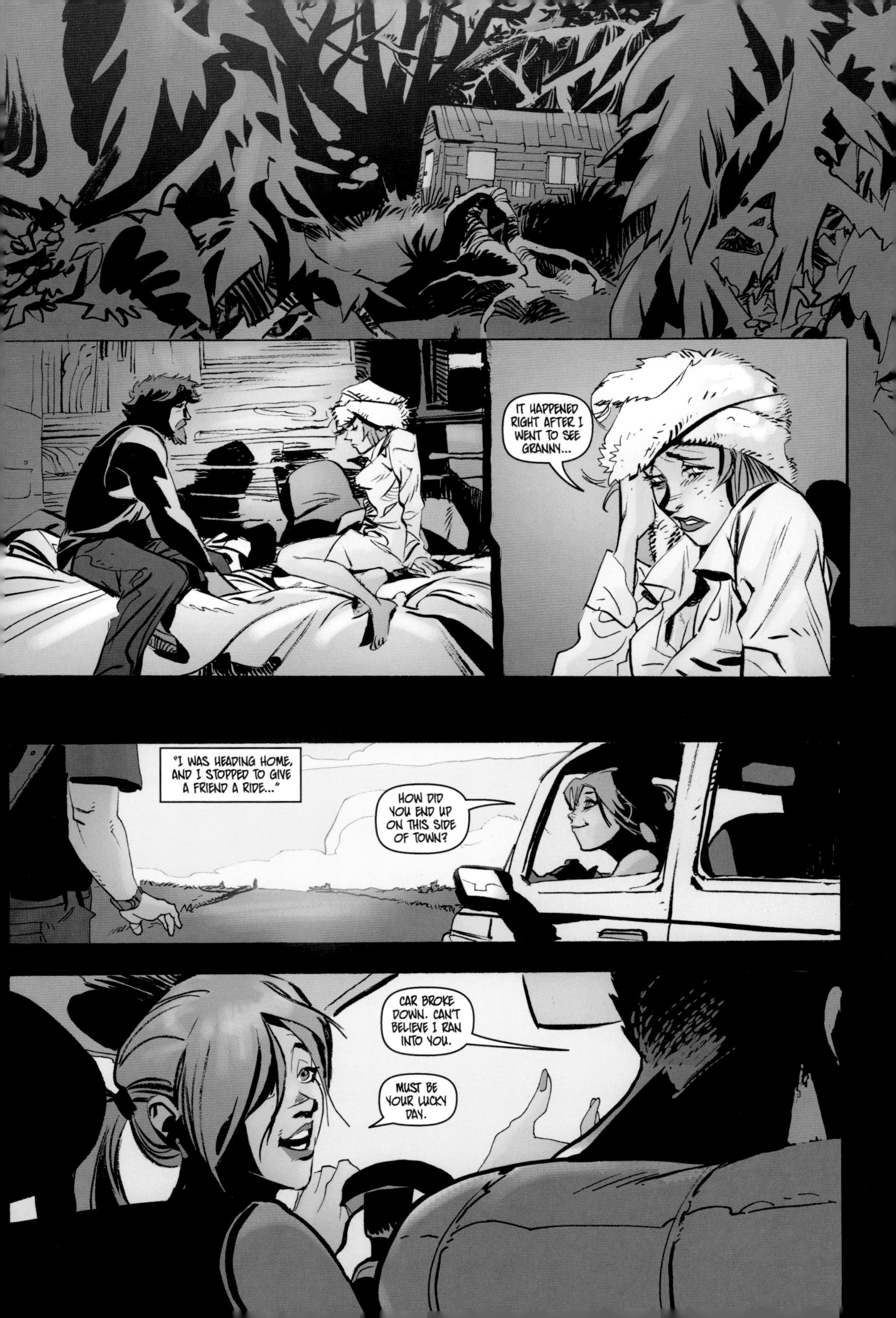
IT HAPPENED RIGHT AFTER I WENT TO SEE GRANNY...
"I WAS HEADING HOME, AND I STOPPED TO GIVE A FRIEND A RIDE..."
HOW DID YOU END UP ON THIS SIDE OF TOWN?
CAR BROKE DOWN. CAN'T BELIEVE I RAN INTO YOU.
MUST BE YOUR LUCKY DAY.

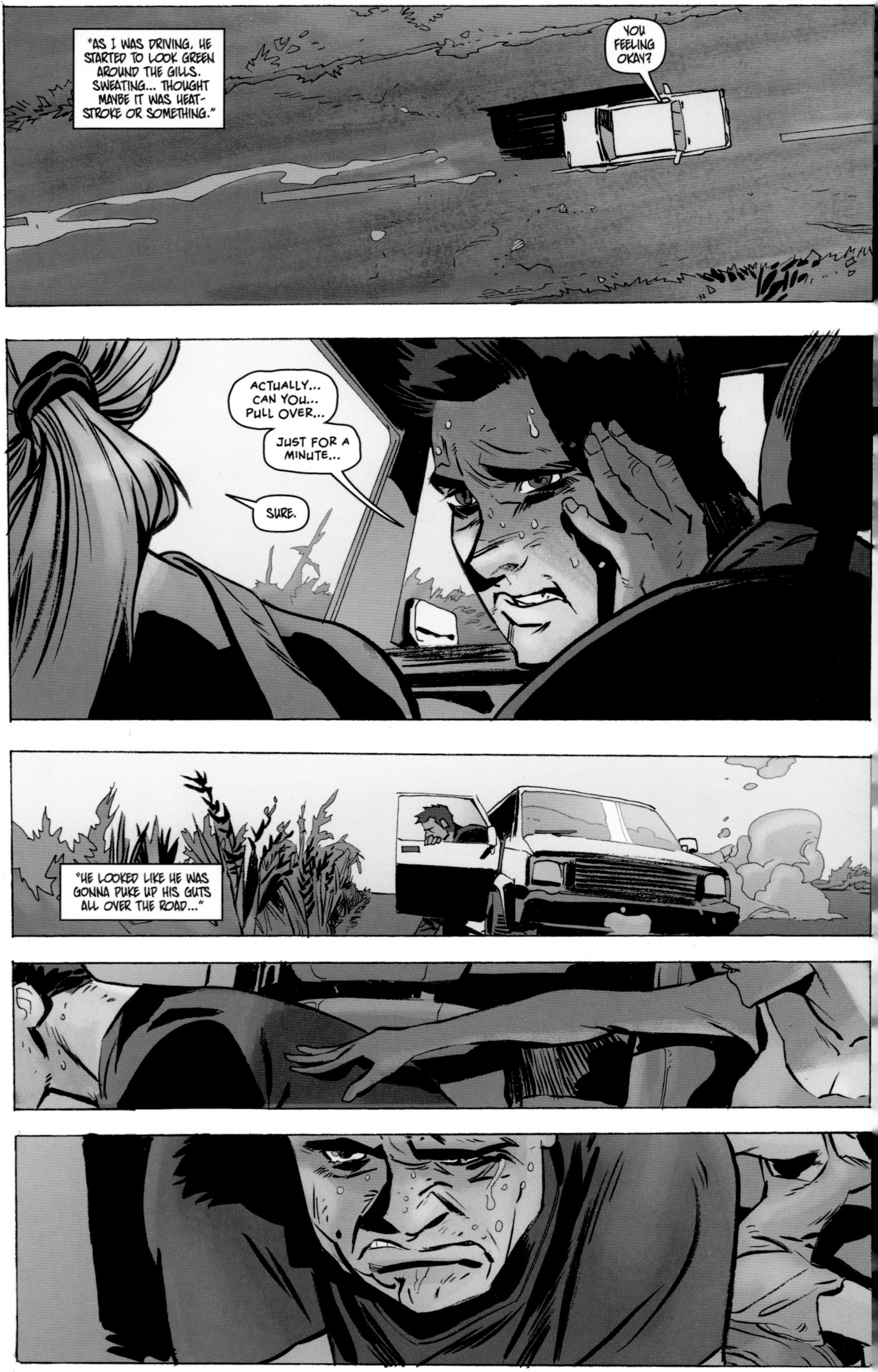
"AS I WAS DRIVING, HE STARTED TO LOOK GREEN AROUND THE GILLS. SWEATING... THOUGHT MAYBE IT WAS HEAT-STROKE OR SOMETHING."
YOU FEELING OKAY?
ACTUALLY... CAN YOU... PULL OVER...
JUST FOR A MINUTE...
SURE.
"HE LOOKED LIKE HE WAS GONNA PUKE UP HIS GUTS ALL OVER THE ROAD..."

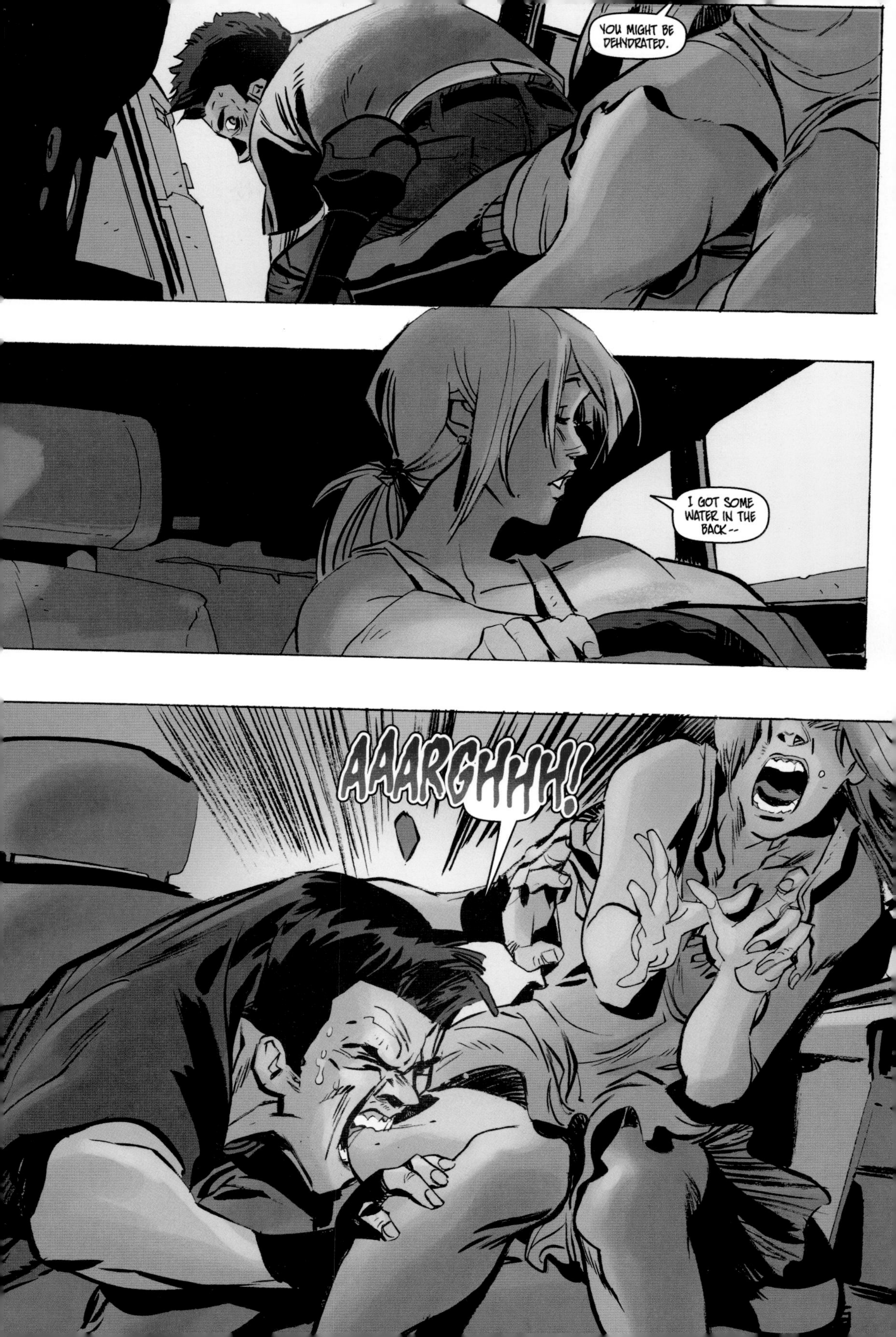
YOU MIGHT BE DEHYDRATED.
I GOT SOME WATER IN THE BACK--
AAARGHHH!

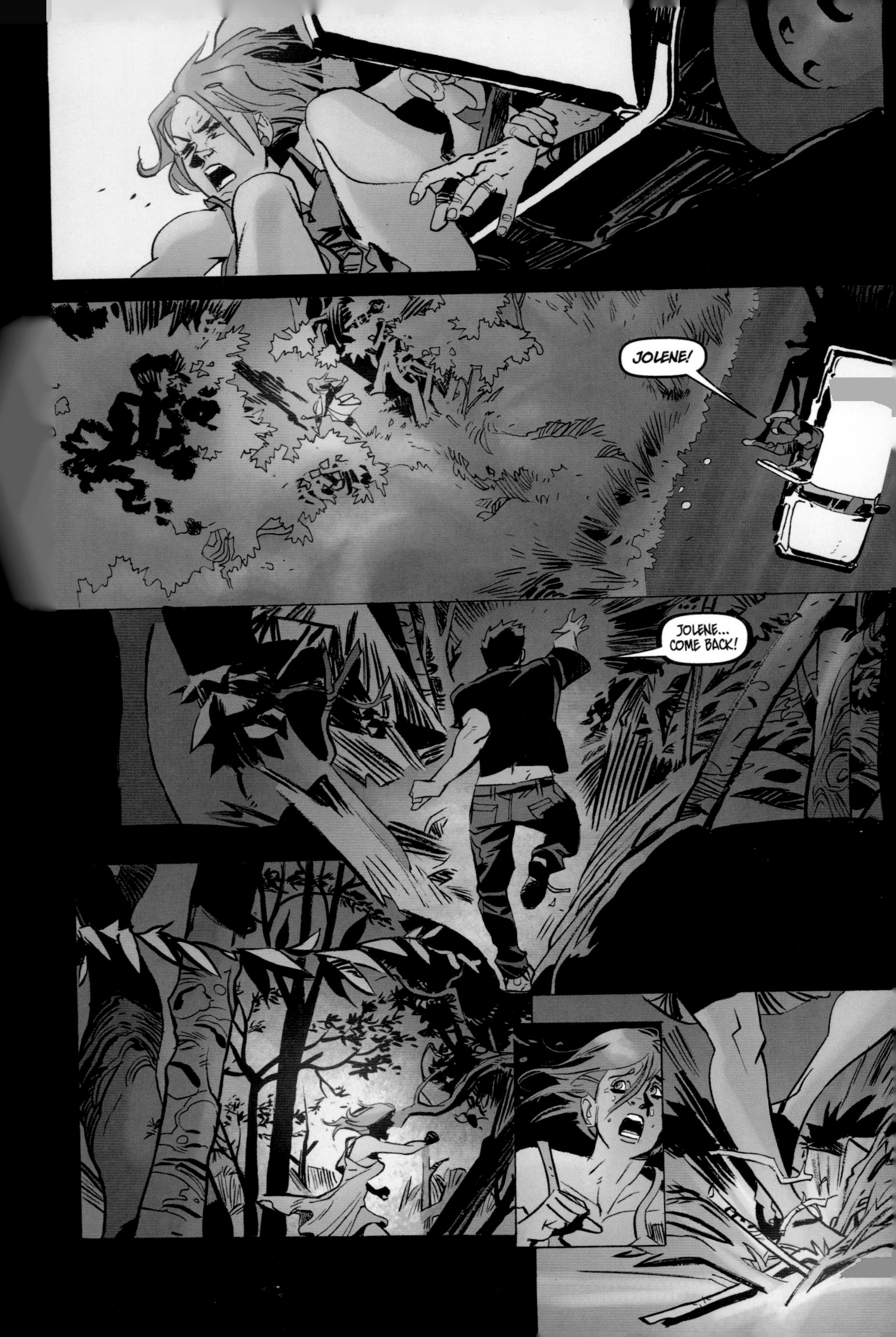
JOLENE!
JOLENE... COME BACK!

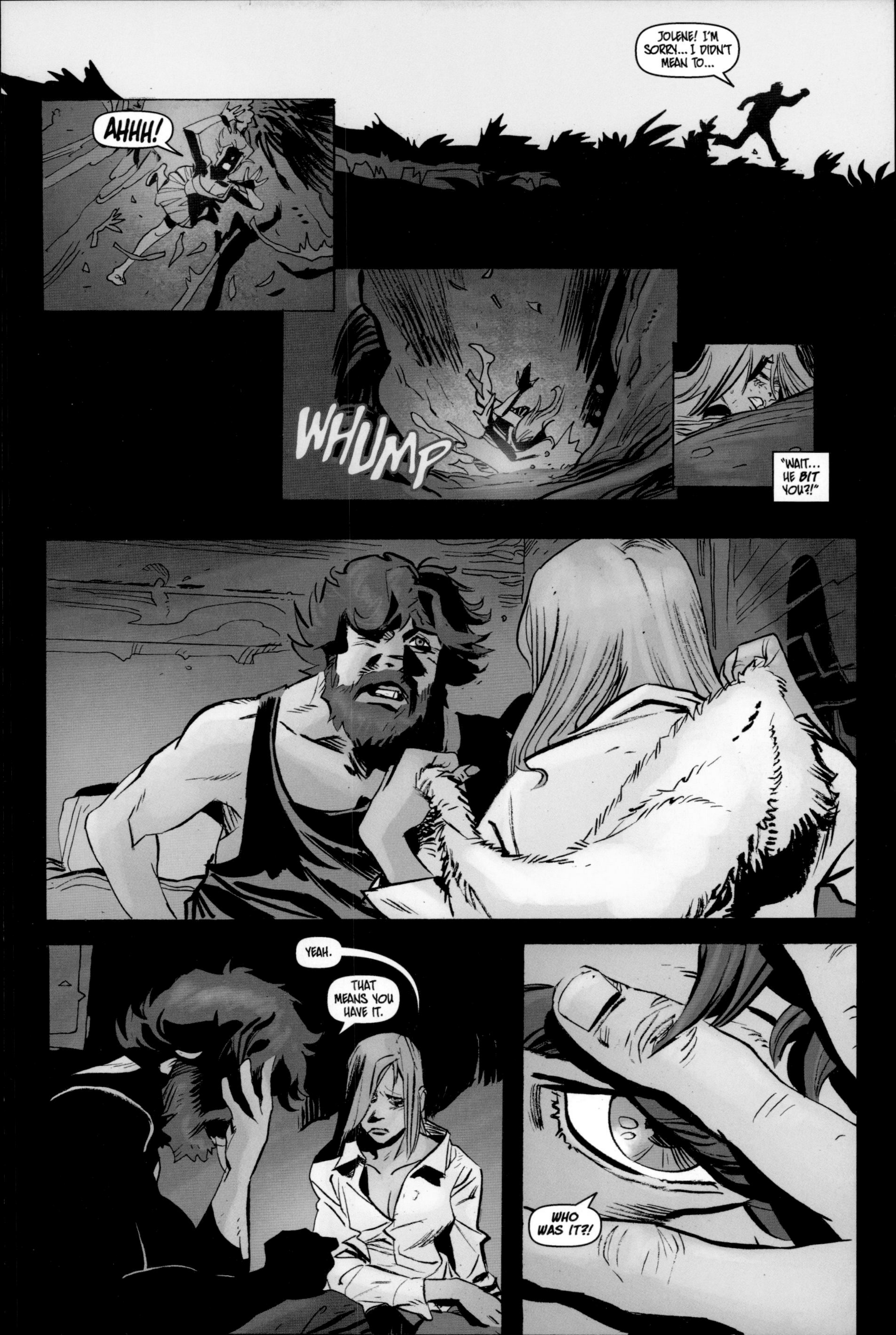
JOLENE! I'M SORRY... I DIDN'T MEAN TO...
AHHH!
WHUMP
"WAIT... HE BIT YOU?!"
YEAH.
THAT MEANS YOU HAVE IT.
WHO WAS IT?!

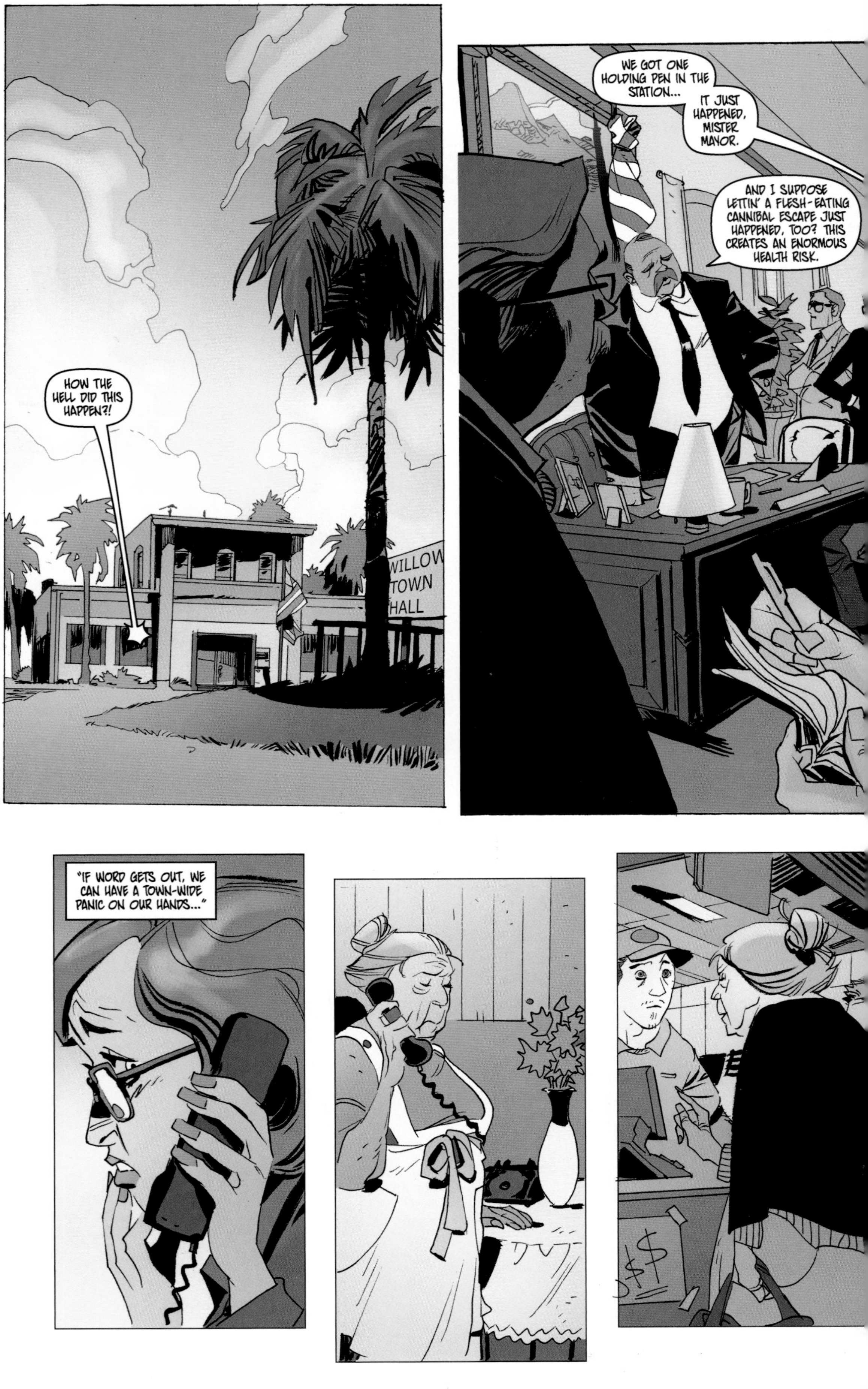

HOW THE HELL DID THIS HAPPEN?!
WILLOW TOWN HALL
WE GOT ONE HOLDING PEN IN THE STATION...
IT JUST HAPPENED, MISTER MAYOR.
AND I SUPPOSE LETTIN' A FLESH-EATING CANNIBAL ESCAPE JUST HAPPENED, TOO? THIS CREATES AN ENORMOUS HEALTH RISK.
"IF WORD GETS OUT, WE CAN HAVE A TOWN-WIDE PANIC ON OUR HANDS..."

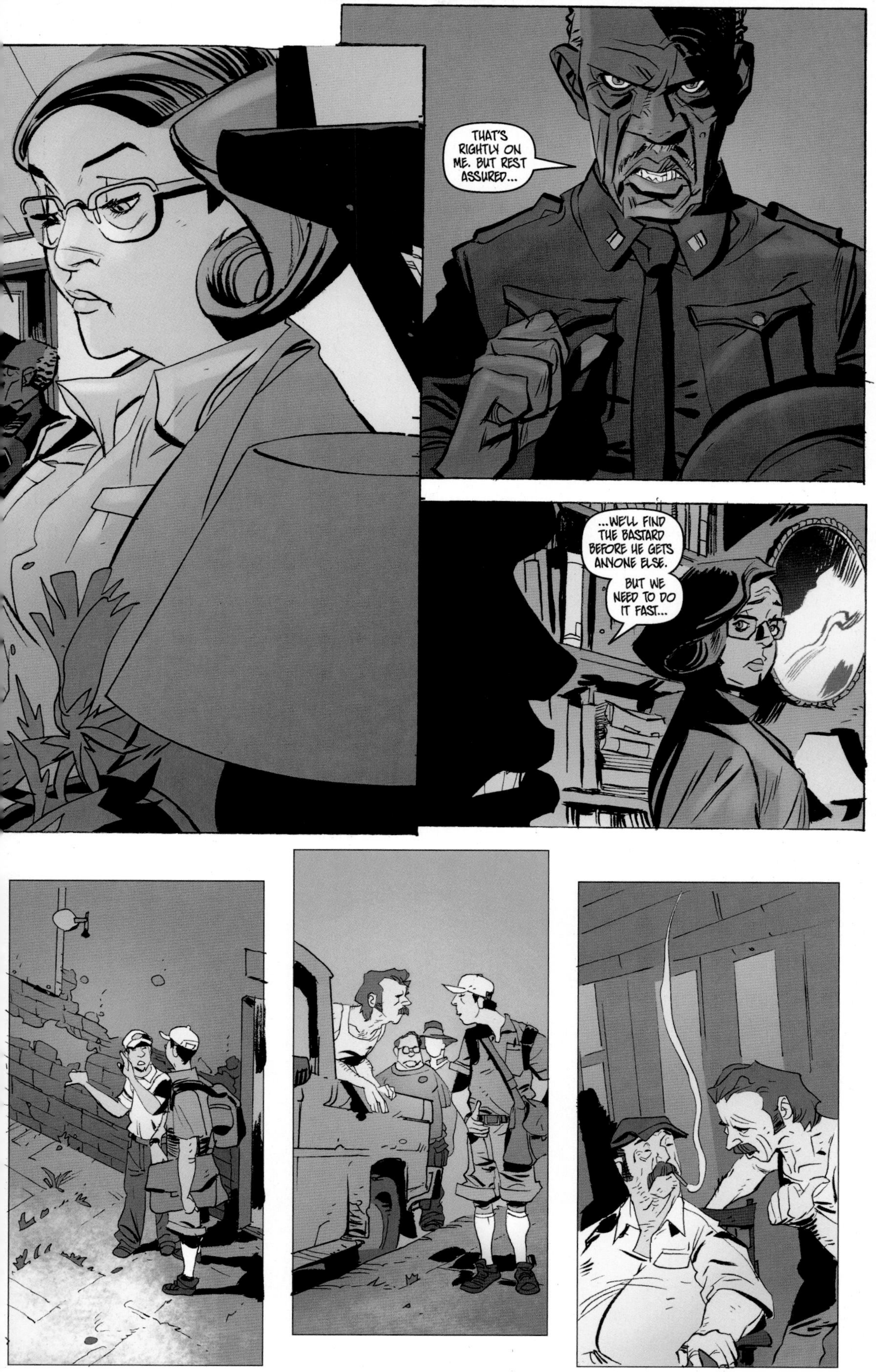
THAT'S RIGHTLY ON ME. BUT REST ASSURED...
...WE'LL FIND THE BASTARD BEFORE HE GETS ANYONE ELSE.
BUT WE NEED TO DO IT FAST...

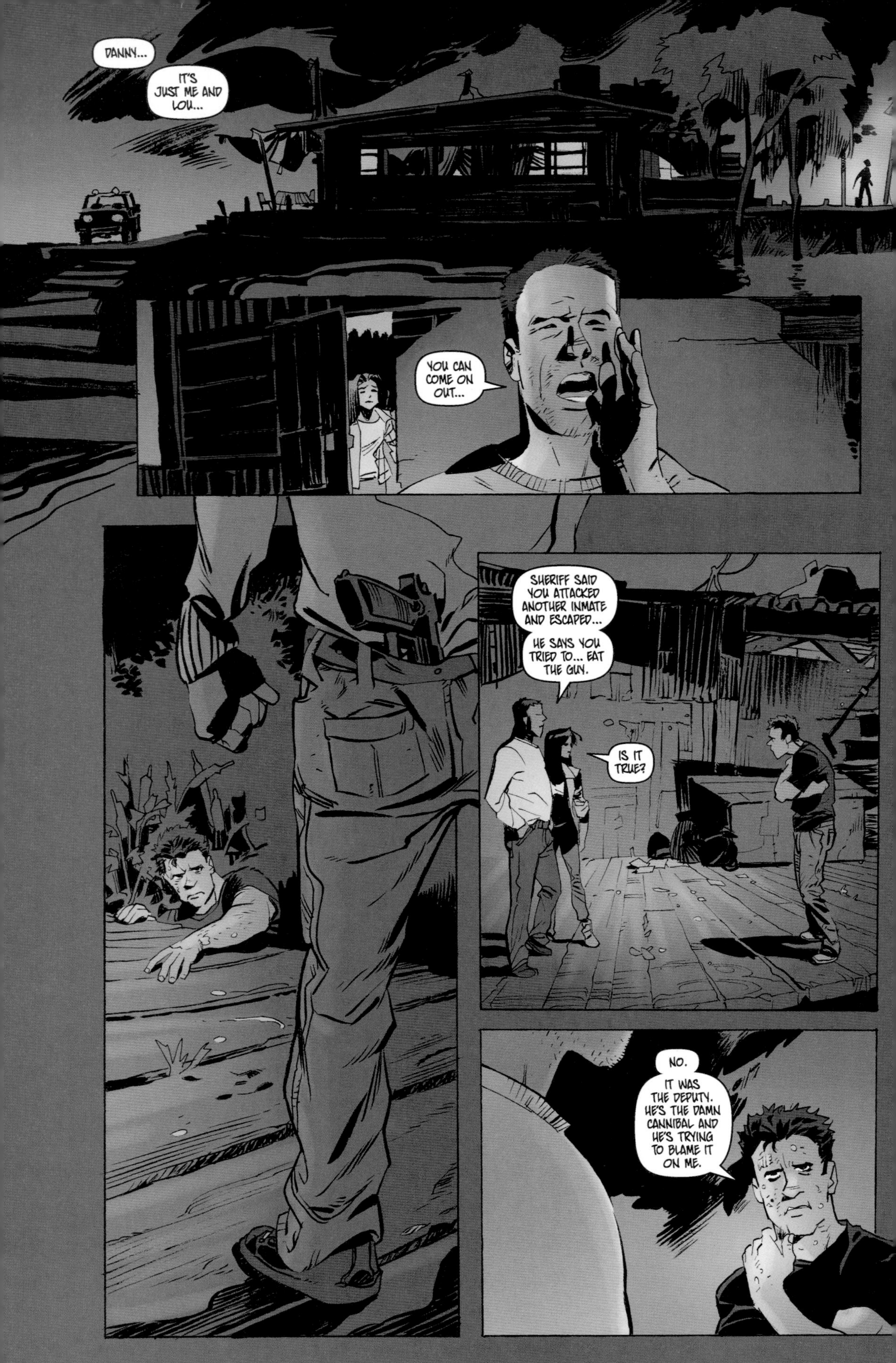
DANNY...
IT'S JUST ME AND LOU...
YOU CAN COME ON OUT...
SHERIFF SAID YOU ATTACKED ANOTHER INMATE AND ESCAPED...
HE SAYS YOU TRIED TO... EAT THE GUY.
IS IT TRUE?
NO.
IT WAS THE DEPUTY. HE'S THE DAMN CANNIBAL AND HE'S TRYING TO BLAME IT ON ME.

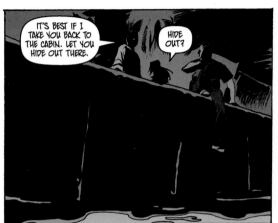

IT'S BEST IF I TAKE YOU BACK TO THE CABIN. LET YOU HIDE OUT THERE.

HIDE OUT?

IF SHERIFF IS GOING AROUND TELLING PEOPLE DANNY'S A CANNIBAL, FOLKS ARE GONNA COME LOOKING FOR HIM.

DAMN MOB MENTALITY GOT ME LOCKED UP IN THE FIRST PLACE.

RIGHT. THEY'LL BE LOOKING FOR SOMEONE TO BLAME.

YOU'RE ACTING LIKE THERE'S GONNA BE SOME HUNT FOR A *WILD BEAST* OR SOMETHING.

THERE IS. I KNOW WHAT THESE FOLKS ARE CAPABLE OF...

I WAS ONE OF THEM.

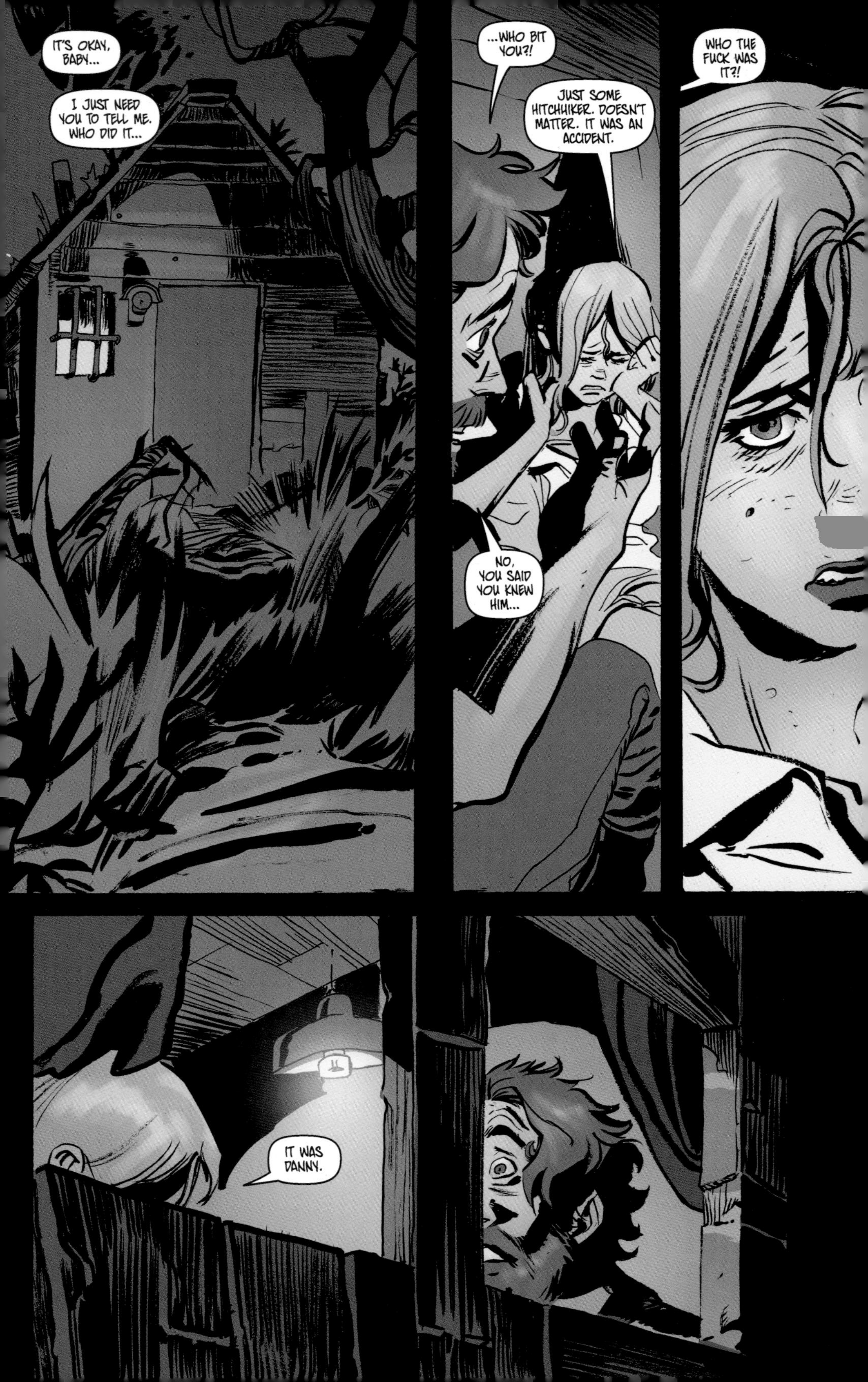
IT'S OKAY, BABY...
I JUST NEED YOU TO TELL ME. WHO DID IT...
...WHO BIT YOU?!
JUST SOME HITCHHIKER. DOESN'T MATTER. IT WAS AN ACCIDENT.
NO, YOU SAID YOU KNEW HIM...
WHO THE FUCK WAS IT?!
IT WAS DANNY.

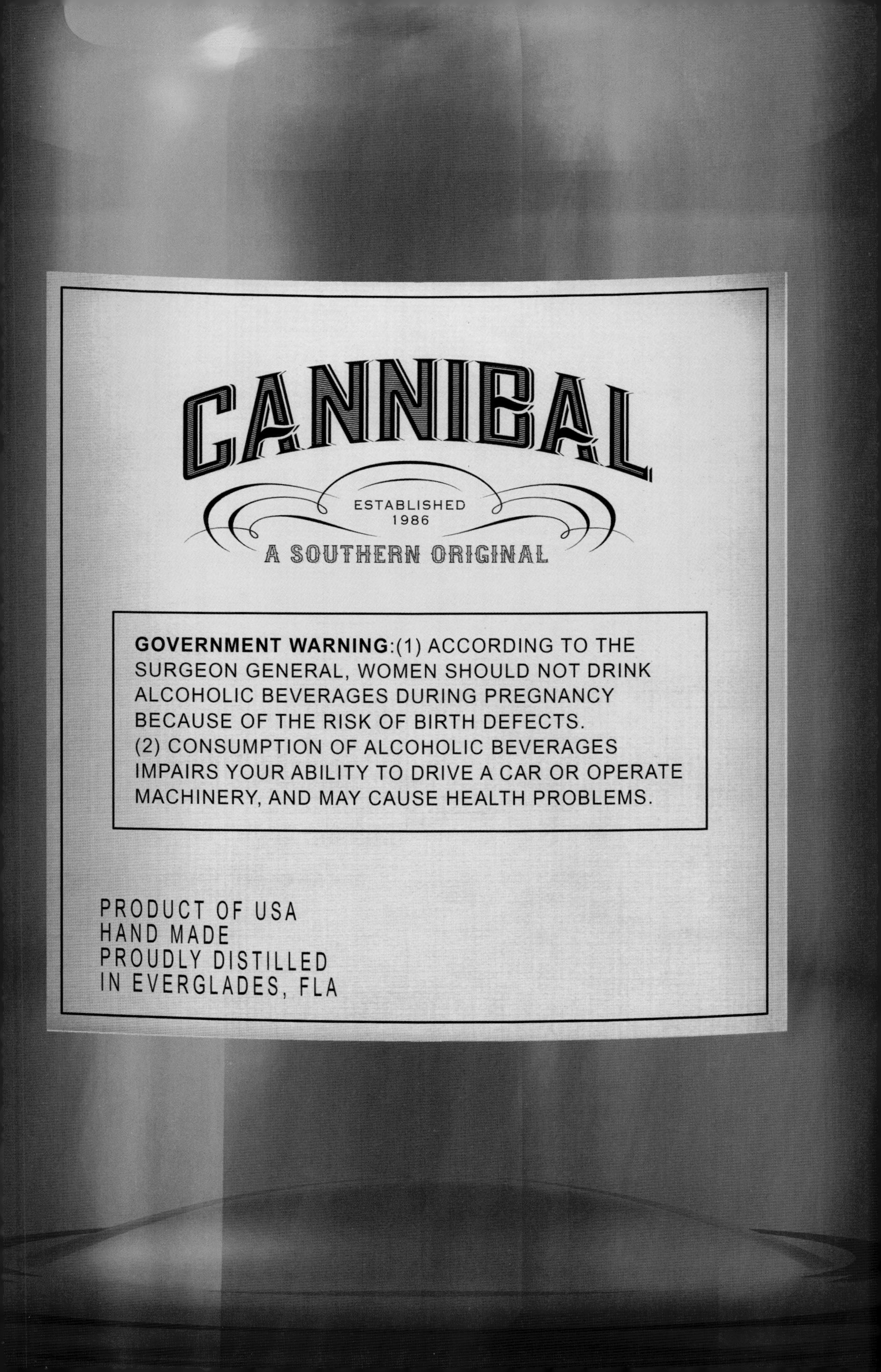
CANNIBAL
ESTABLISHED
1986
A SOUTHERN ORIGINAL
GOVERNMENT WARNING:(1) ACCORDING TO THE SURGEON GENERAL, WOMEN SHOULD NOT DRINK ALCOHOLIC BEVERAGES DURING PREGNANCY BECAUSE OF THE RISK OF BIRTH DEFECTS.
(2) CONSUMPTION OF ALCOHOLIC BEVERAGES IMPAIRS YOUR ABILITY TO DRIVE A CAR OR OPERATE MACHINERY, AND MAY CAUSE HEALTH PROBLEMS.
PRODUCT OF USA
HAND MADE
PROUDLY DISTILLED
IN EVERGLADES, FLA

ESTABLISHED
1986

A SOUTHERN ORIGINAL

CANNIBAL

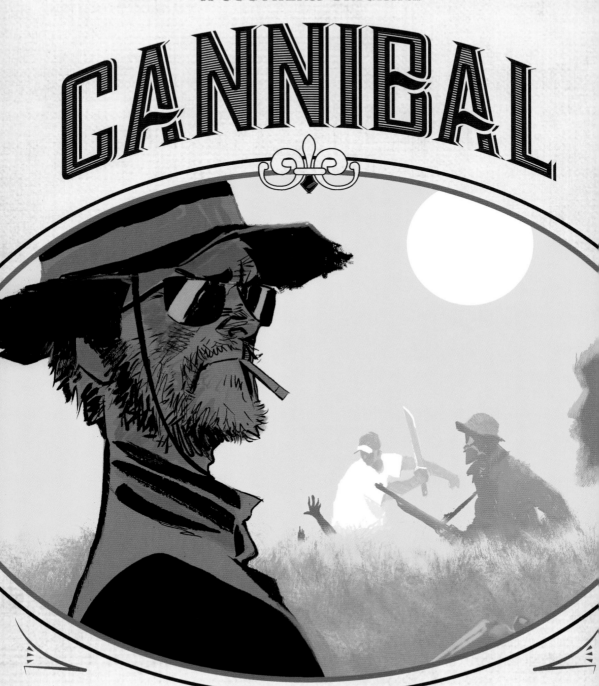

70 cl e

40% Vol.

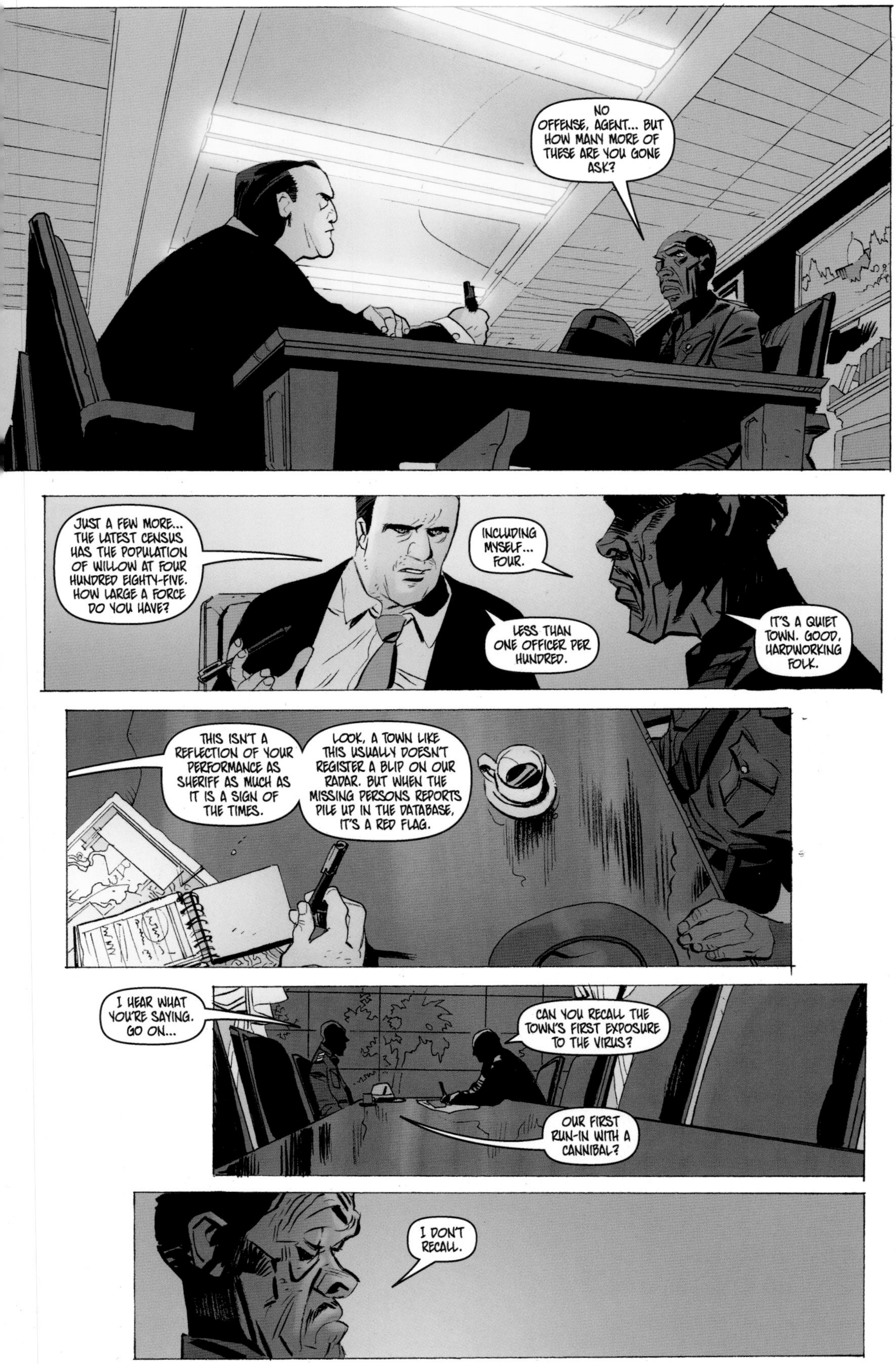
NO OFFENSE, AGENT... BUT HOW MANY MORE OF THESE ARE YOU GONE ASK?
JUST A FEW MORE... THE LATEST CENSUS HAS THE POPULATION OF WILLOW AT FOUR HUNDRED EIGHTY-FIVE. HOW LARGE A FORCE DO YOU HAVE?
INCLUDING MYSELF... FOUR.
LESS THAN ONE OFFICER PER HUNDRED.
IT'S A QUIET TOWN. GOOD, HARDWORKING FOLK.
THIS ISN'T A REFLECTION OF YOUR PERFORMANCE AS SHERIFF AS MUCH AS IT IS A SIGN OF THE TIMES.
LOOK, A TOWN LIKE THIS USUALLY DOESN'T REGISTER A BLIP ON OUR RADAR. BUT WHEN THE MISSING PERSONS REPORTS PILE UP IN THE DATABASE, IT'S A RED FLAG.
I HEAR WHAT YOU'RE SAYING. GO ON...
CAN YOU RECALL THE TOWN'S FIRST EXPOSURE TO THE VIRUS?
OUR FIRST RUN-IN WITH A CANNIBAL?
I DON'T RECALL.

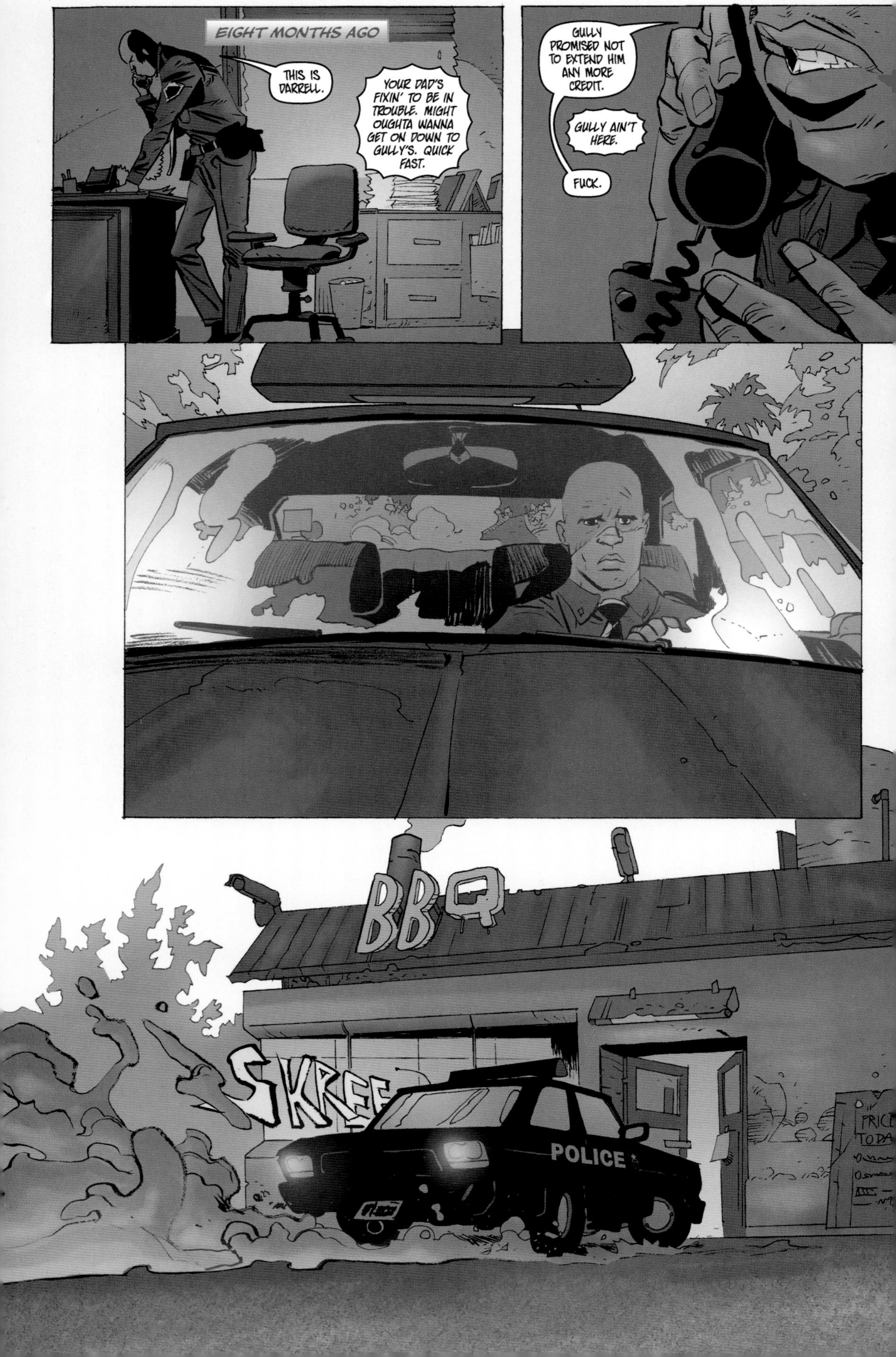
EIGHT MONTHS AGO
THIS IS DARRELL.
YOUR DAD'S FIXIN' TO BE IN TROUBLE. MIGHT OUGHTA WANNA GET ON DOWN TO GULLY'S. QUICK FAST.
GULLY PROMISED NOT TO EXTEND HIM ANY MORE CREDIT.
GULLY AIN'T HERE.
FUCK.
BBQ
SKREE
POLICE

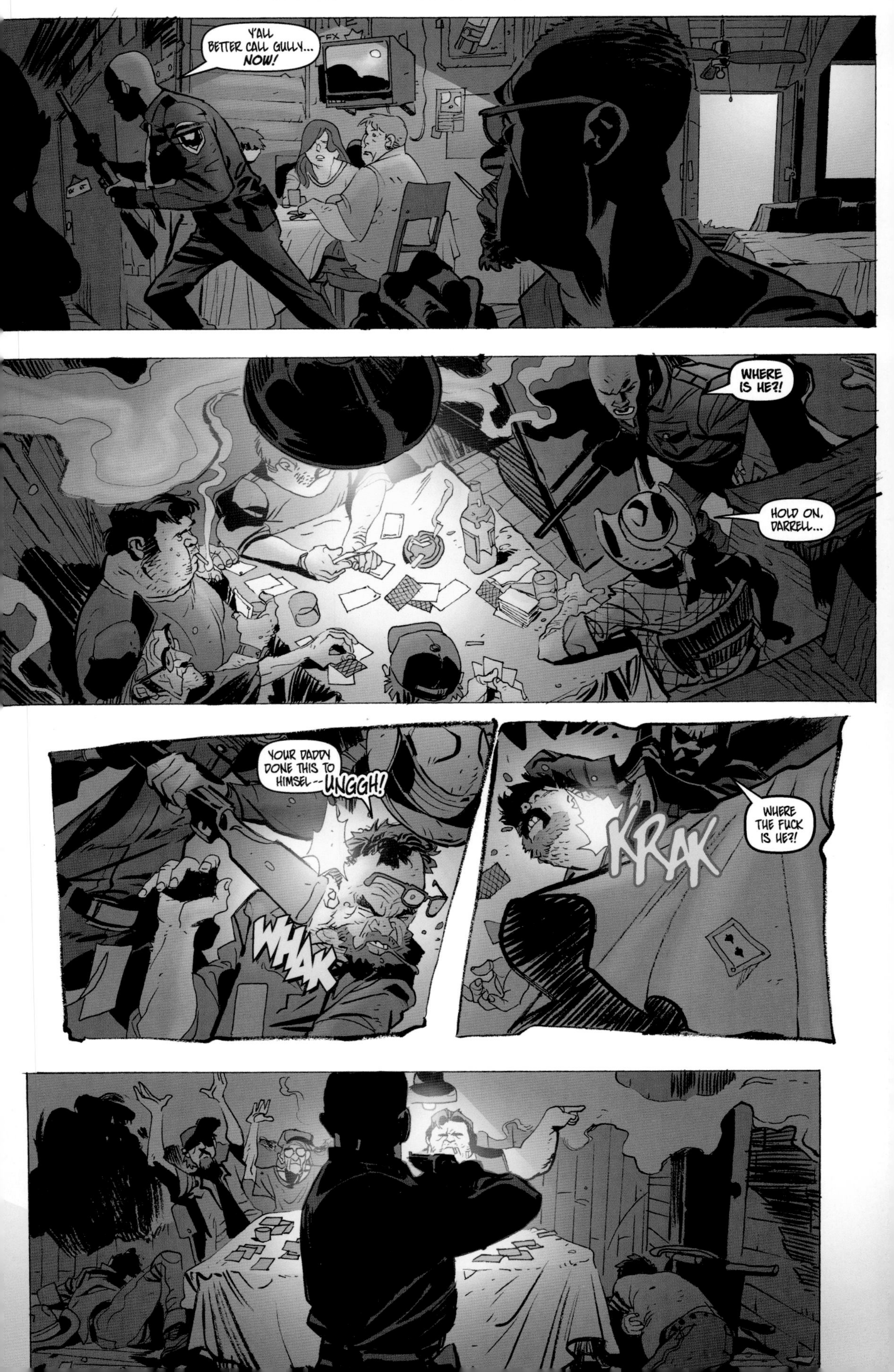
Y'ALL BETTER CALL GULLY... NOW!
WHERE IS HE?!
HOLD ON, DARRELL...
YOUR DADDY DONE THIS TO HIMSEL-- UNGGH!
WHAK
KRAK
WHERE THE FUCK IS HE?!

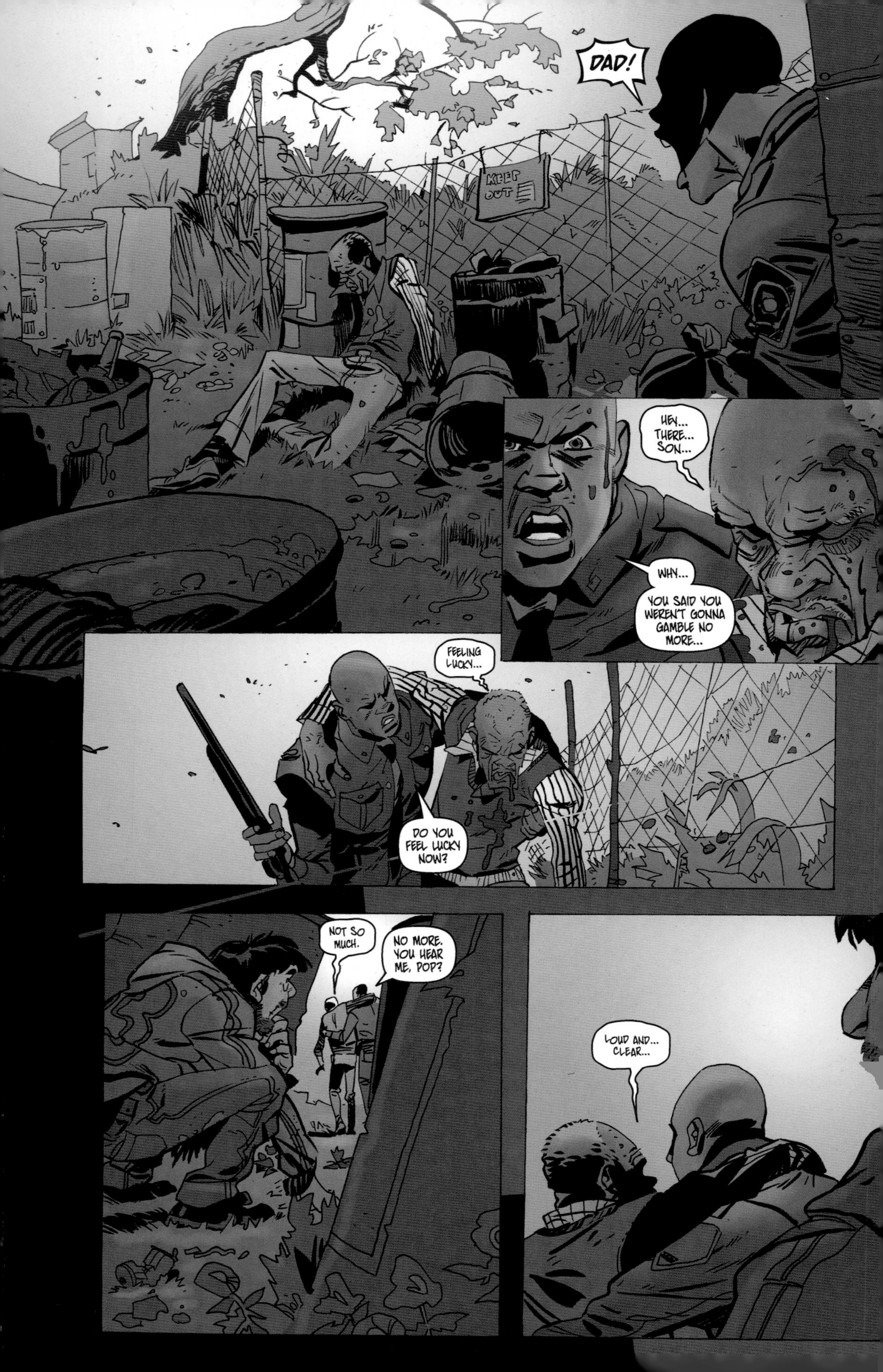
DAD!
HEY... THERE... SON...
WHY...
YOU SAID YOU WEREN'T GONNA GAMBLE NO MORE...
FEELING LUCKY...
DO YOU FEEL LUCKY NOW?
NOT SO MUCH.
NO MORE. YOU HEAR ME, POP?
LOUD AND... CLEAR...

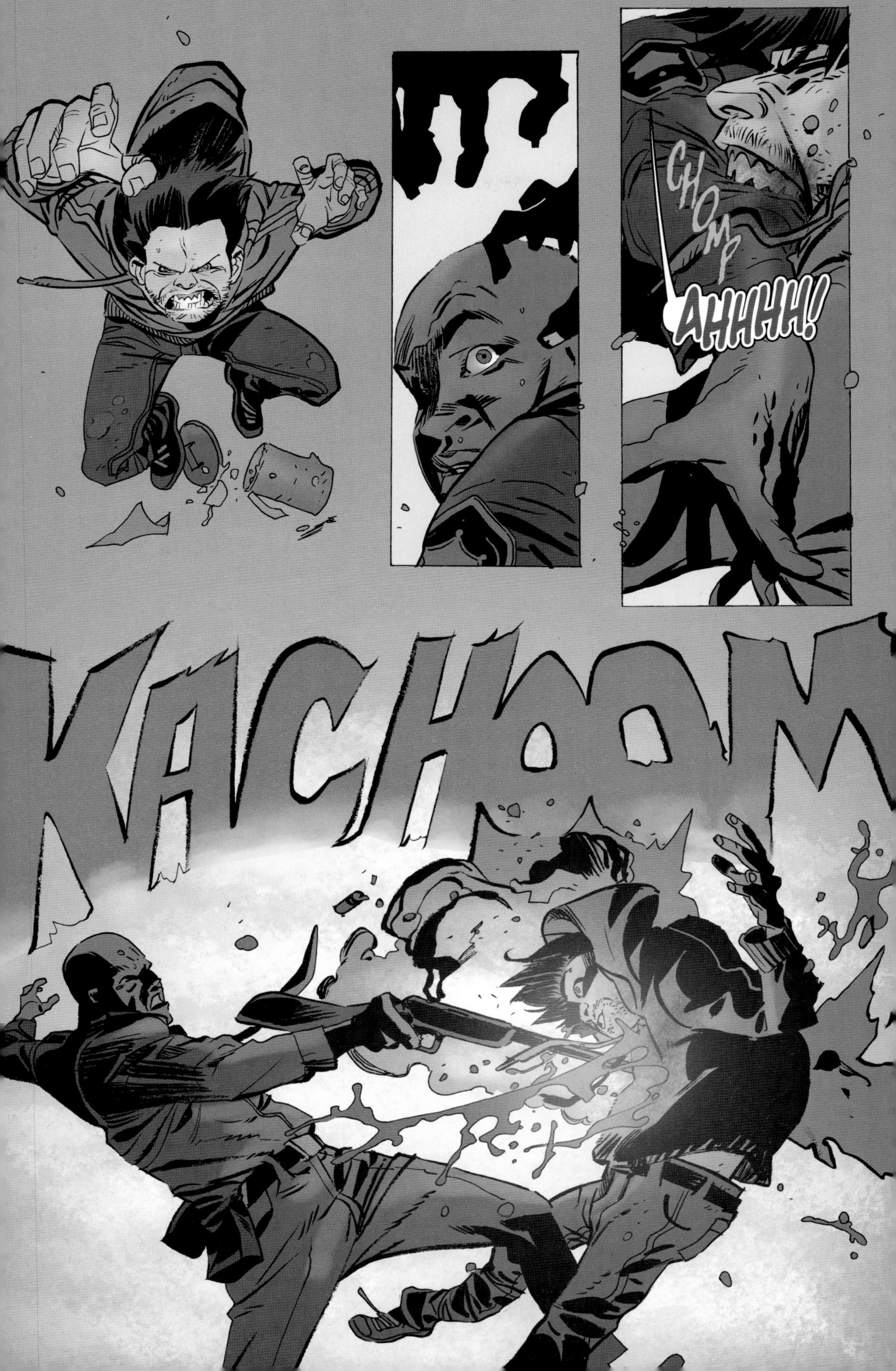
CHOMP
AHHHH!
KACHOOM

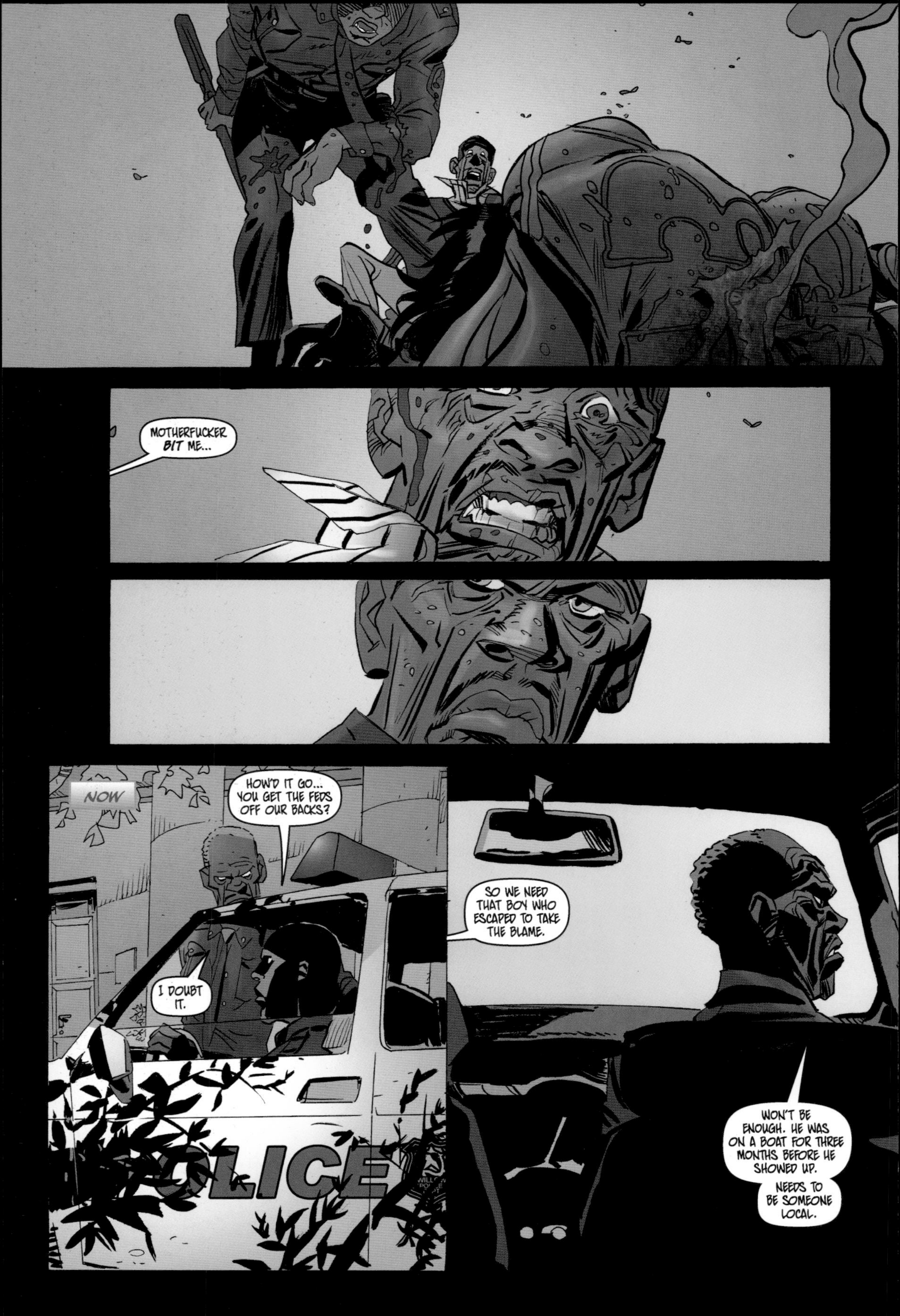
MOTHERFUCKER BIT ME...
NOW
HOW'D IT GO... YOU GET THE FEDS OFF OUR BACKS?
I DOUBT IT.
POLICE
SO WE NEED THAT BOY WHO ESCAPED TO TAKE THE BLAME.
WON'T BE ENOUGH. HE WAS ON A BOAT FOR THREE MONTHS BEFORE HE SHOWED UP.
NEEDS TO BE SOMEONE LOCAL.

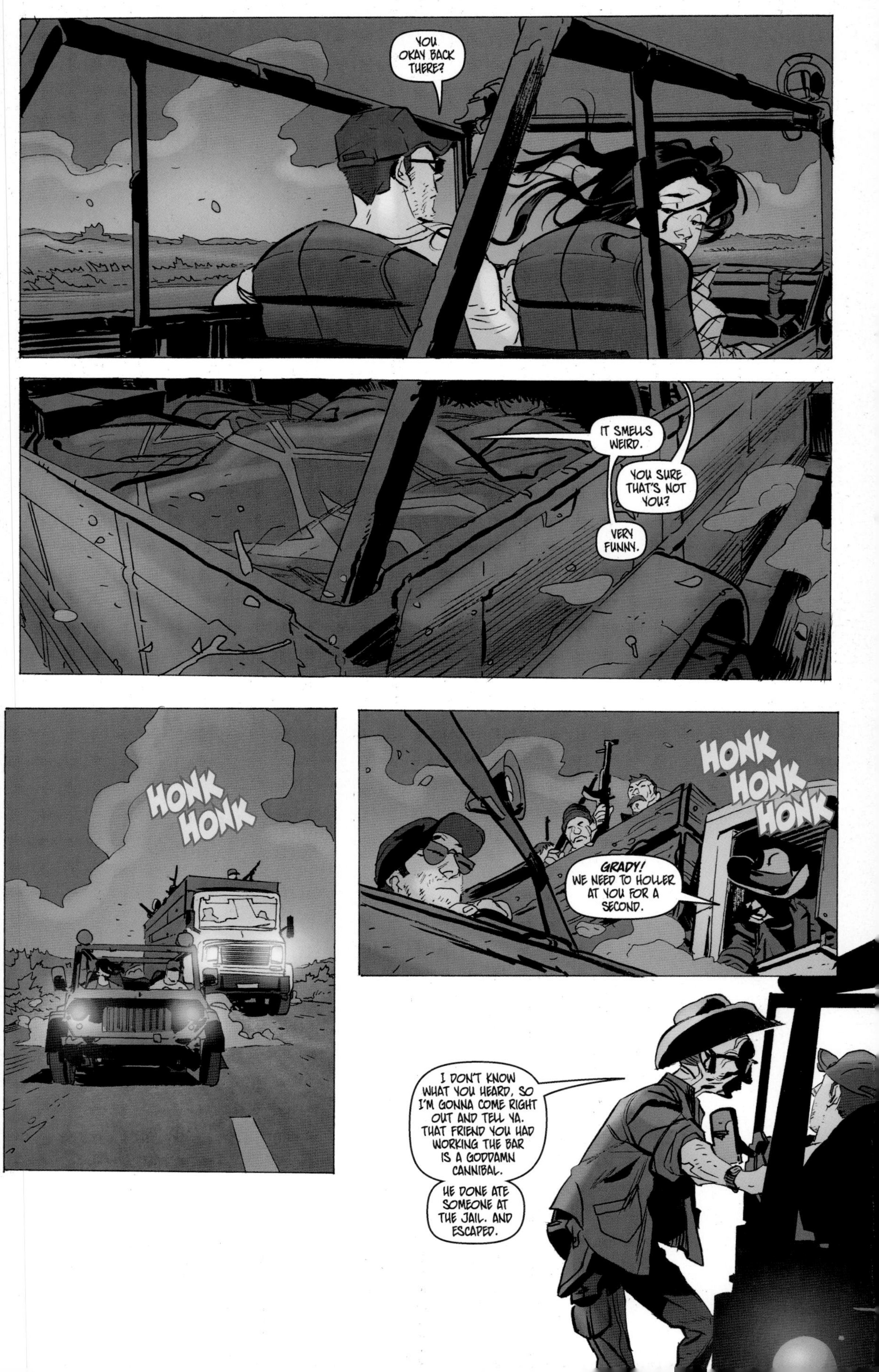

YOU OKAY BACK THERE?
IT SMELLS WEIRD.
YOU SURE THAT'S NOT YOU?
VERY FUNNY.
HONK HONK
HONK HONK HONK
GRADY! WE NEED TO HOLLER AT YOU FOR A SECOND.
I DON'T KNOW WHAT YOU HEARD, SO I'M GONNA COME RIGHT OUT AND TELL YA. THAT FRIEND YOU HAD WORKING THE BAR IS A GODDAMN CANNIBAL.
HE DONE ATE SOMEONE AT THE JAIL. AND ESCAPED.

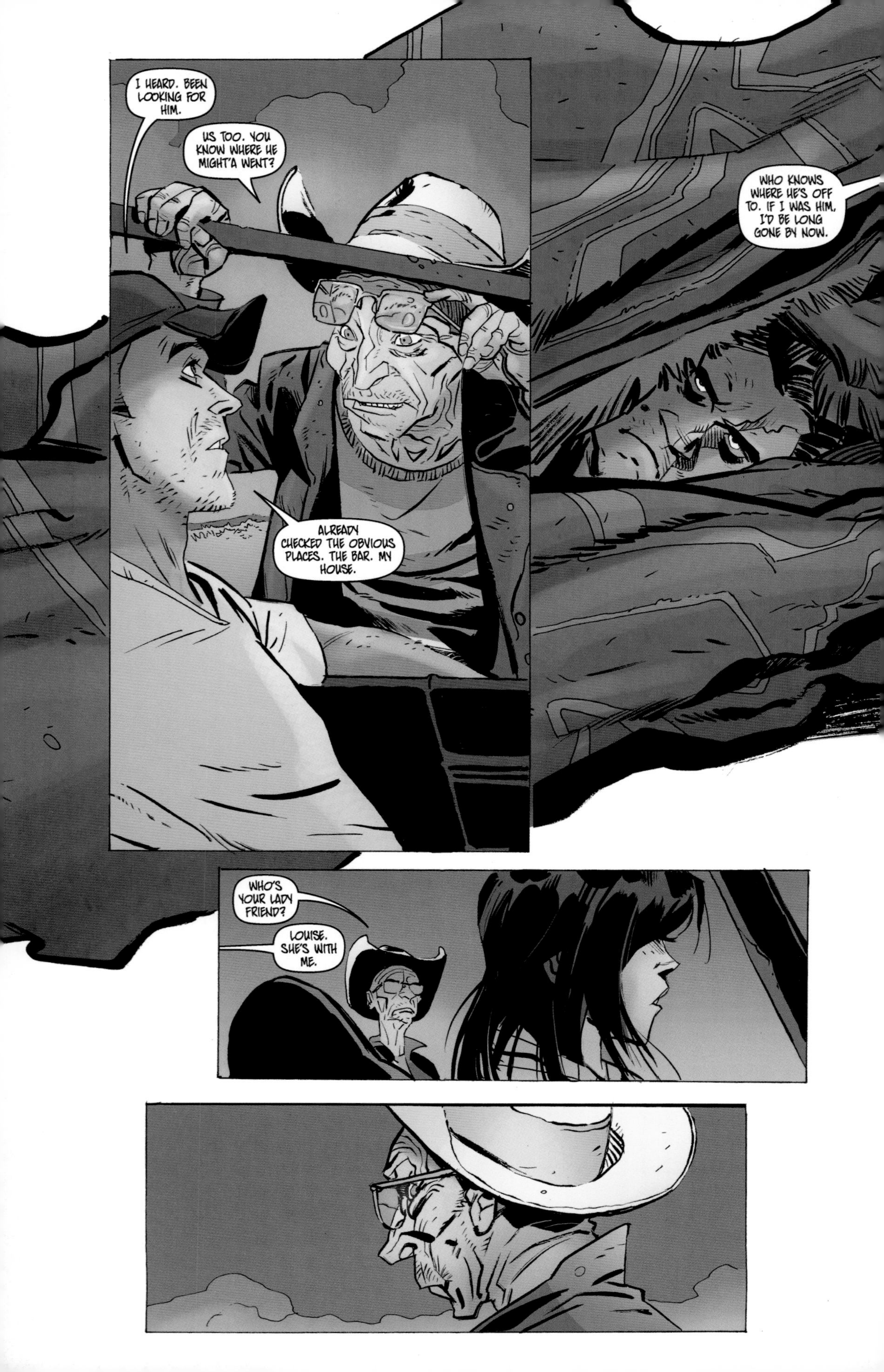
I HEARD. BEEN LOOKING FOR HIM.
US TOO. YOU KNOW WHERE HE MIGHT'A WENT?
ALREADY CHECKED THE OBVIOUS PLACES. THE BAR. MY HOUSE.
WHO KNOWS WHERE HE'S OFF TO. IF I WAS HIM, I'D BE LONG GONE BY NOW.
WHO'S YOUR LADY FRIEND?
LOUISE. SHE'S WITH ME.

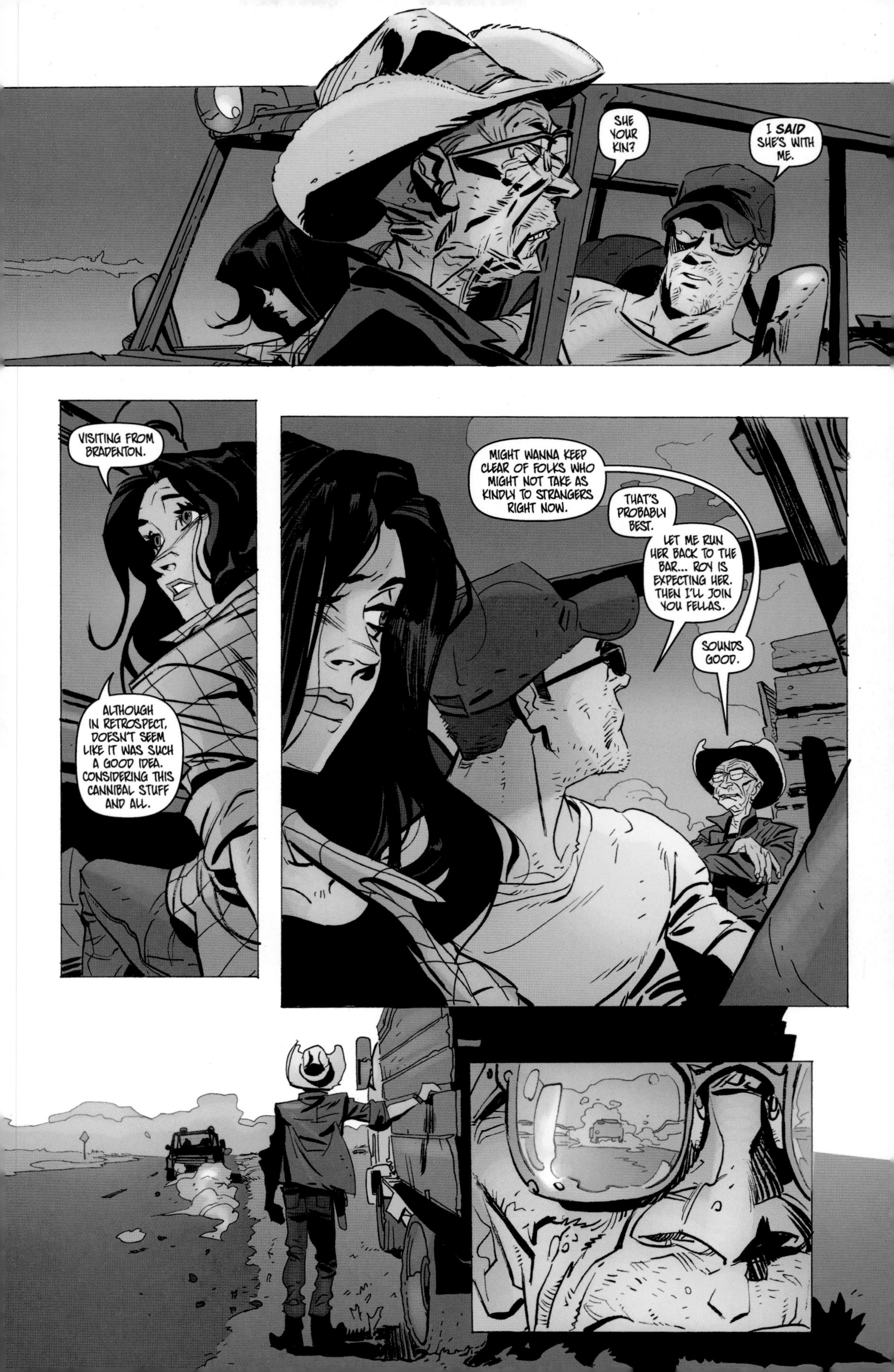
SHE YOUR KIN?
I *SAID* SHE'S WITH ME.
VISITING FROM BRADENTON.
ALTHOUGH IN RETROSPECT, DOESN'T SEEM LIKE IT WAS SUCH A GOOD IDEA. CONSIDERING THIS CANNIBAL STUFF AND ALL.
MIGHT WANNA KEEP CLEAR OF FOLKS WHO MIGHT NOT TAKE AS KINDLY TO STRANGERS RIGHT NOW.
THAT'S PROBABLY BEST.
LET ME RUN HER BACK TO THE BAR... ROY IS EXPECTING HER. THEN I'LL JOIN YOU FELLAS.
SOUNDS GOOD.

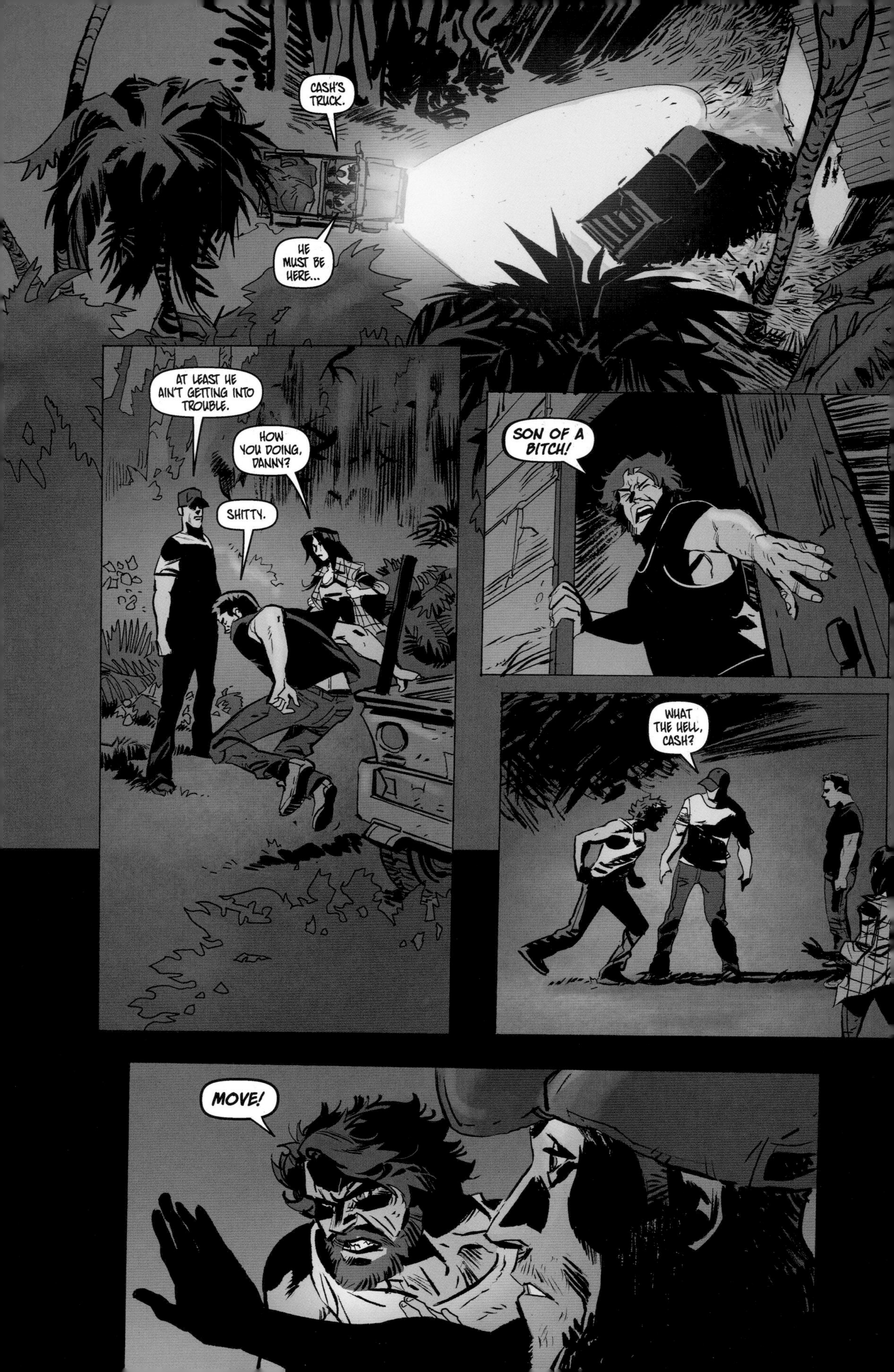
CASH'S TRUCK.
HE MUST BE HERE...
AT LEAST HE AIN'T GETTING INTO TROUBLE.
HOW YOU DOING, DANNY?
SHITTY.
SON OF A BITCH!
WHAT THE HELL, CASH?
MOVE!

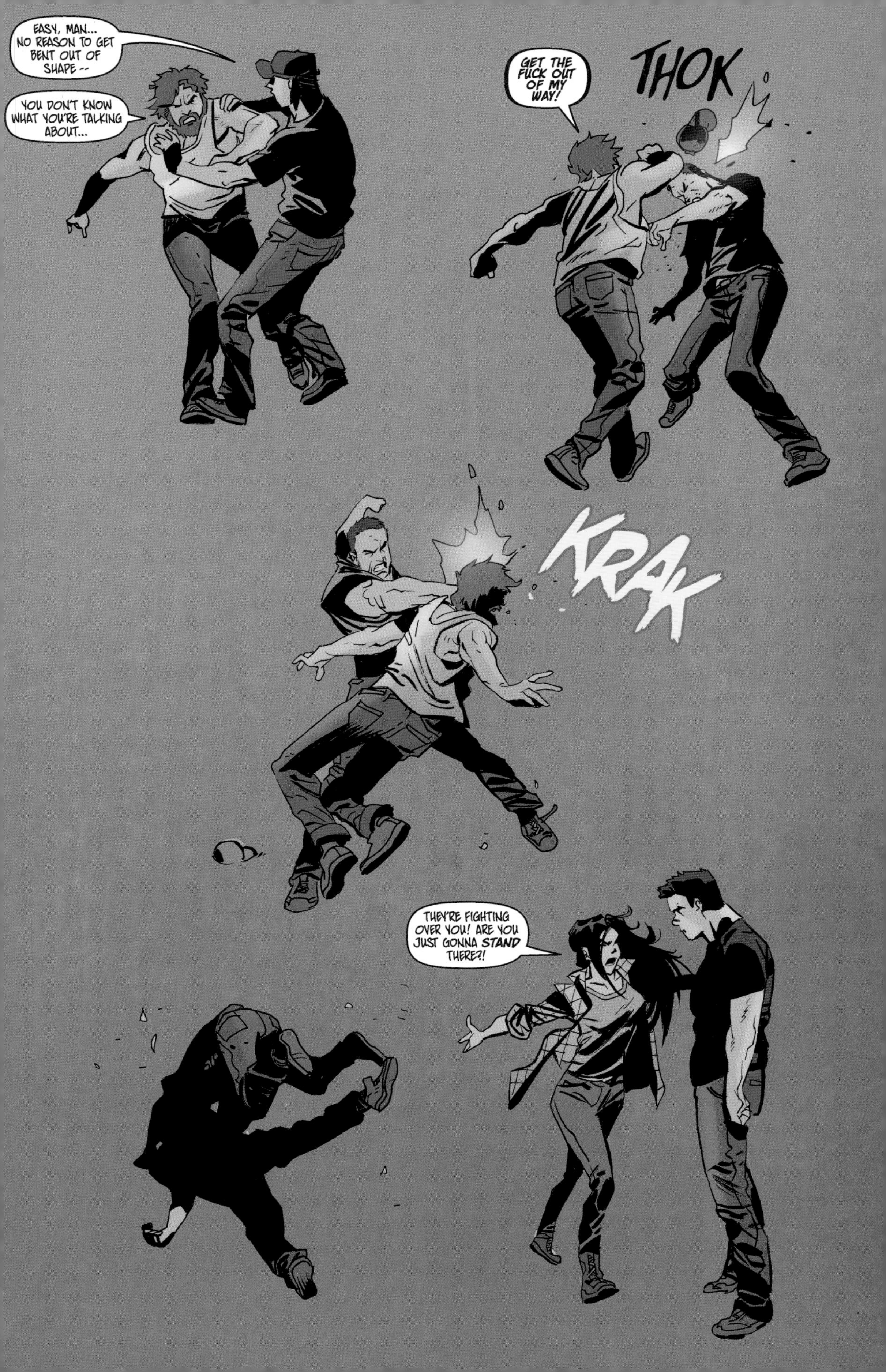
EASY, MAN... NO REASON TO GET BENT OUT OF SHAPE --
YOU DON'T KNOW WHAT YOU'RE TALKING ABOUT...
GET THE FUCK OUT OF MY WAY!
THOK
KRAK
THEY'RE FIGHTING OVER YOU! ARE YOU JUST GONNA **STAND** THERE?!

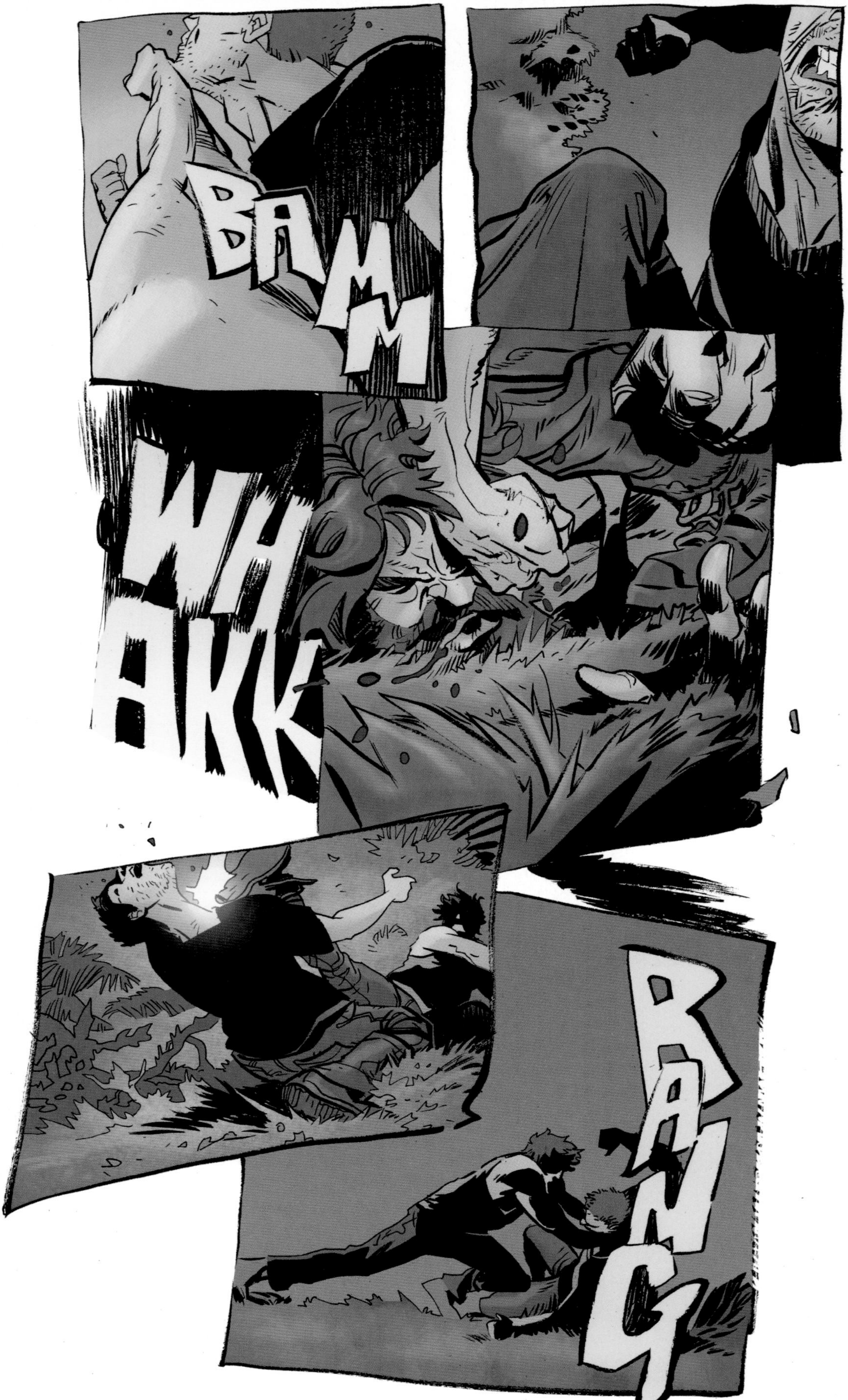
BAMM
WHAKK
BANG

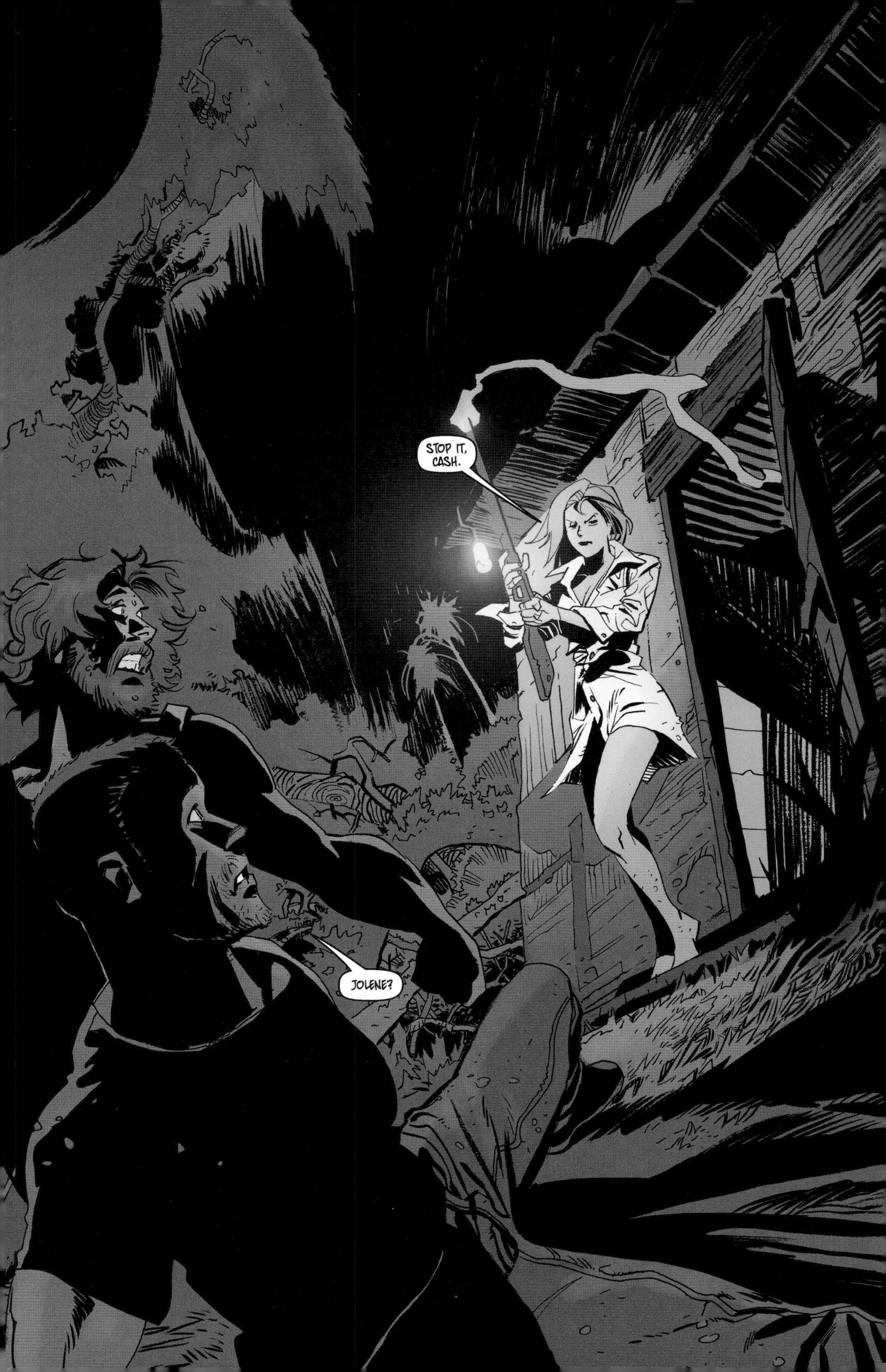
STOP IT, CASH.
JOLENE?

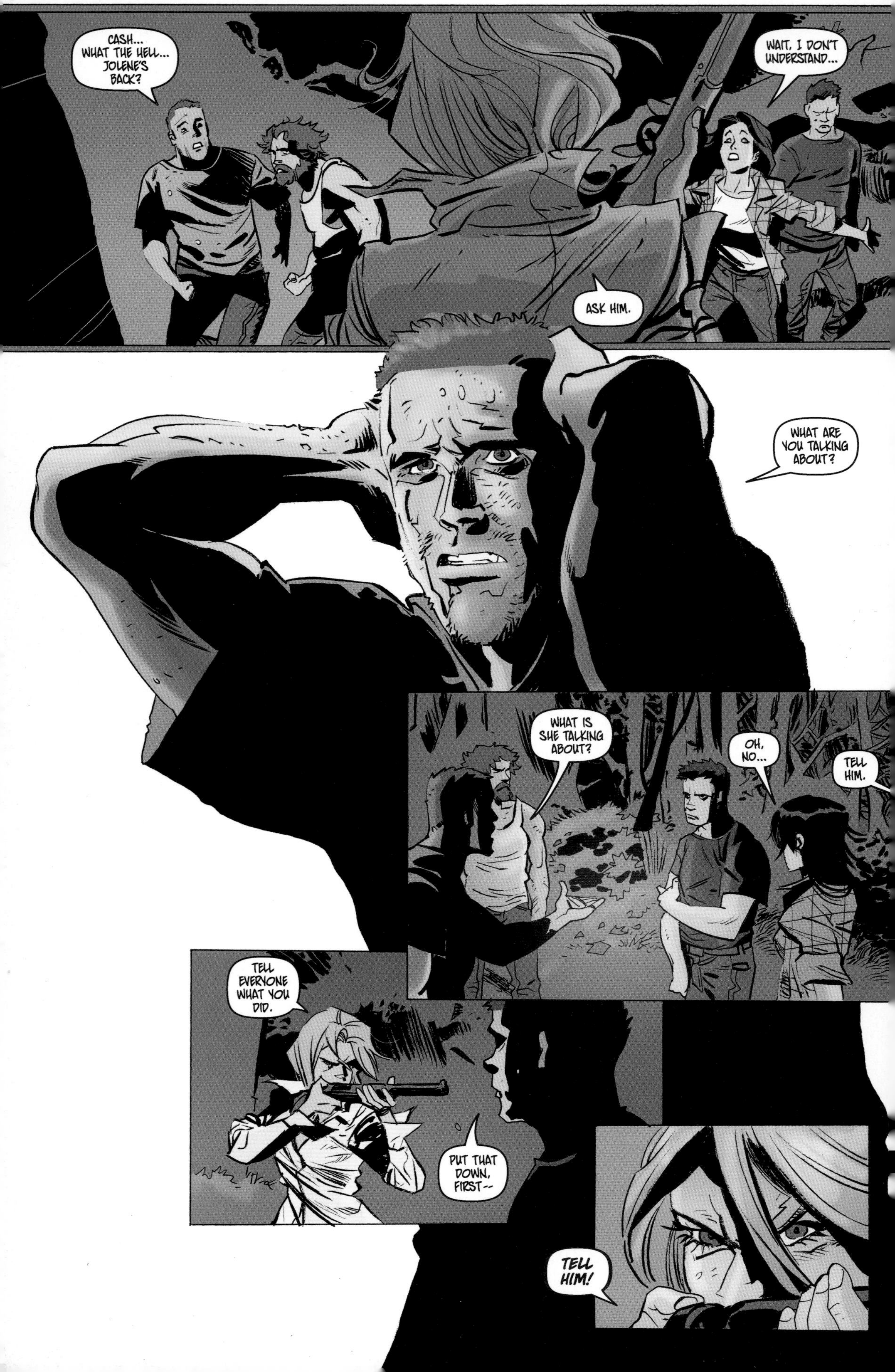
CASH... WHAT THE HELL... JOLENE'S BACK?
WAIT, I DON'T UNDERSTAND...
ASK HIM.
WHAT ARE YOU TALKING ABOUT?
WHAT IS SHE TALKING ABOUT?
OH, NO...
TELL HIM.
TELL EVERYONE WHAT YOU DID.
PUT THAT DOWN, FIRST--
TELL HIM!

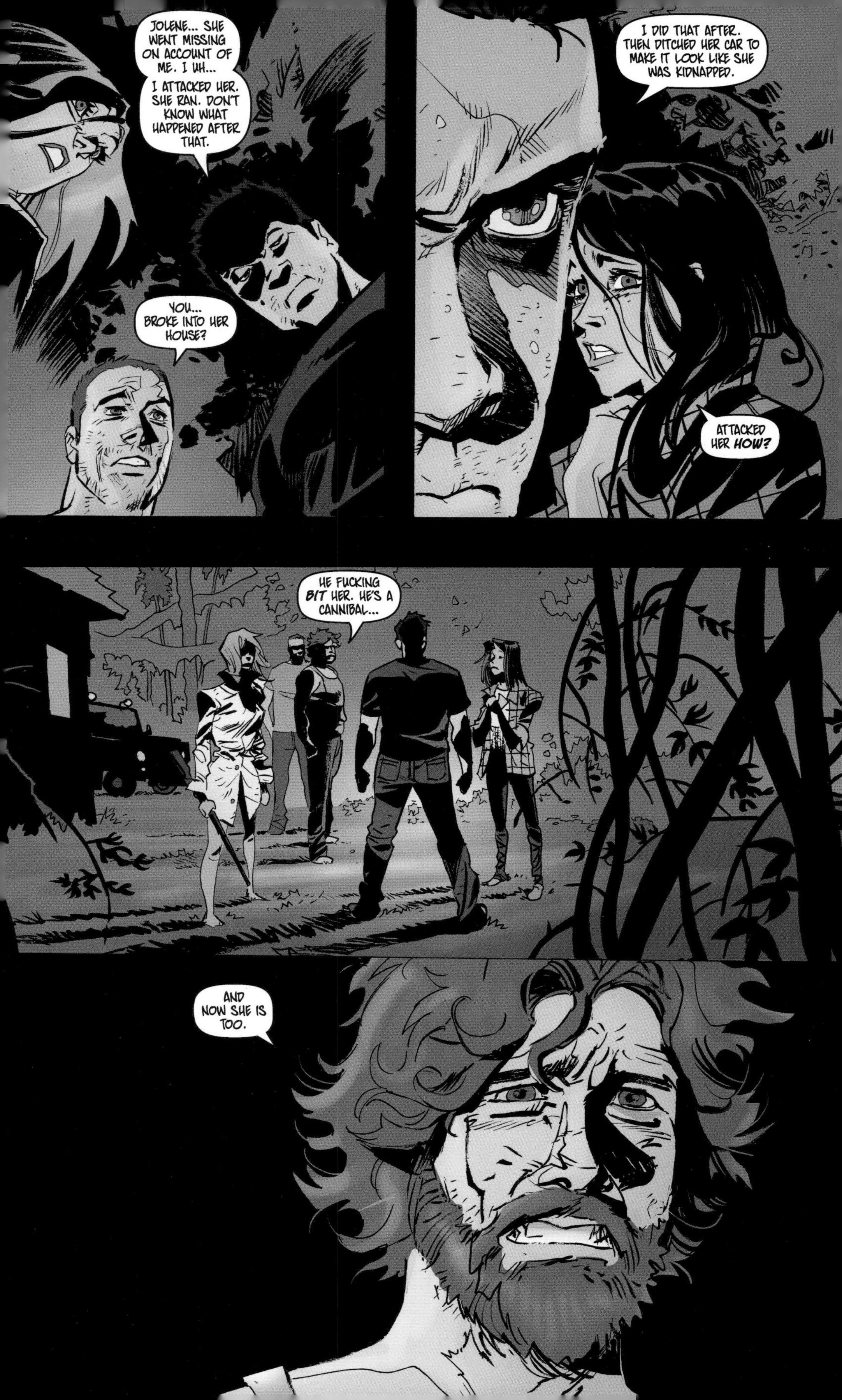
JOLENE... SHE WENT MISSING ON ACCOUNT OF ME. I UH...
I ATTACKED HER. SHE RAN. DON'T KNOW WHAT HAPPENED AFTER THAT.
YOU... BROKE INTO HER HOUSE?
I DID THAT AFTER. THEN DITCHED HER CAR TO MAKE IT LOOK LIKE SHE WAS KIDNAPPED.
ATTACKED HER HOW?
HE FUCKING BIT HER. HE'S A CANNIBAL...
AND NOW SHE IS TOO.

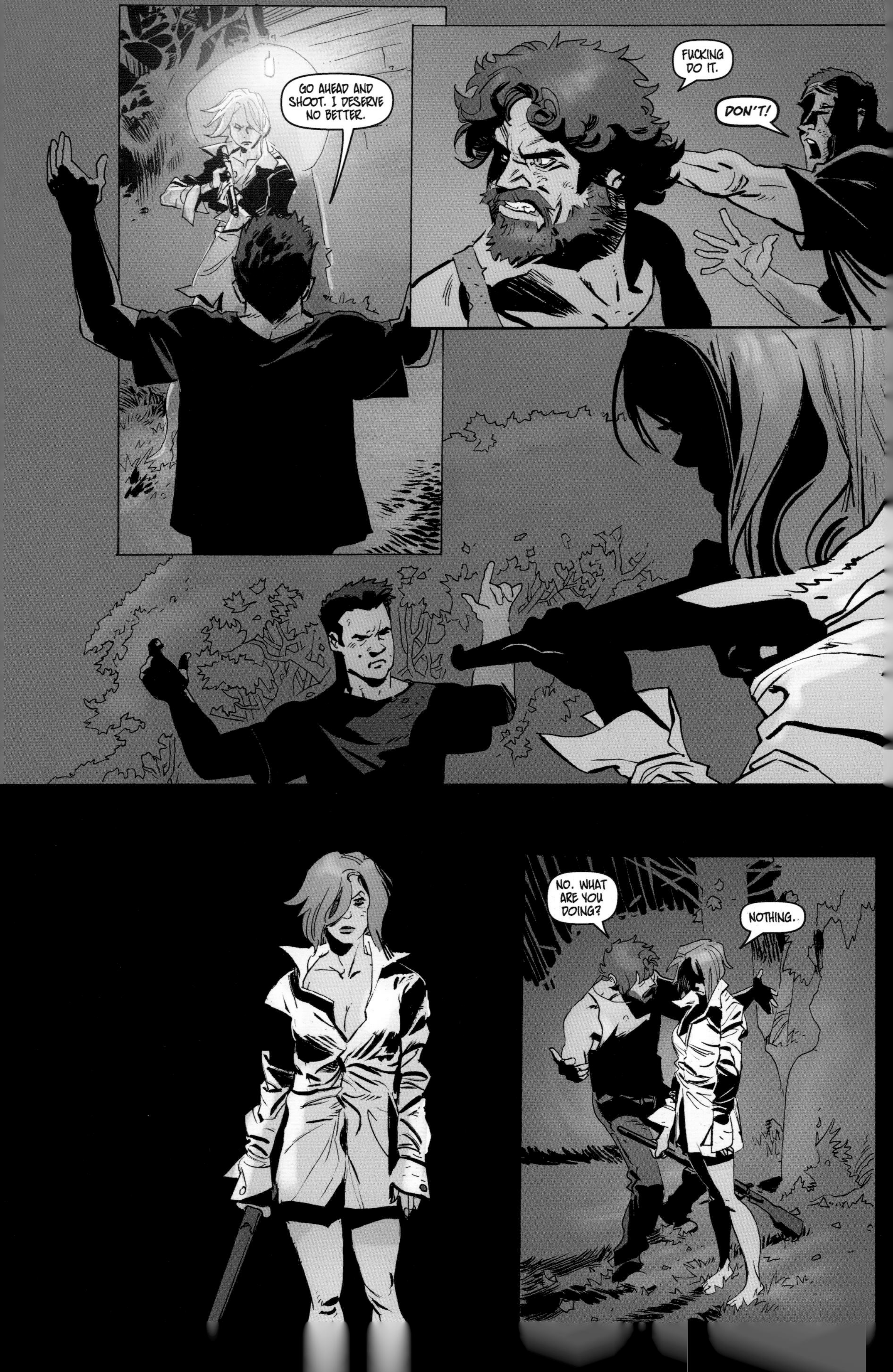
GO AHEAD AND SHOOT. I DESERVE NO BETTER.
FUCKING DO IT.
DON'T!
NO. WHAT ARE YOU DOING?
NOTHING.

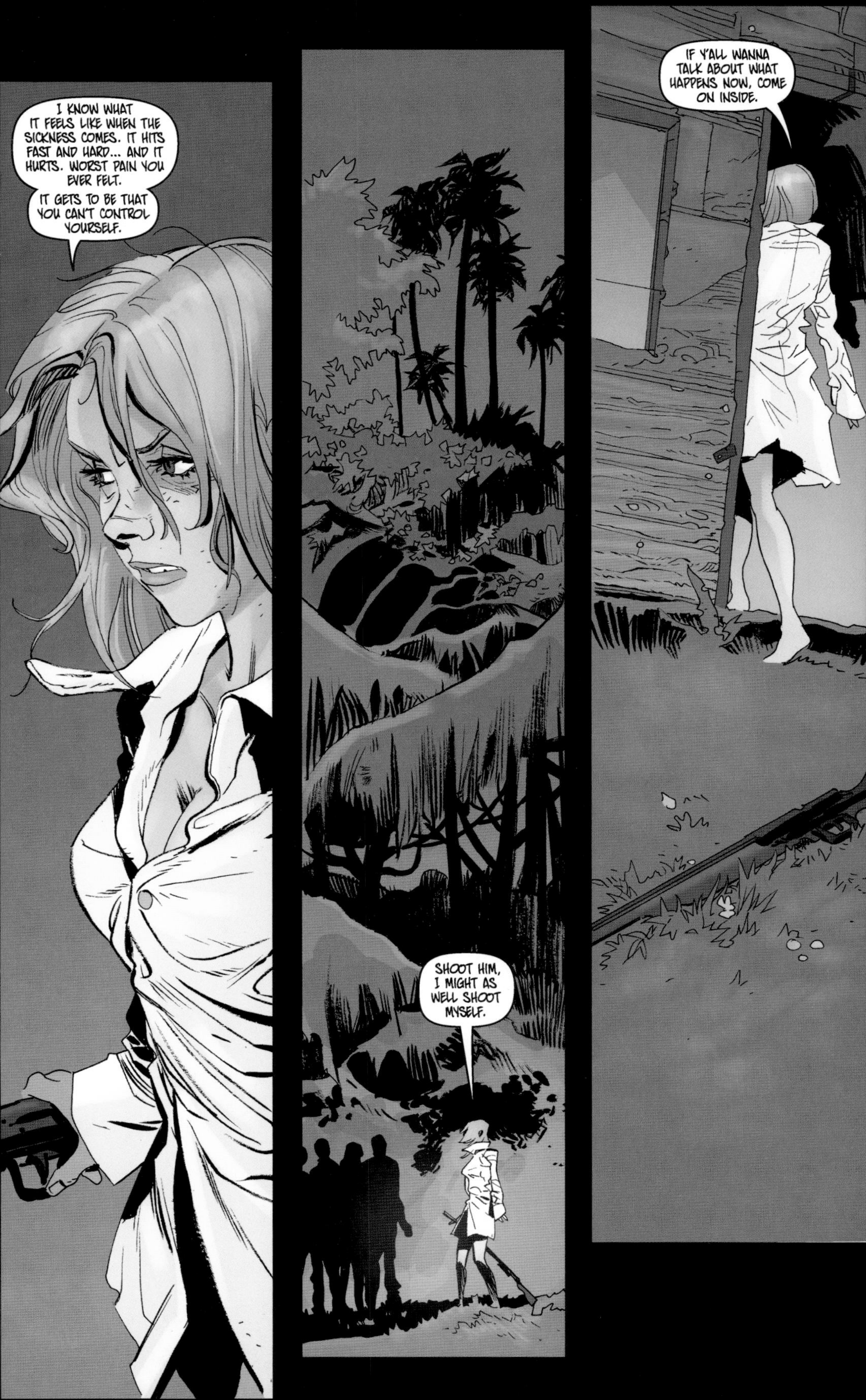
I KNOW WHAT IT FEELS LIKE WHEN THE SICKNESS COMES. IT HITS FAST AND HARD... AND IT HURTS. WORST PAIN YOU EVER FELT.
IT GETS TO BE THAT YOU CAN'T CONTROL YOURSELF.
SHOOT HIM, I MIGHT AS WELL SHOOT MYSELF.
IF Y'ALL WANNA TALK ABOUT WHAT HAPPENS NOW, COME ON INSIDE.

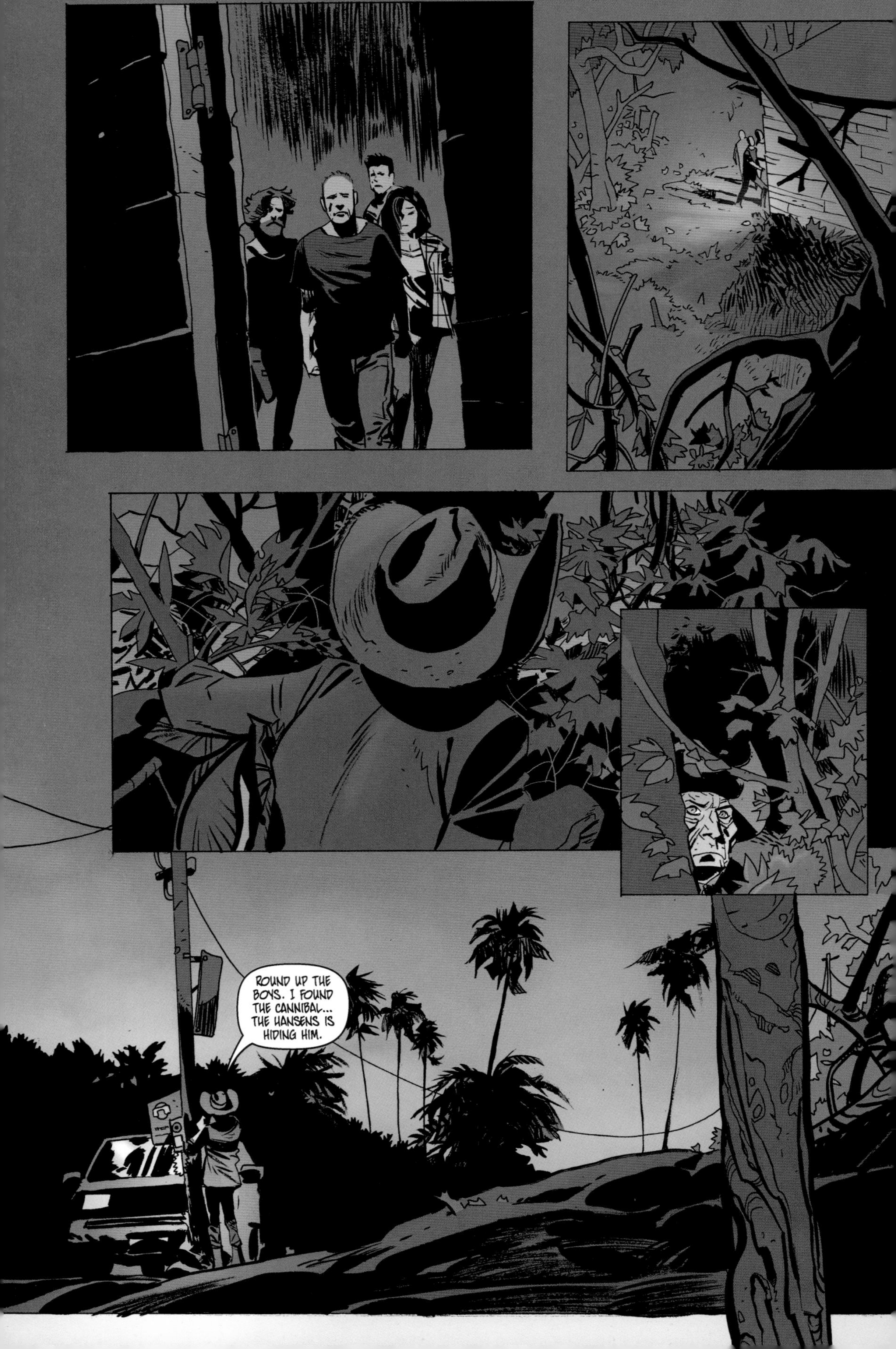
ROUND UP THE BOYS. I FOUND THE CANNIBAL... THE HANSENS IS HIDING HIM.

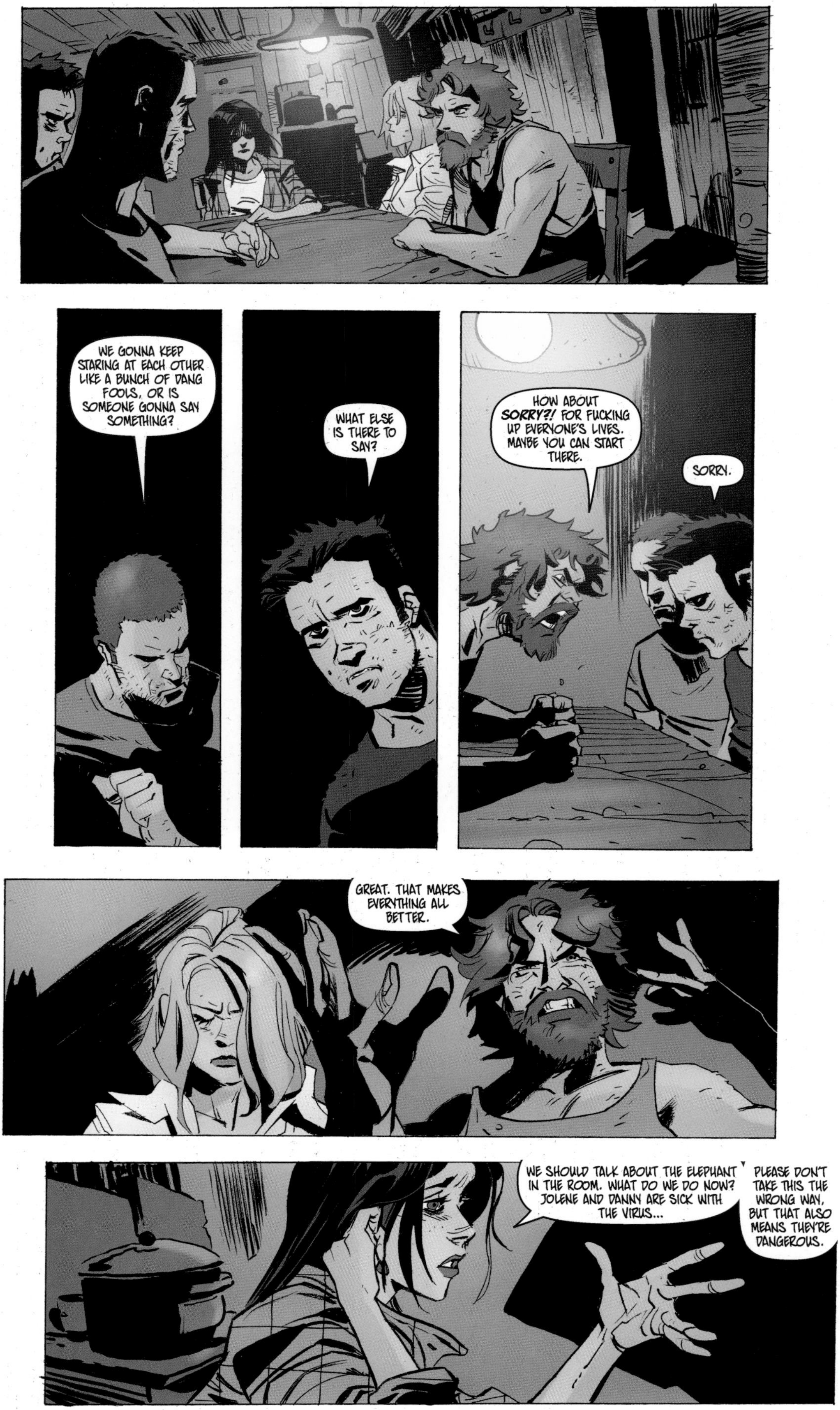
WE GONNA KEEP STARING AT EACH OTHER LIKE A BUNCH OF DANG FOOLS, OR IS SOMEONE GONNA SAY SOMETHING?
WHAT ELSE IS THERE TO SAY?
HOW ABOUT SORRY?! FOR FUCKING UP EVERYONE'S LIVES. MAYBE YOU CAN START THERE.
SORRY.
GREAT. THAT MAKES EVERYTHING ALL BETTER.
WE SHOULD TALK ABOUT THE ELEPHANT IN THE ROOM. WHAT DO WE DO NOW? JOLENE AND DANNY ARE SICK WITH THE VIRUS...
PLEASE DON'T TAKE THIS THE WRONG WAY, BUT THAT ALSO MEANS THEY'RE DANGEROUS.

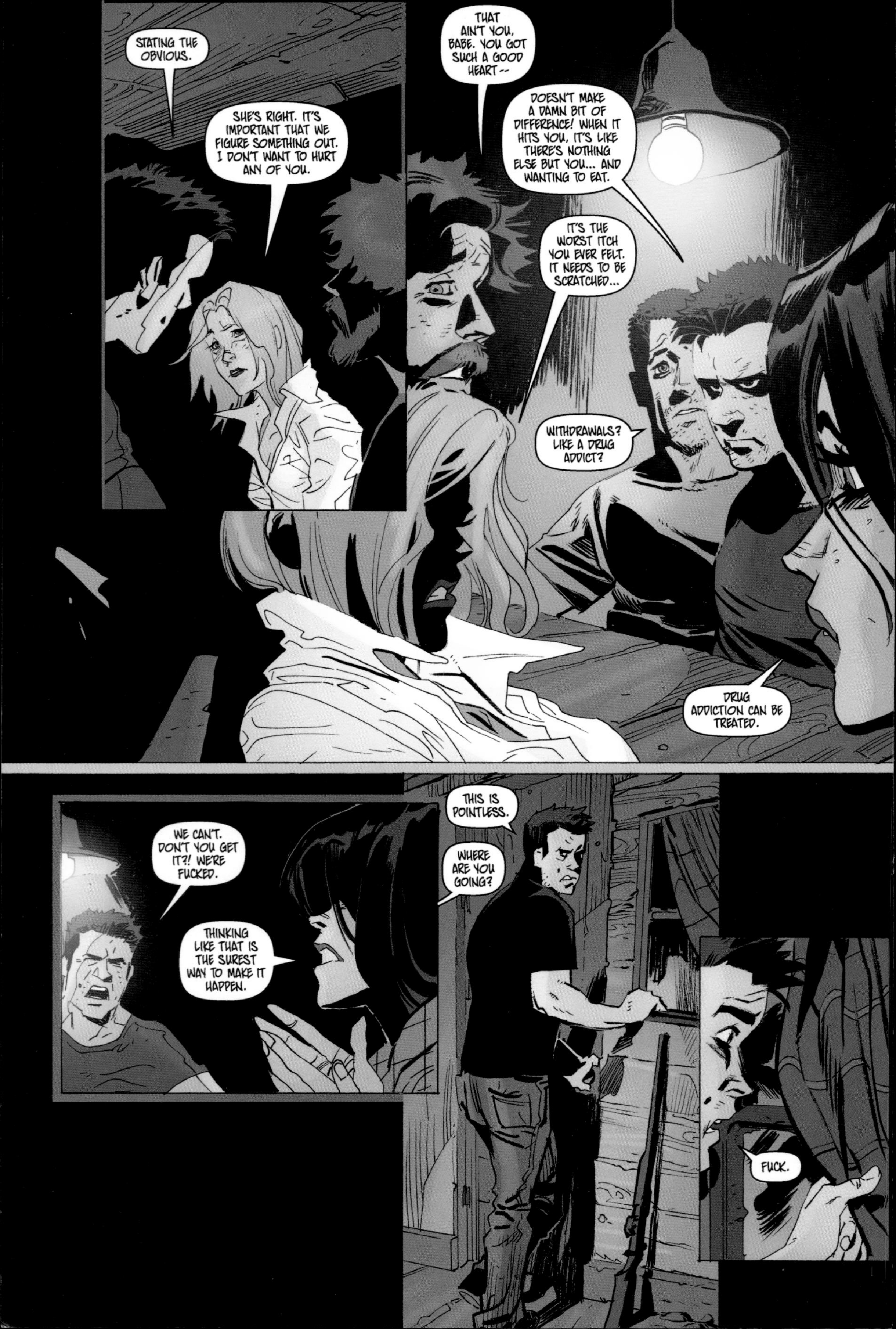
STATING THE OBVIOUS.
SHE'S RIGHT. IT'S IMPORTANT THAT WE FIGURE SOMETHING OUT. I DON'T WANT TO HURT ANY OF YOU.
THAT AIN'T YOU, BABE. YOU GOT SUCH A GOOD HEART --
DOESN'T MAKE A DAMN BIT OF DIFFERENCE! WHEN IT HITS YOU, IT'S LIKE THERE'S NOTHING ELSE BUT YOU... AND WANTING TO EAT.
IT'S THE WORST ITCH YOU EVER FELT. IT NEEDS TO BE SCRATCHED...
WITHDRAWALS? LIKE A DRUG ADDICT?
DRUG ADDICTION CAN BE TREATED.
WE CAN'T. DON'T YOU GET IT?! WE'RE FUCKED.
THINKING LIKE THAT IS THE SUREST WAY TO MAKE IT HAPPEN.
THIS IS POINTLESS.
WHERE ARE YOU GOING?
FUCK.

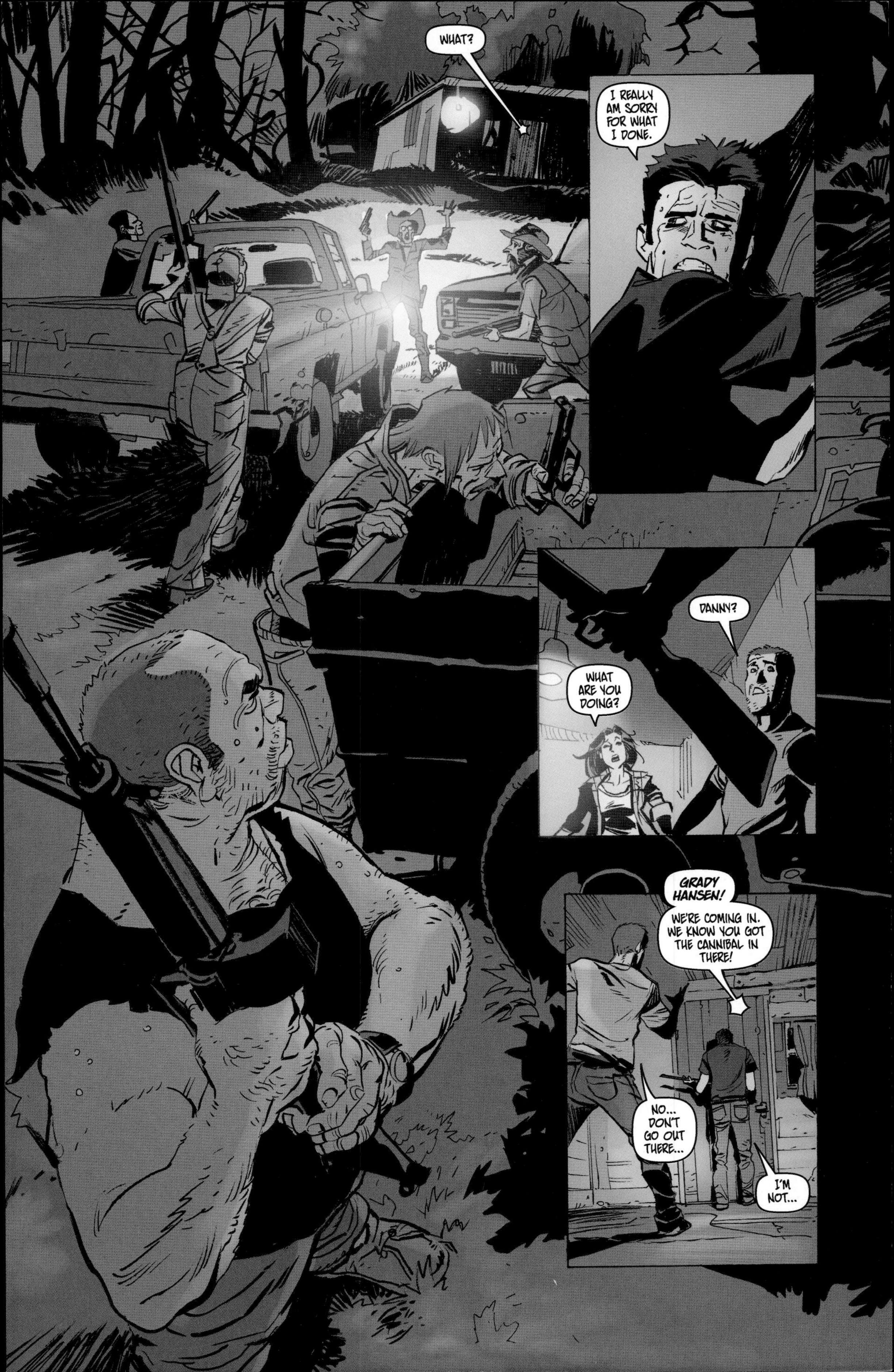
WHAT?
I REALLY AM SORRY FOR WHAT I DONE.
DANNY?
WHAT ARE YOU DOING?
GRADY HANSEN!
WE'RE COMING IN. WE KNOW YOU GOT THE CANNIBAL IN THERE!
NO... DON'T GO OUT THERE...
I'M NOT...

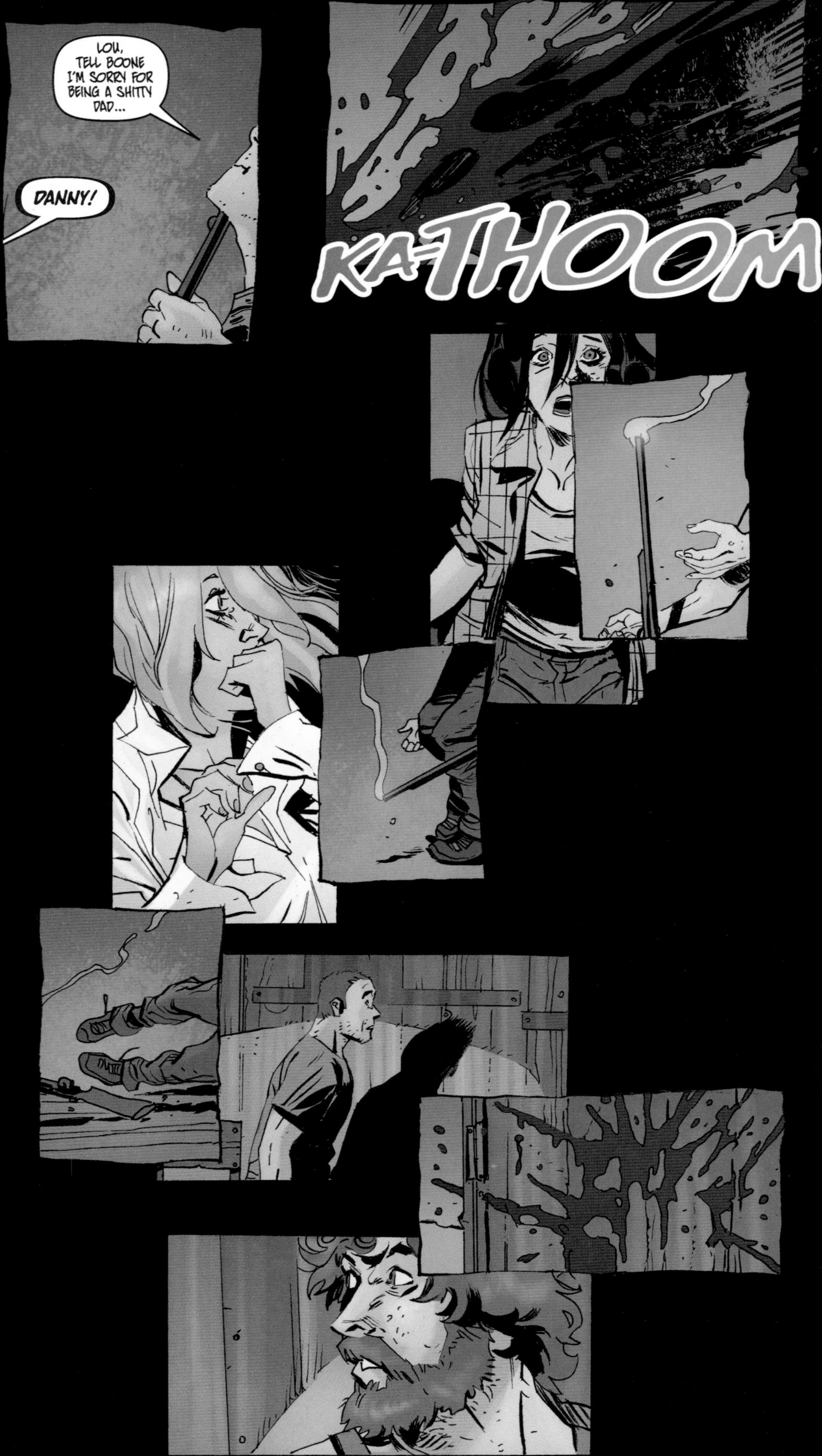

LOU, TELL BOONE I'M SORRY FOR BEING A SHITTY DAD...
DANNY!
KA-THOOM

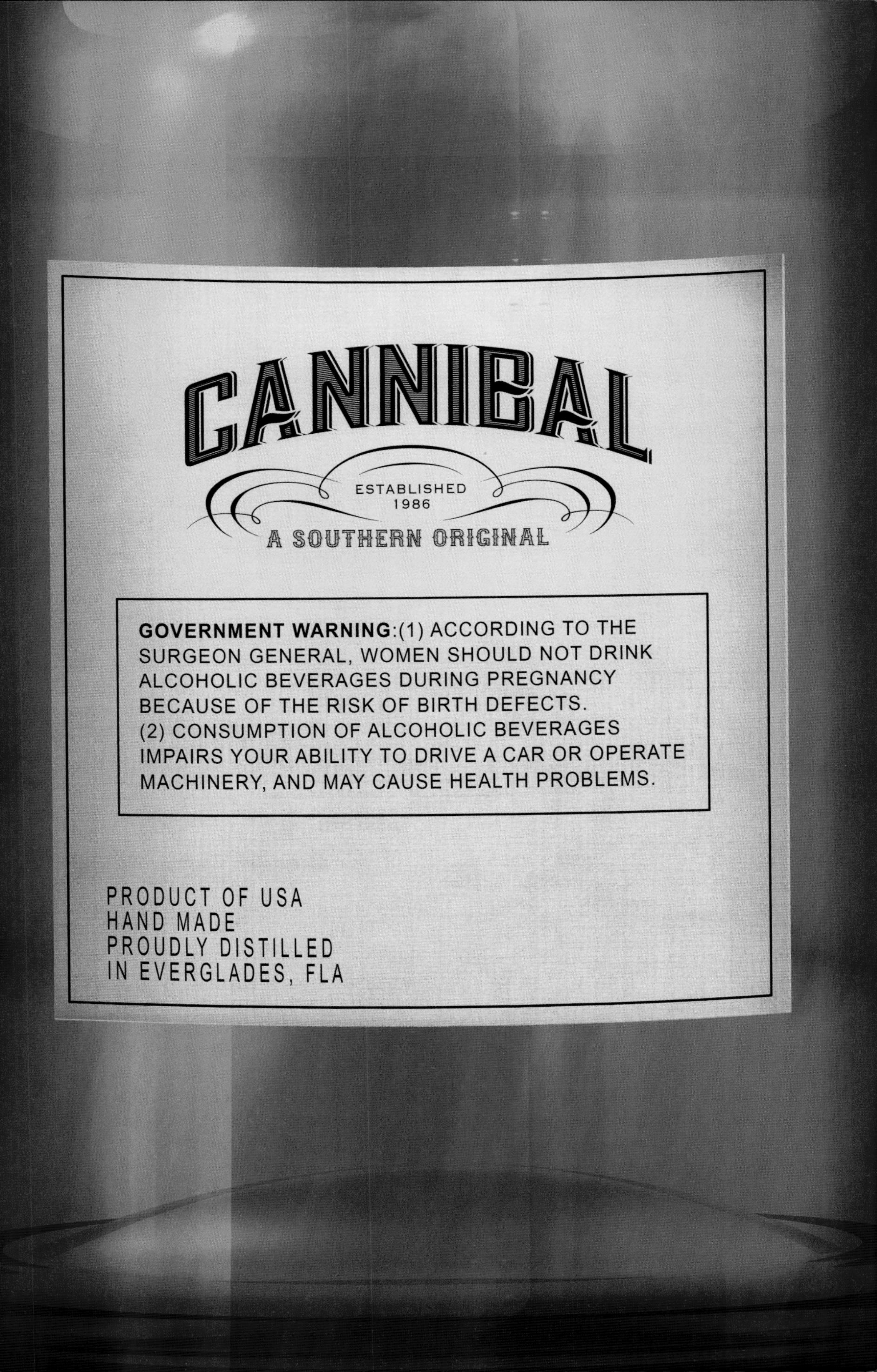
CANNIBAL
ESTABLISHED
1986
A SOUTHERN ORIGINAL
GOVERNMENT WARNING:(1) ACCORDING TO THE SURGEON GENERAL, WOMEN SHOULD NOT DRINK ALCOHOLIC BEVERAGES DURING PREGNANCY BECAUSE OF THE RISK OF BIRTH DEFECTS. (2) CONSUMPTION OF ALCOHOLIC BEVERAGES IMPAIRS YOUR ABILITY TO DRIVE A CAR OR OPERATE MACHINERY, AND MAY CAUSE HEALTH PROBLEMS.
PRODUCT OF USA
HAND MADE
PROUDLY DISTILLED
IN EVERGLADES, FLA

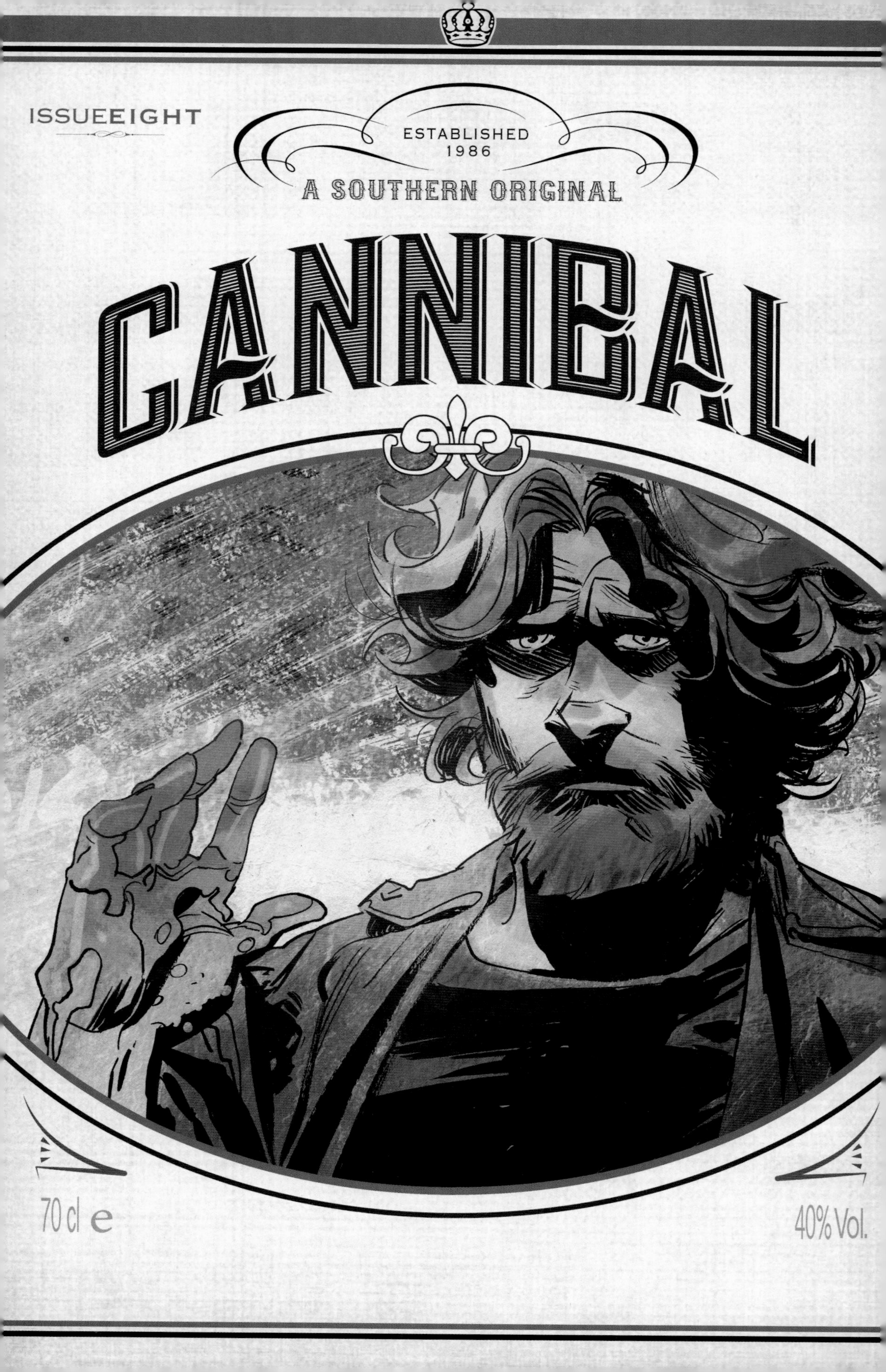
ISSUEEIGHT
ESTABLISHED 1986
A SOUTHERN ORIGINAL
CANNIBAL
70 cl e
40% Vol.

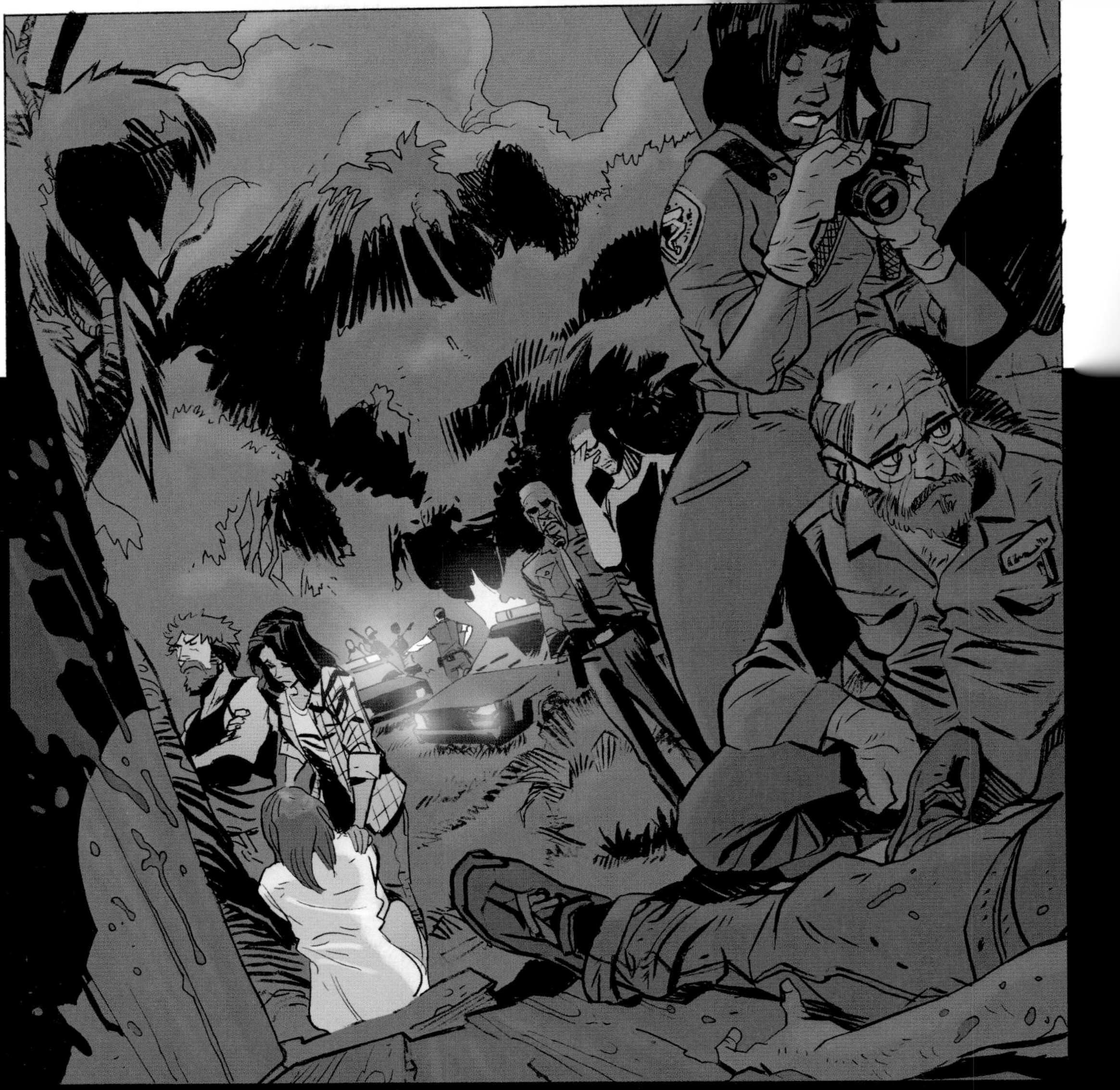
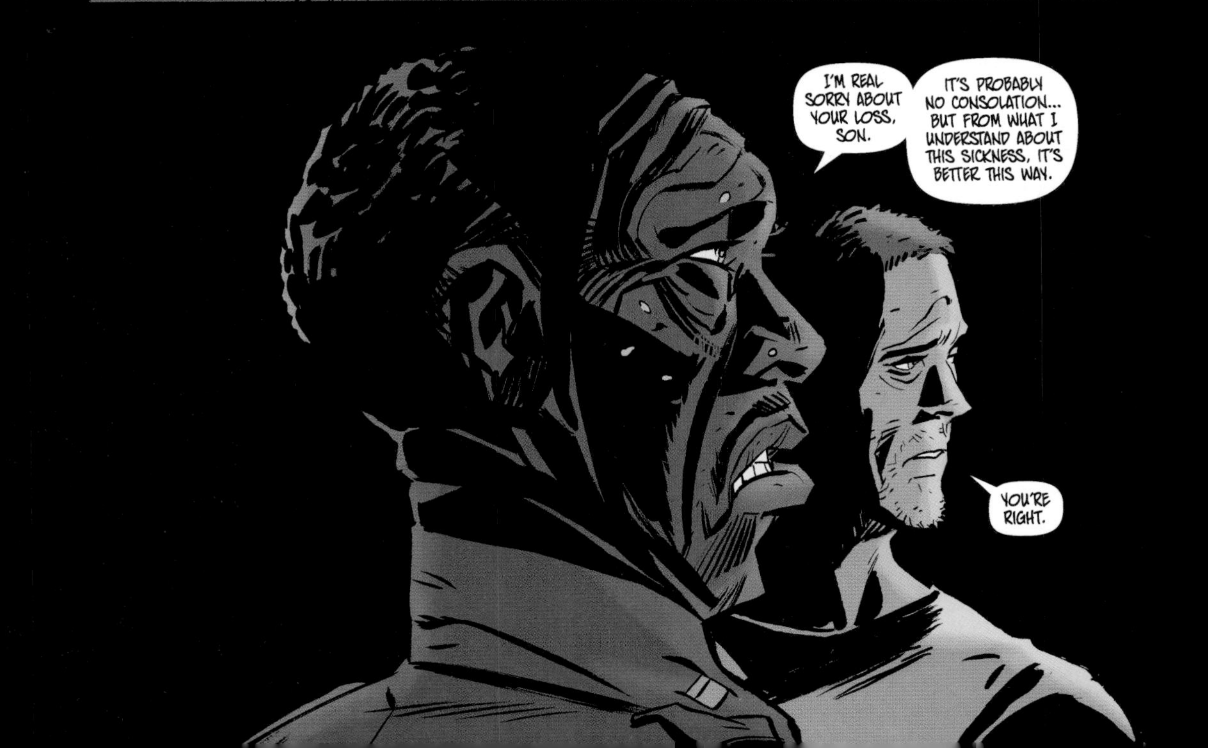
I'M REAL SORRY ABOUT YOUR LOSS, SON.
IT'S PROBABLY NO CONSOLATION... BUT FROM WHAT I UNDERSTAND ABOUT THIS SICKNESS, IT'S BETTER THIS WAY.
YOU'RE RIGHT.

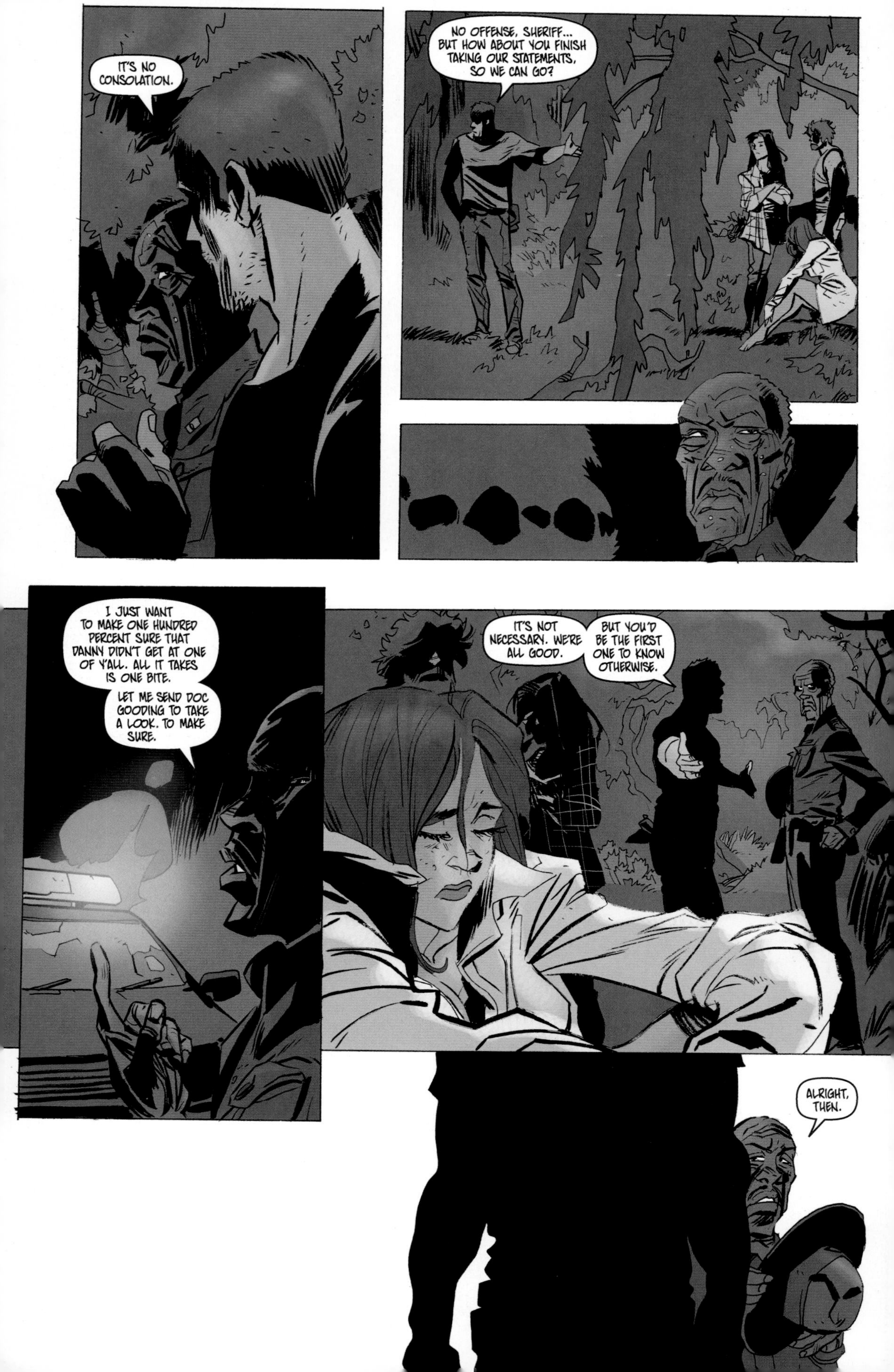
IT'S NO CONSOLATION.
NO OFFENSE, SHERIFF... BUT HOW ABOUT YOU FINISH TAKING OUR STATEMENTS, SO WE CAN GO?
I JUST WANT TO MAKE ONE HUNDRED PERCENT SURE THAT DANNY DIDN'T GET AT ONE OF Y'ALL. ALL IT TAKES IS ONE BITE.
LET ME SEND DOC GOODING TO TAKE A LOOK. TO MAKE SURE.
IT'S NOT NECESSARY. WE'RE ALL GOOD.
BUT YOU'D BE THE FIRST ONE TO KNOW OTHERWISE.
ALRIGHT, THEN.

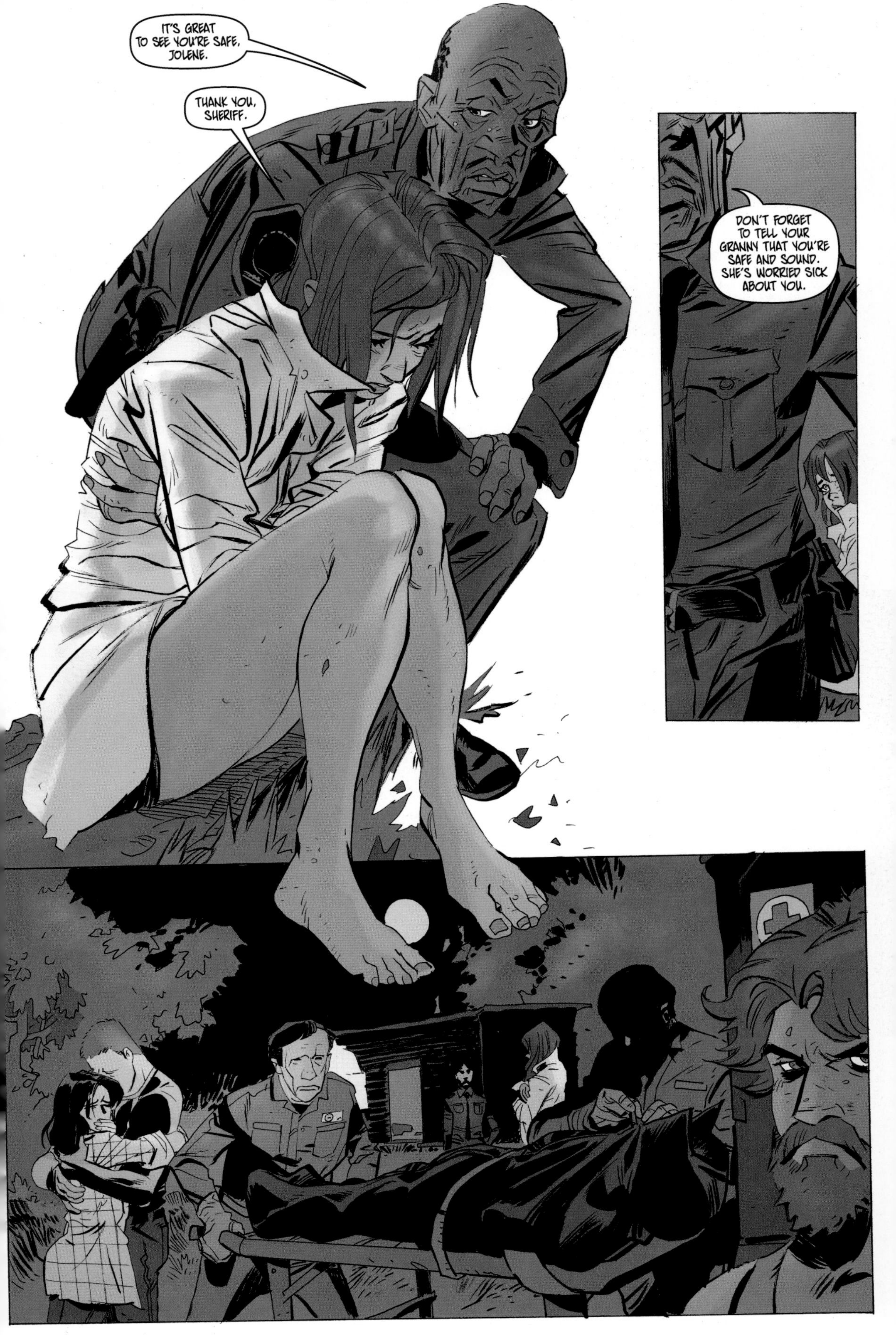
IT'S GREAT TO SEE YOU'RE SAFE, JOLENE.
THANK YOU, SHERIFF.
DON'T FORGET TO TELL YOUR GRANNY THAT YOU'RE SAFE AND SOUND. SHE'S WORRIED SICK ABOUT YOU.

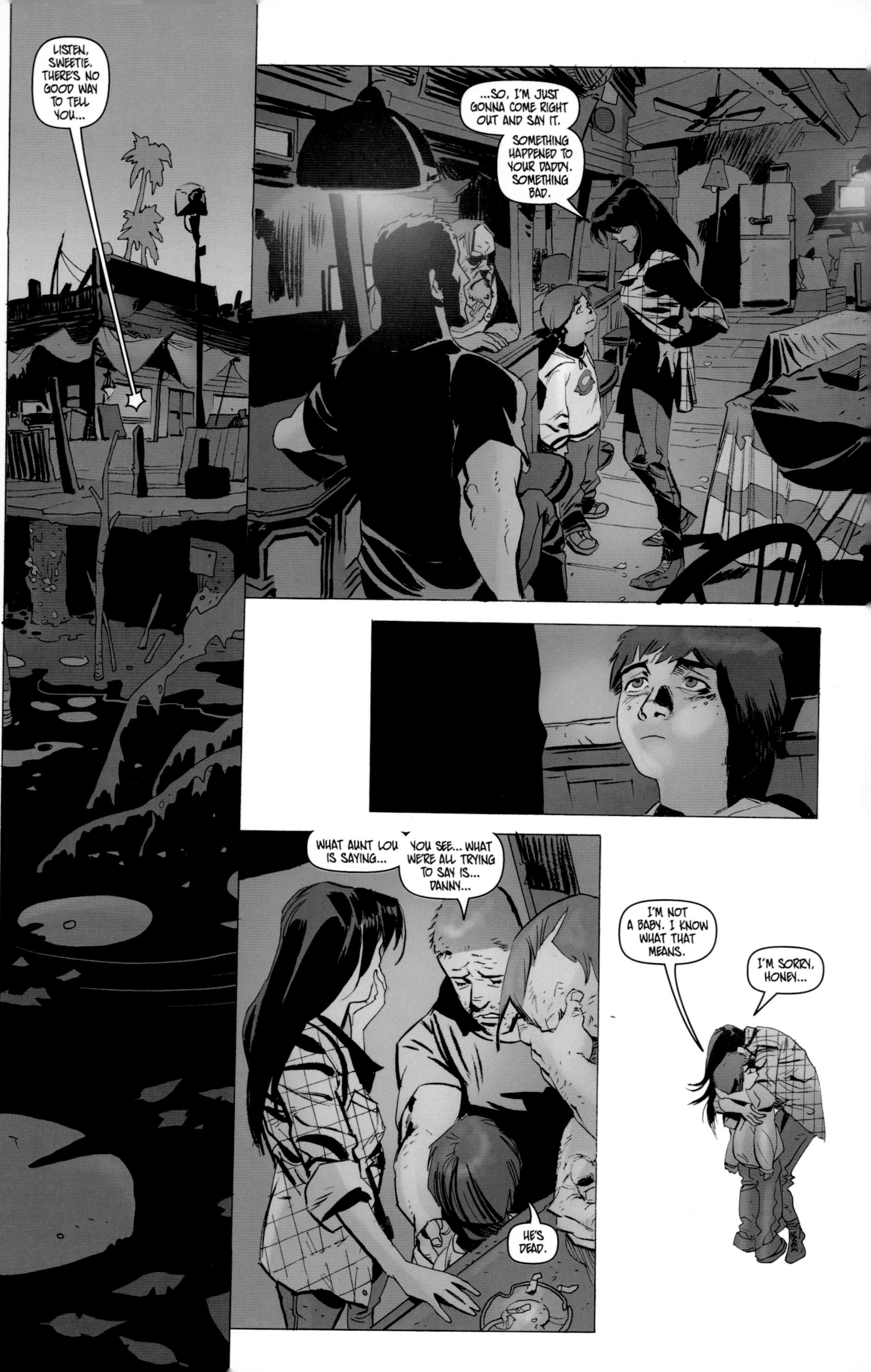

LISTEN, SWEETIE. THERE'S NO GOOD WAY TO TELL YOU...
...SO, I'M JUST GONNA COME RIGHT OUT AND SAY IT.
SOMETHING HAPPENED TO YOUR DADDY. SOMETHING BAD.
WHAT AUNT LOU IS SAYING...
YOU SEE... WHAT WE'RE ALL TRYING TO SAY IS... DANNY...
HE'S DEAD.
I'M NOT A BABY. I KNOW WHAT THAT MEANS.
I'M SORRY, HONEY...

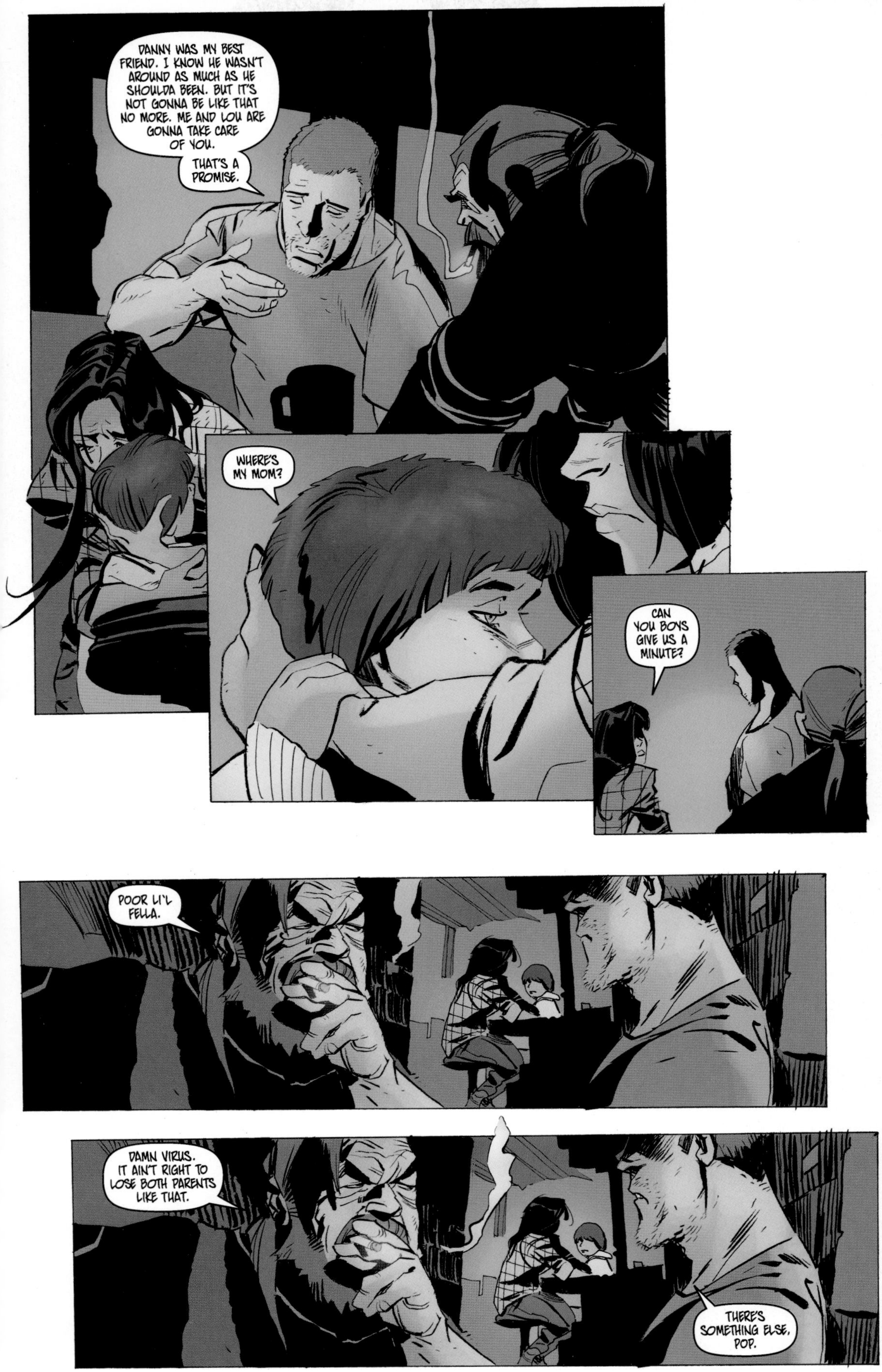
DANNY WAS MY BEST FRIEND. I KNOW HE WASN'T AROUND AS MUCH AS HE SHOULDA BEEN. BUT IT'S NOT GONNA BE LIKE THAT NO MORE. ME AND LOU ARE GONNA TAKE CARE OF YOU.
THAT'S A PROMISE.
WHERE'S MY MOM?
CAN YOU BOYS GIVE US A MINUTE?
POOR LI'L FELLA.
DAMN VIRUS. IT AIN'T RIGHT TO LOSE BOTH PARENTS LIKE THAT.
THERE'S SOMETHING ELSE, POP.

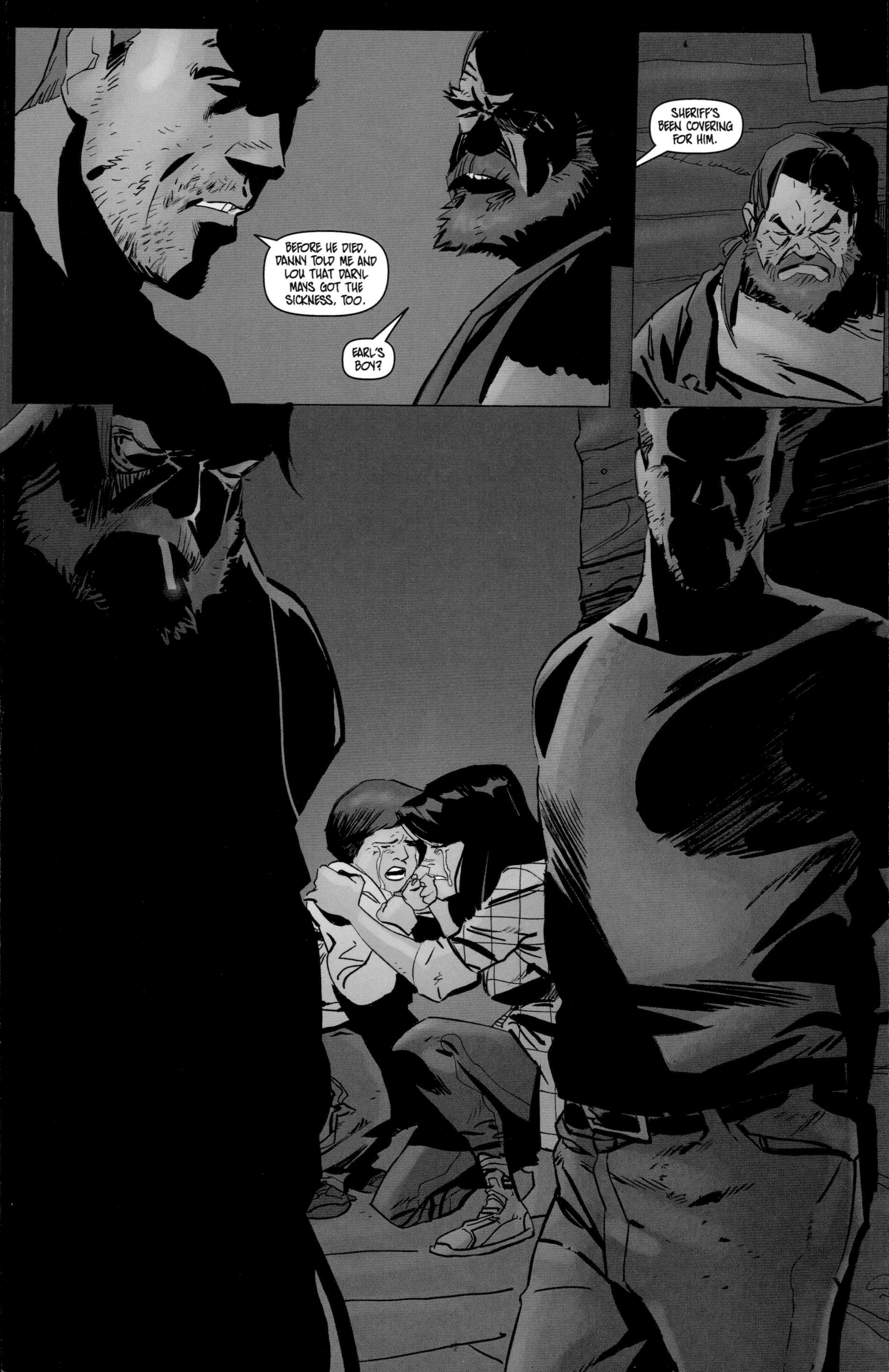
BEFORE HE DIED, DANNY TOLD ME AND LOU THAT DARYL MAYS GOT THE SICKNESS, TOO.
EARL'S BOY?
SHERIFF'S BEEN COVERING FOR HIM.

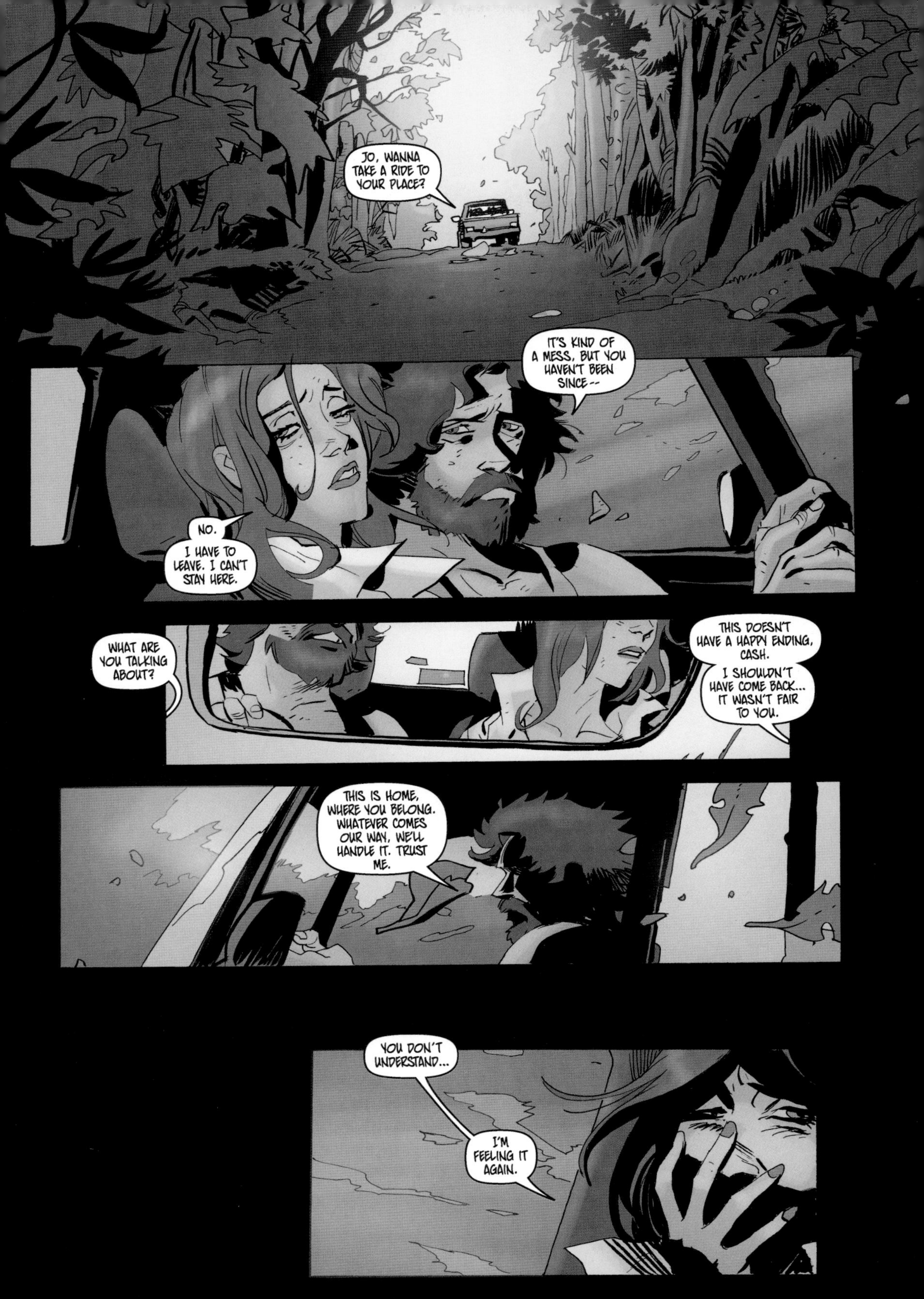
JO, WANNA TAKE A RIDE TO YOUR PLACE?
IT'S KIND OF A MESS, BUT YOU HAVEN'T BEEN SINCE--
NO.
I HAVE TO LEAVE. I CAN'T STAY HERE.
WHAT ARE YOU TALKING ABOUT?
THIS DOESN'T HAVE A HAPPY ENDING, CASH.
I SHOULDN'T HAVE COME BACK... IT WASN'T FAIR TO YOU.
THIS IS HOME, WHERE YOU BELONG. WHATEVER COMES OUR WAY, WE'LL HANDLE IT. TRUST ME.
YOU DON'T UNDERSTAND...
I'M FEELING IT AGAIN.

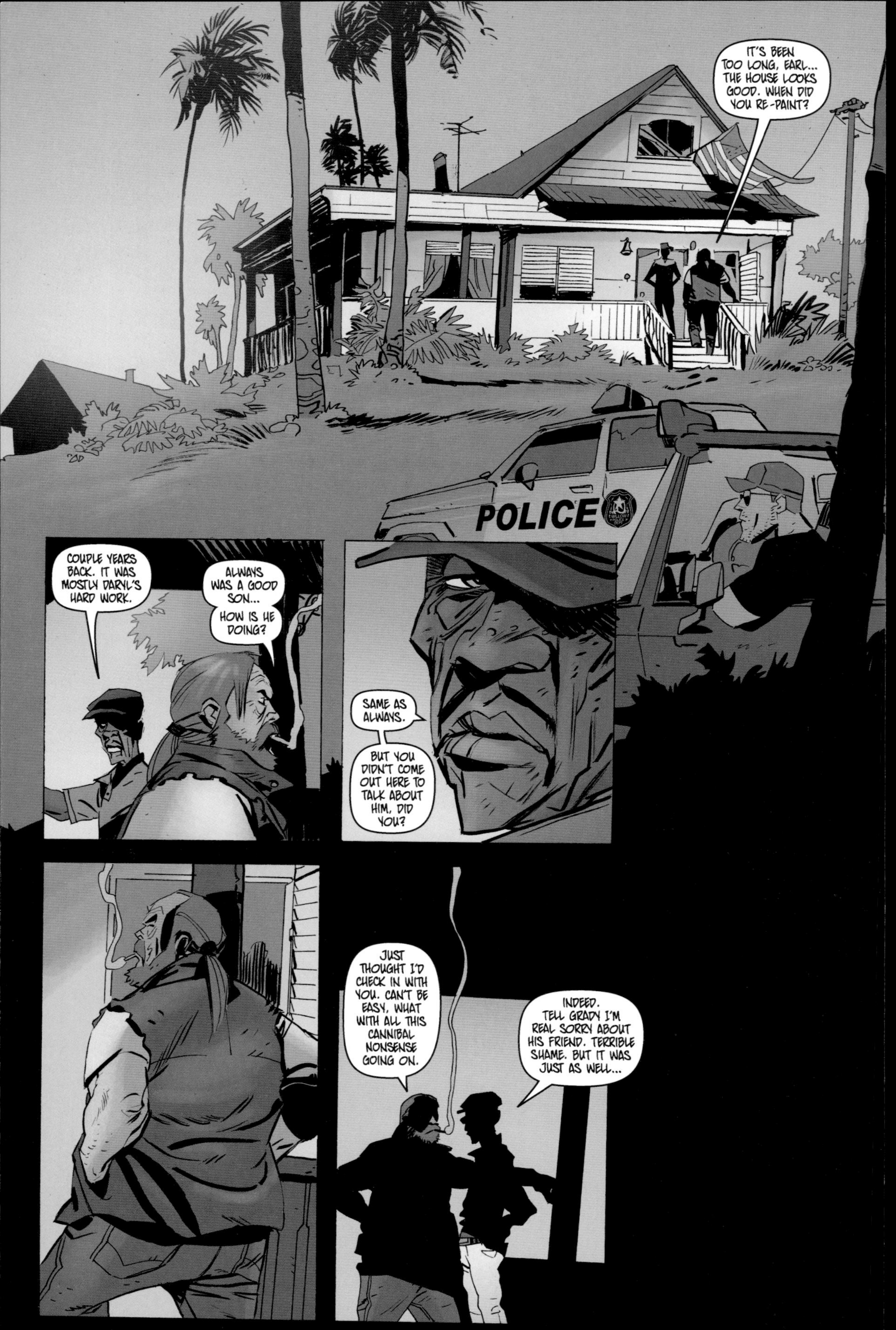
IT'S BEEN TOO LONG, EARL... THE HOUSE LOOKS GOOD. WHEN DID YOU RE-PAINT?
POLICE
COUPLE YEARS BACK. IT WAS MOSTLY DARYL'S HARD WORK.
ALWAYS WAS A GOOD SON...
HOW IS HE DOING?
SAME AS ALWAYS.
BUT YOU DIDN'T COME OUT HERE TO TALK ABOUT HIM, DID YOU?
JUST THOUGHT I'D CHECK IN WITH YOU. CAN'T BE EASY, WHAT WITH ALL THIS CANNIBAL NONSENSE GOING ON.
INDEED. TELL GRADY I'M REAL SORRY ABOUT HIS FRIEND. TERRIBLE SHAME. BUT IT WAS JUST AS WELL...

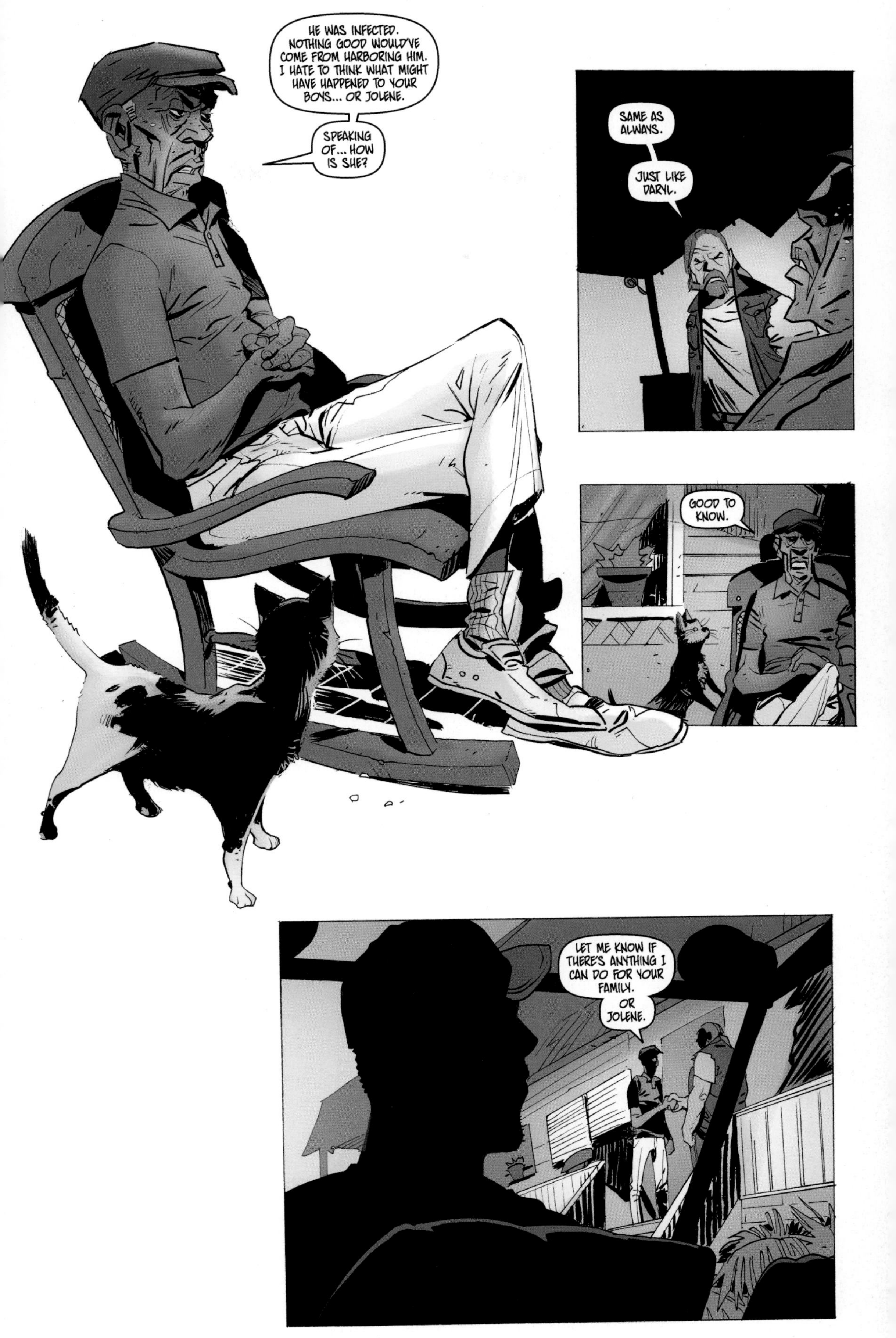
HE WAS INFECTED. NOTHING GOOD WOULD'VE COME FROM HARBORING HIM. I HATE TO THINK WHAT MIGHT HAVE HAPPENED TO YOUR BOYS... OR JOLENE.
SPEAKING OF... HOW IS SHE?
SAME AS ALWAYS.
JUST LIKE DARYL.
GOOD TO KNOW.
LET ME KNOW IF THERE'S ANYTHING I CAN DO FOR YOUR FAMILY.
OR JOLENE.

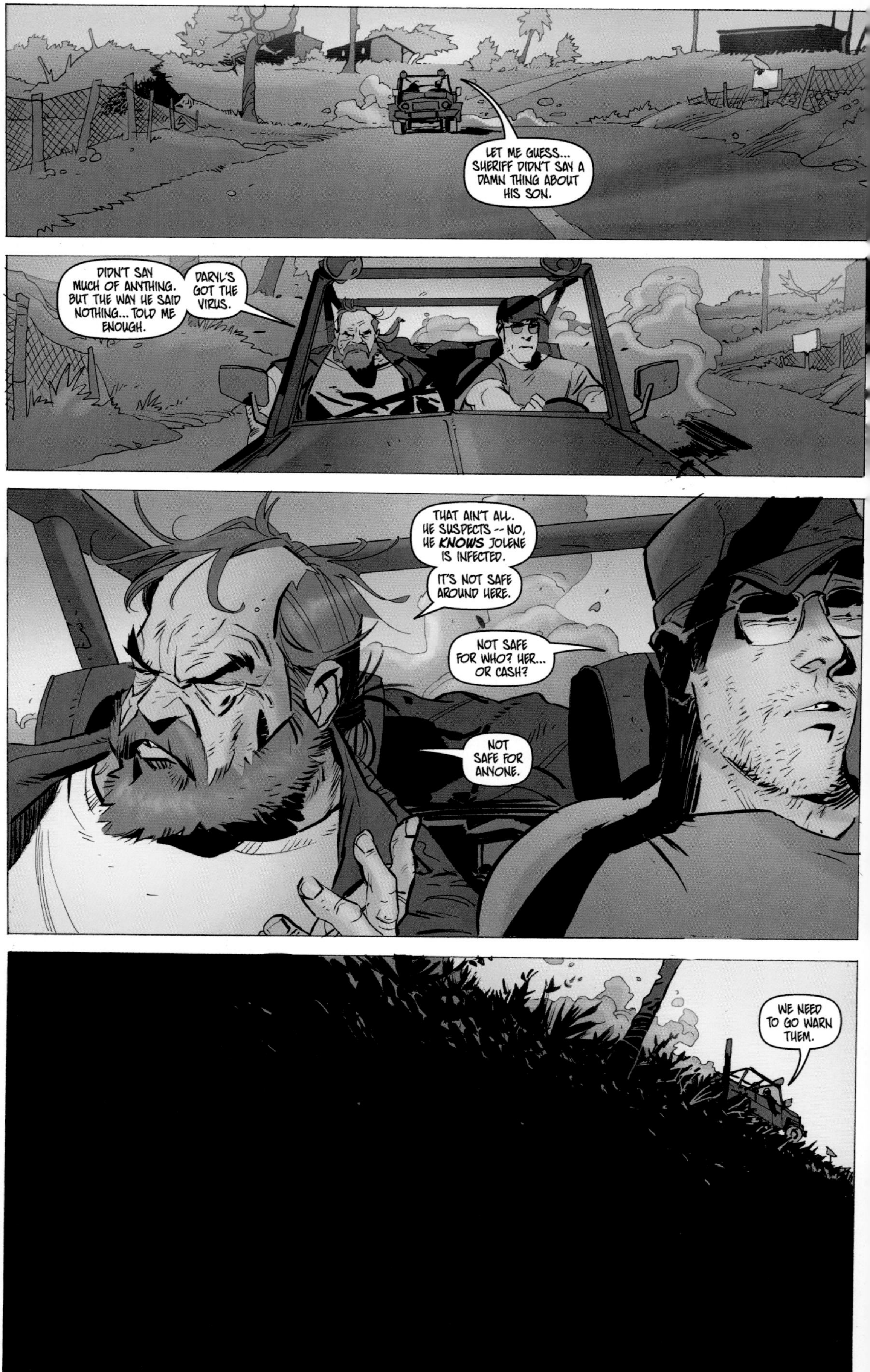
LET ME GUESS... SHERIFF DIDN'T SAY A DAMN THING ABOUT HIS SON.
DIDN'T SAY MUCH OF ANYTHING. BUT THE WAY HE SAID NOTHING... TOLD ME ENOUGH.
DARYL'S GOT THE VIRUS.
THAT AIN'T ALL. HE SUSPECTS -- NO, HE KNOWS JOLENE IS INFECTED.
IT'S NOT SAFE AROUND HERE.
NOT SAFE FOR WHO? HER... OR CASH?
NOT SAFE FOR ANYONE.
WE NEED TO GO WARN THEM.

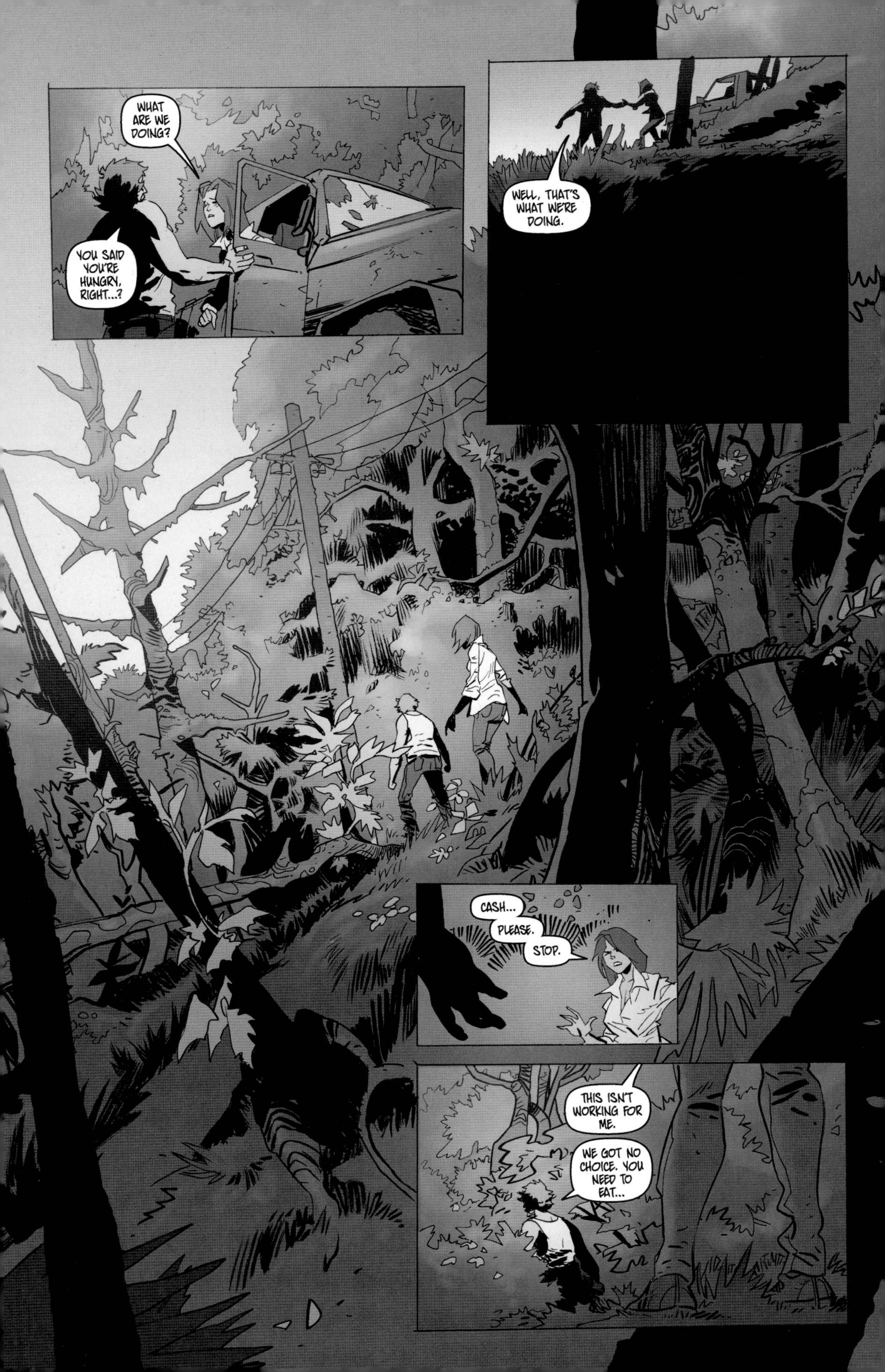
WHAT ARE WE DOING?
YOU SAID YOU'RE HUNGRY, RIGHT...?
WELL, THAT'S WHAT WE'RE DOING.
CASH...
PLEASE.
STOP.
THIS ISN'T WORKING FOR ME.
WE GOT NO CHOICE. YOU NEED TO EAT...

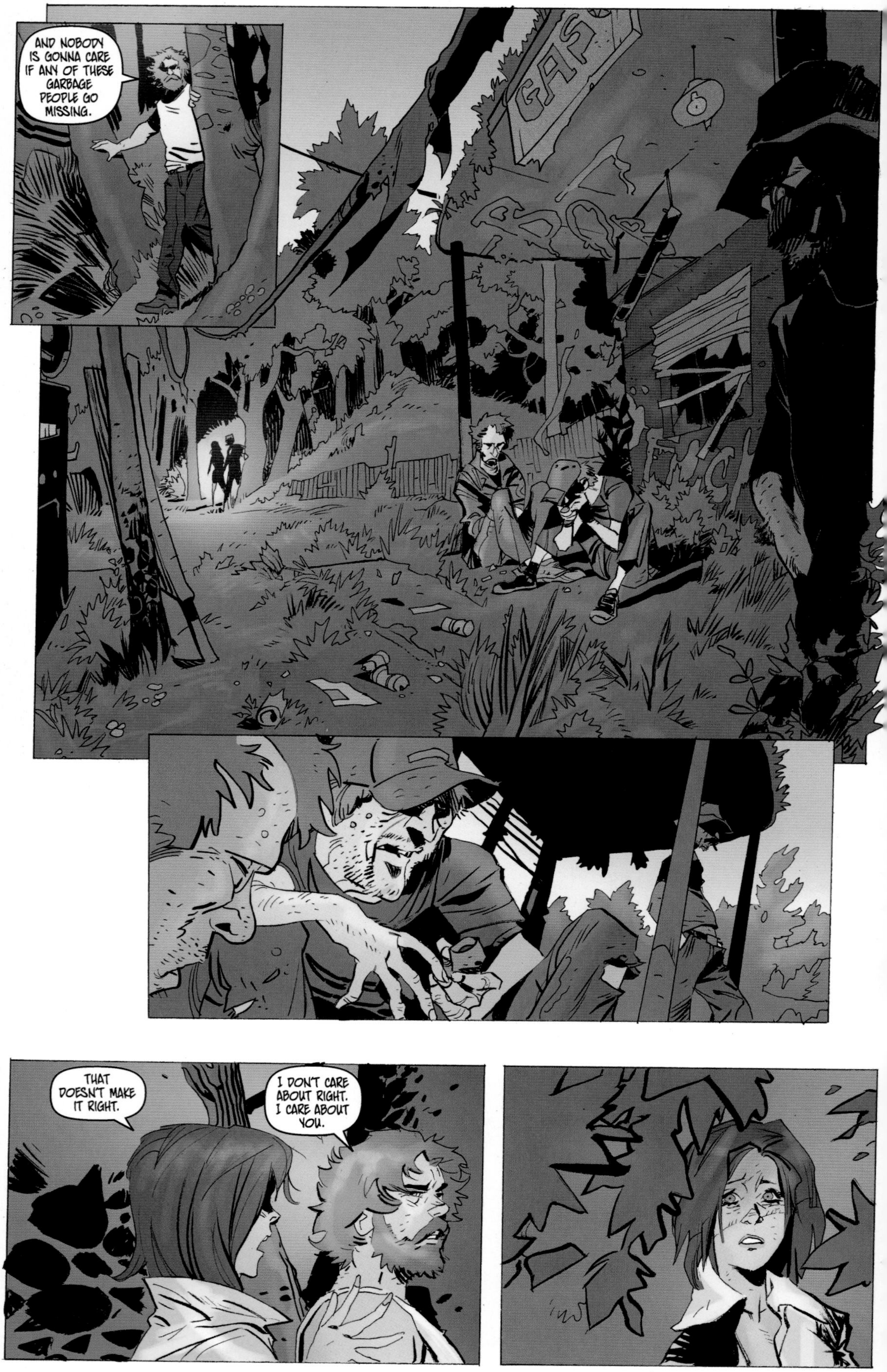
AND NOBODY IS GONNA CARE IF ANY OF THESE GARBAGE PEOPLE GO MISSING.
GAS
THAT DOESN'T MAKE IT RIGHT.
I DON'T CARE ABOUT RIGHT. I CARE ABOUT YOU.

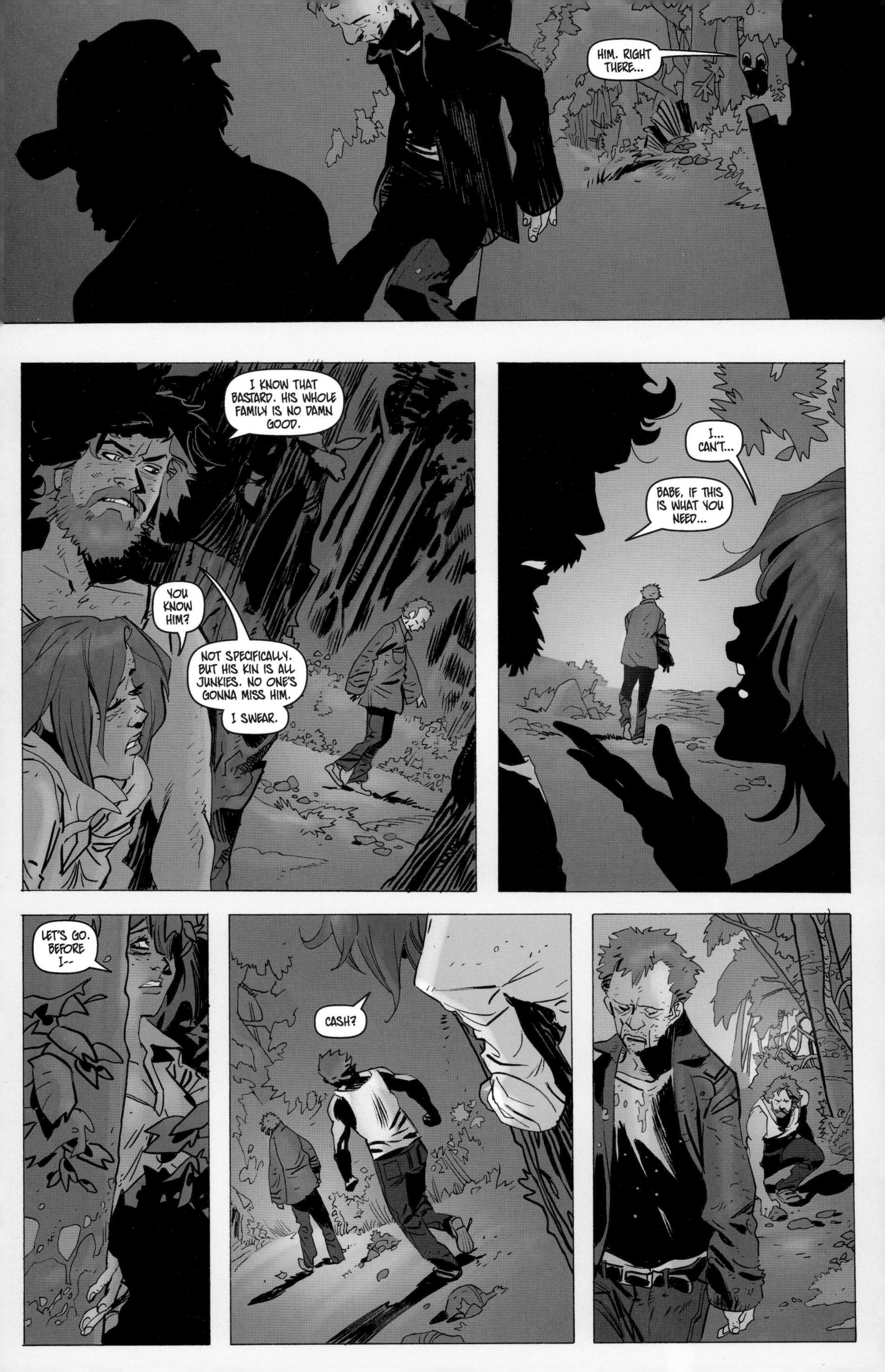
HIM. RIGHT THERE...
I KNOW THAT BASTARD. HIS WHOLE FAMILY IS NO DAMN GOOD.
YOU KNOW HIM?
NOT SPECIFICALLY. BUT HIS KIN IS ALL JUNKIES. NO ONE'S GONNA MISS HIM.
I SWEAR.
I... CAN'T...
BABE, IF THIS IS WHAT YOU NEED...
LET'S GO. BEFORE I--
CASH?

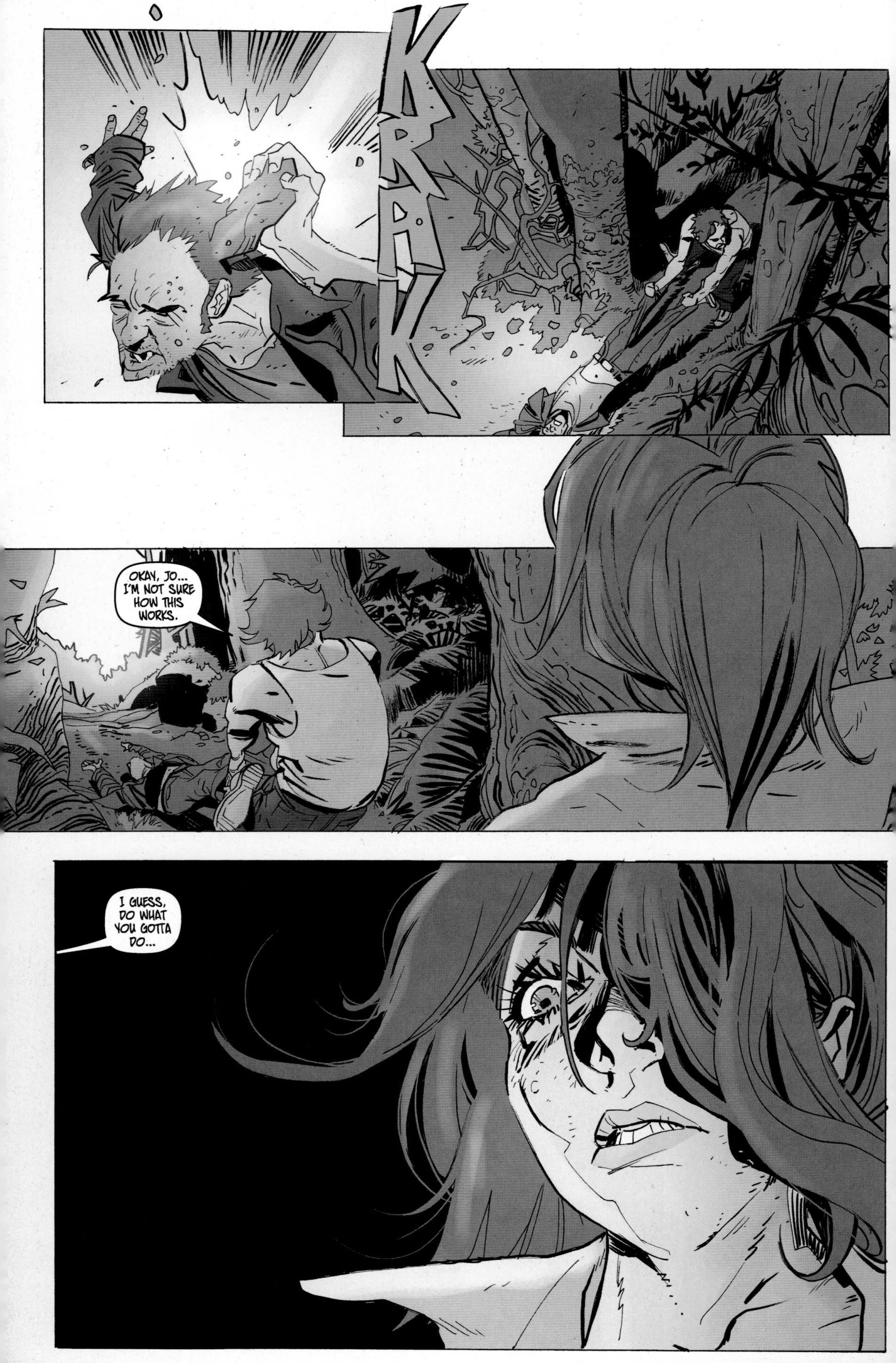
KRAK
OKAY, JO... I'M NOT SURE HOW THIS WORKS.
I GUESS, DO WHAT YOU GOTTA DO...

YOU WANT ME TO TAKE A WALK OR SOMETHING--
JO?
JOLENE?!

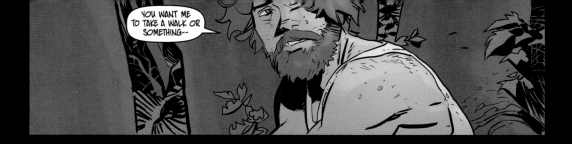

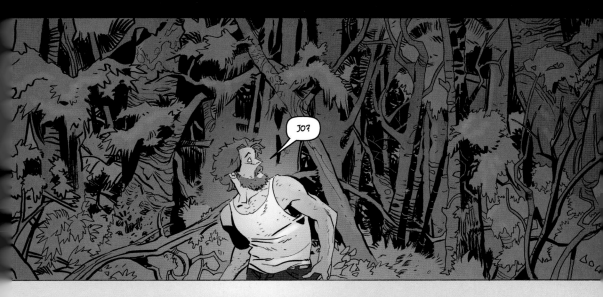

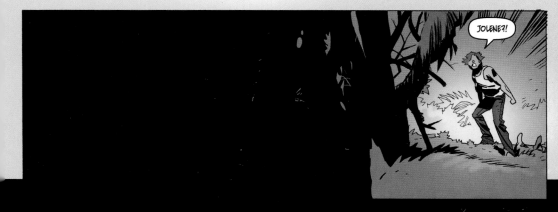

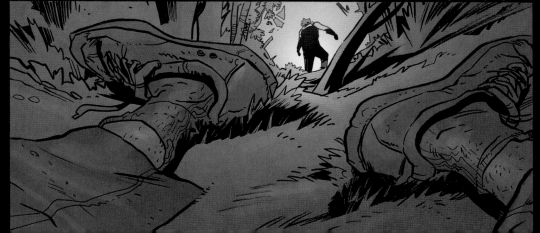

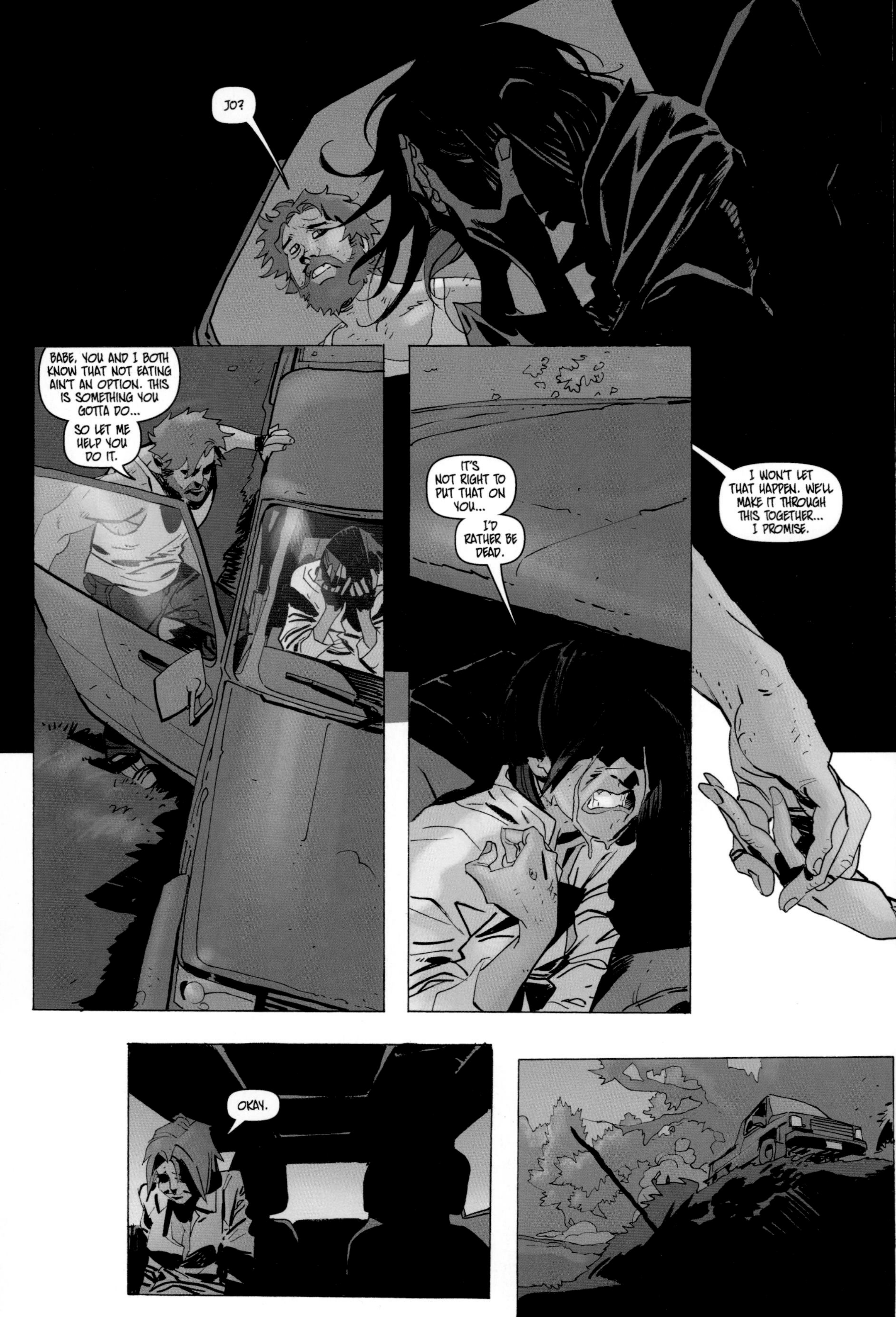
JO?
BABE, YOU AND I BOTH KNOW THAT NOT EATING AIN'T AN OPTION. THIS IS SOMETHING YOU GOTTA DO...
SO LET ME HELP YOU DO IT.
IT'S NOT RIGHT TO PUT THAT ON YOU...
I'D RATHER BE DEAD.
I WON'T LET THAT HAPPEN. WE'LL MAKE IT THROUGH THIS TOGETHER... I PROMISE.
OKAY.

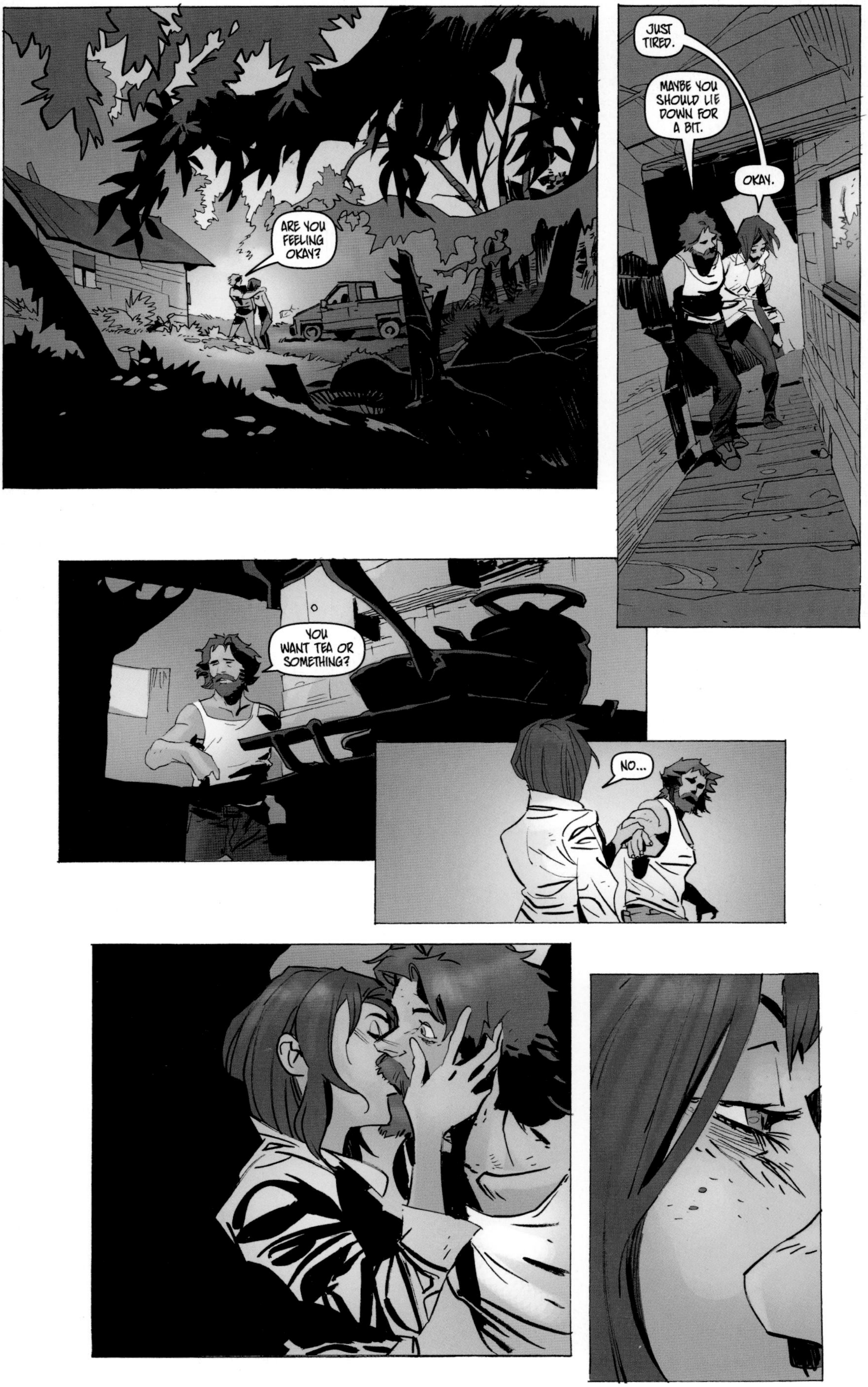
ARE YOU FEELING OKAY?
JUST TIRED.
MAYBE YOU SHOULD LIE DOWN FOR A BIT.
OKAY.
YOU WANT TEA OR SOMETHING?
NO...

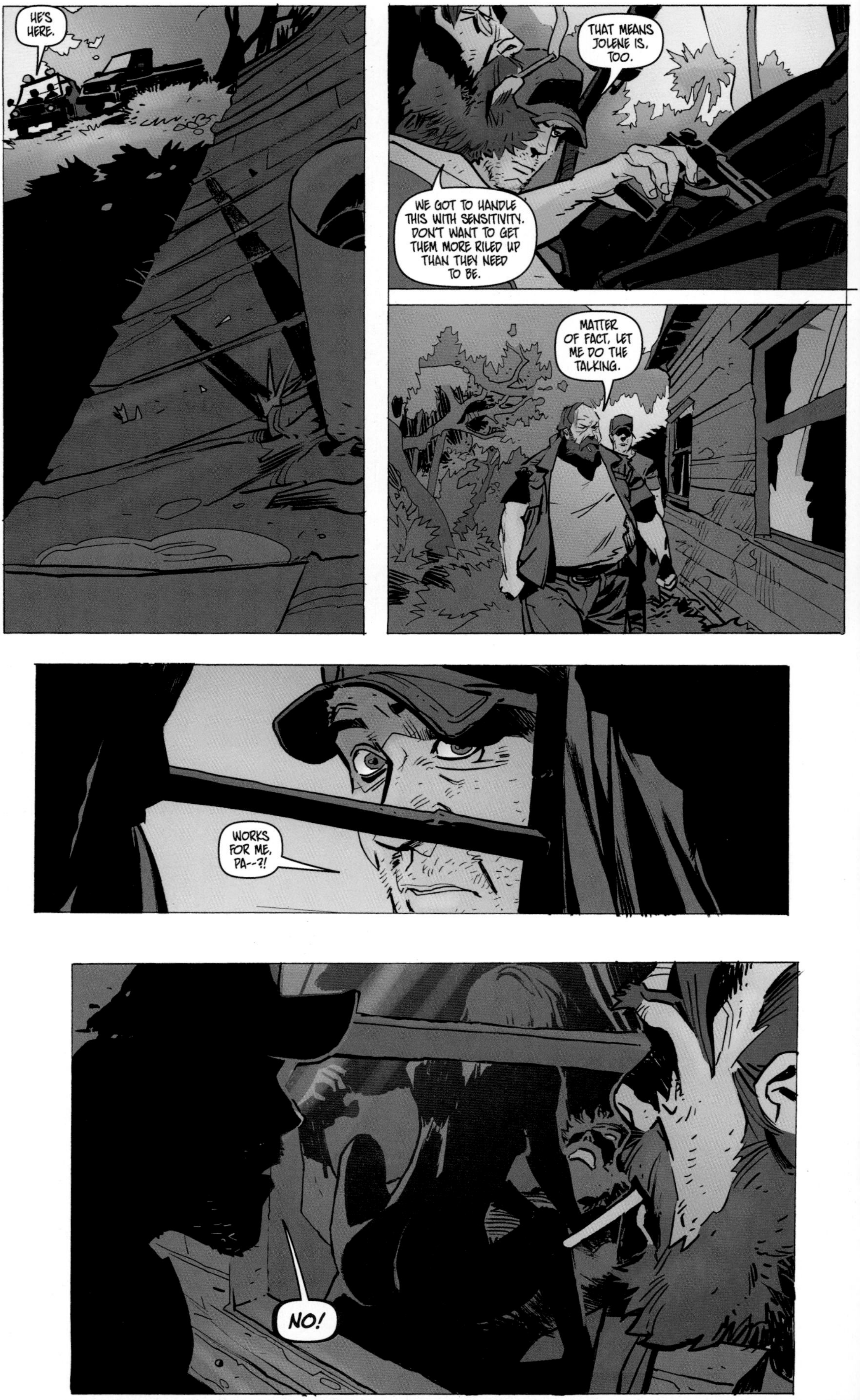
HE'S HERE.
THAT MEANS JOLENE IS, TOO.
WE GOT TO HANDLE THIS WITH SENSITIVITY. DON'T WANT TO GET THEM MORE RILED UP THAN THEY NEED TO BE.
MATTER OF FACT, LET ME DO THE TALKING.
WORKS FOR ME, PA--?!
NO!

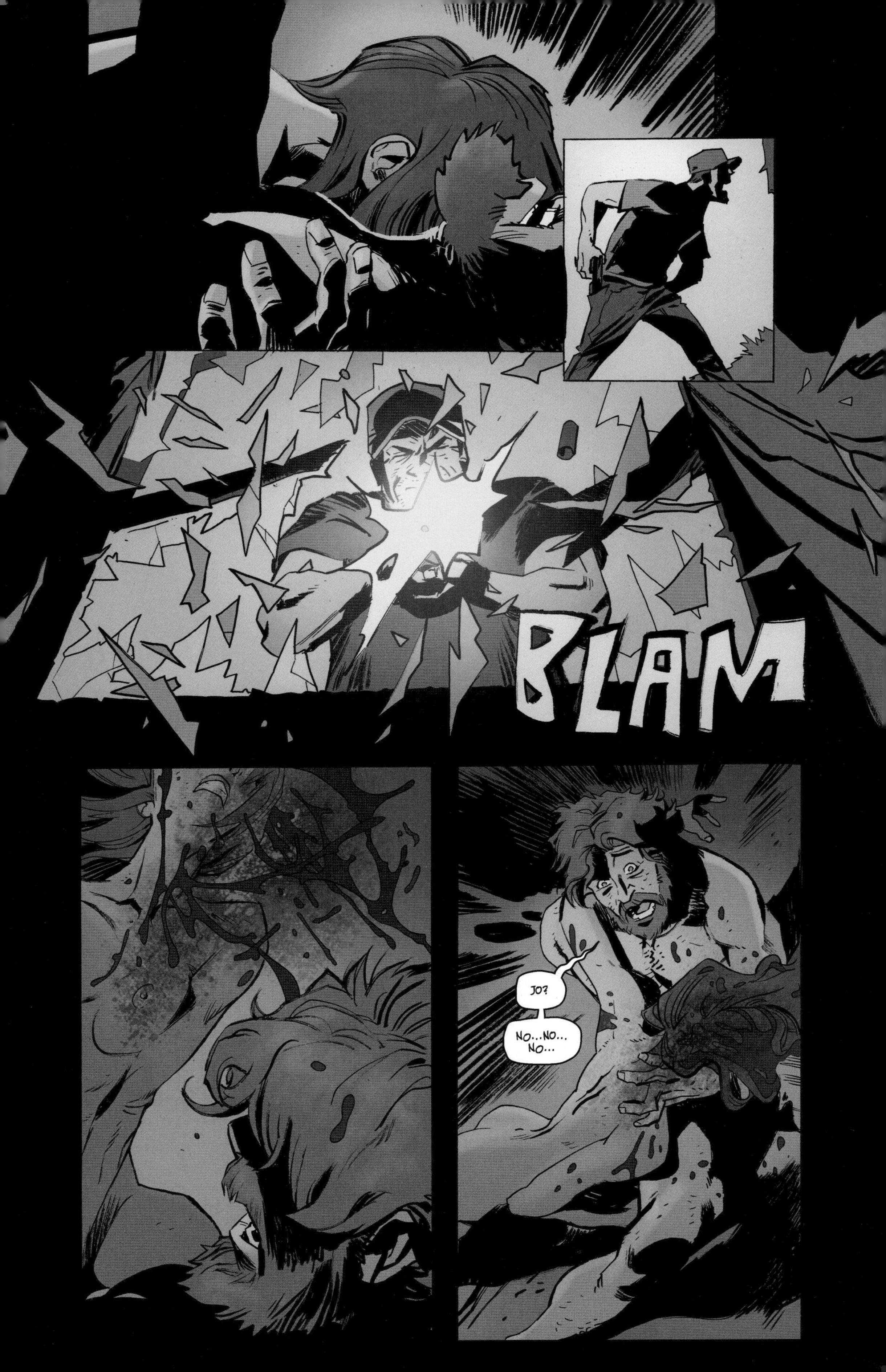
BLAM
JO?
NO...NO... NO...

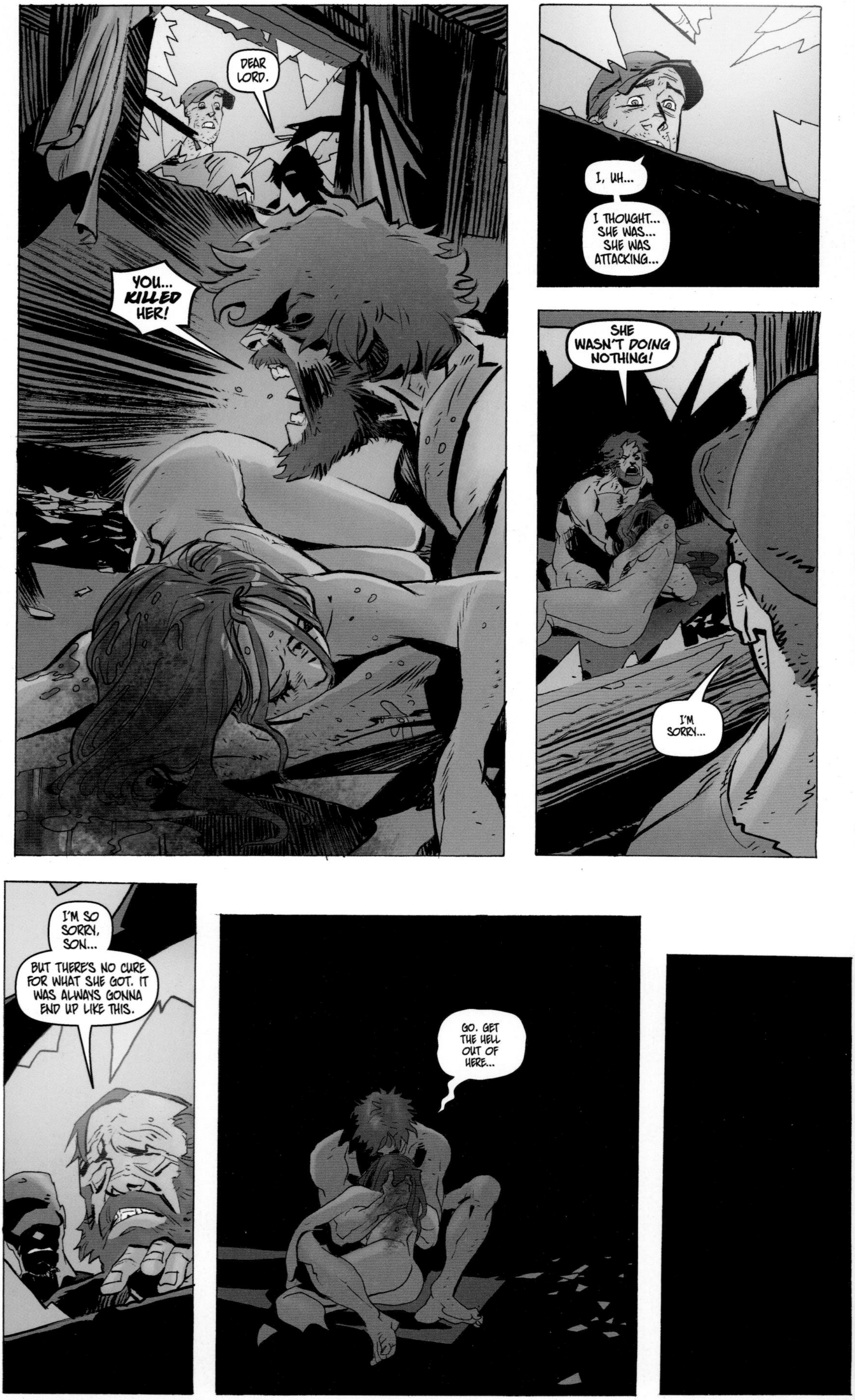
DEAR LORD.
YOU... KILLED HER!
I, UH...
I THOUGHT... SHE WAS... SHE WAS ATTACKING...
SHE WASN'T DOING NOTHING!
I'M SORRY...
I'M SO SORRY, SON...
BUT THERE'S NO CURE FOR WHAT SHE GOT. IT WAS ALWAYS GONNA END UP LIKE THIS.
GO. GET THE HELL OUT OF HERE...

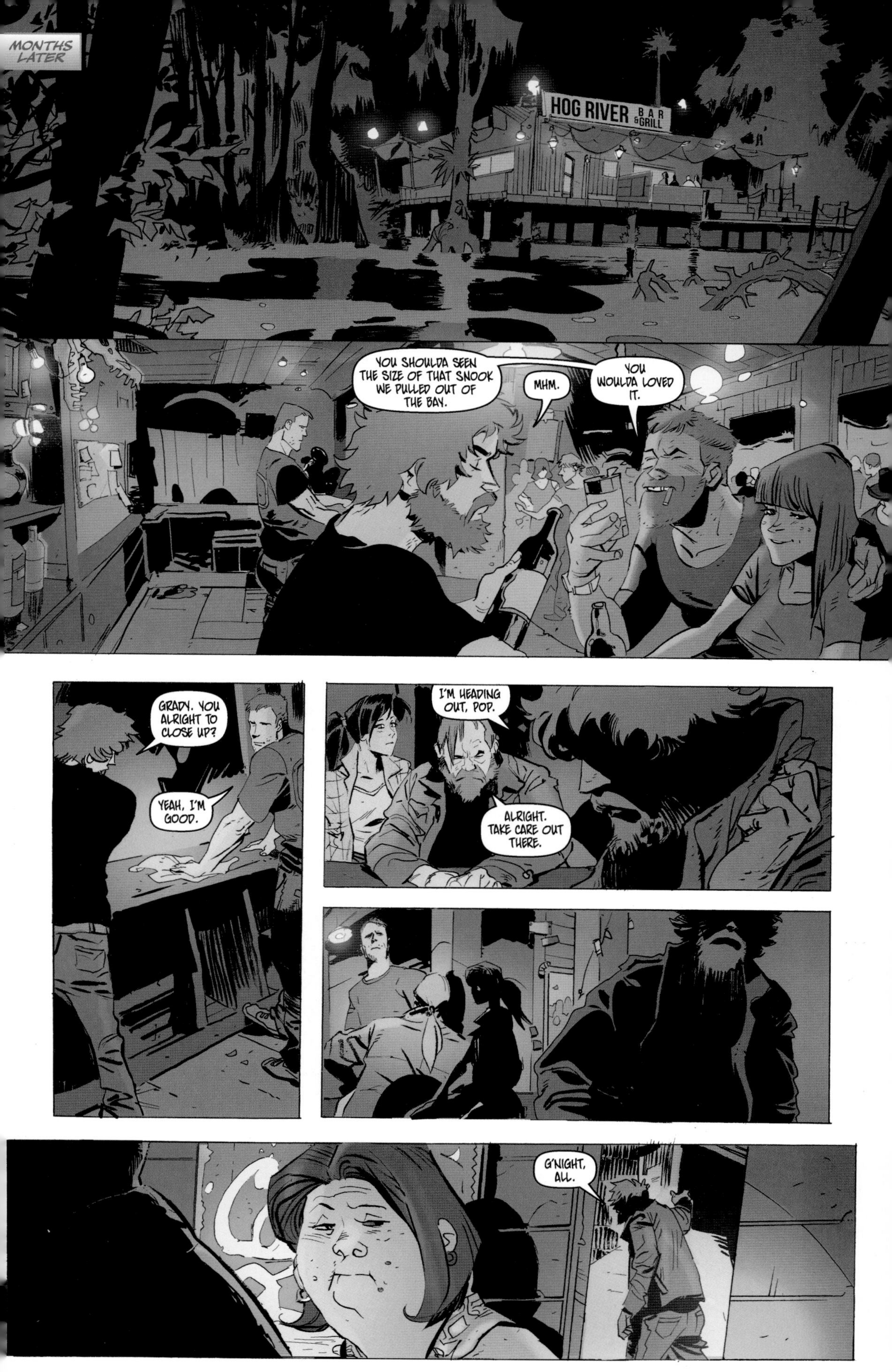
MONTHS LATER
HOG RIVER BAR & GRILL
YOU SHOULDA SEEN THE SIZE OF THAT SNOOK WE PULLED OUT OF THE BAY.
MHM.
YOU WOULDA LOVED IT.
GRADY. YOU ALRIGHT TO CLOSE UP?
YEAH, I'M GOOD.
I'M HEADING OUT, POP.
ALRIGHT. TAKE CARE OUT THERE.
G'NIGHT, ALL.

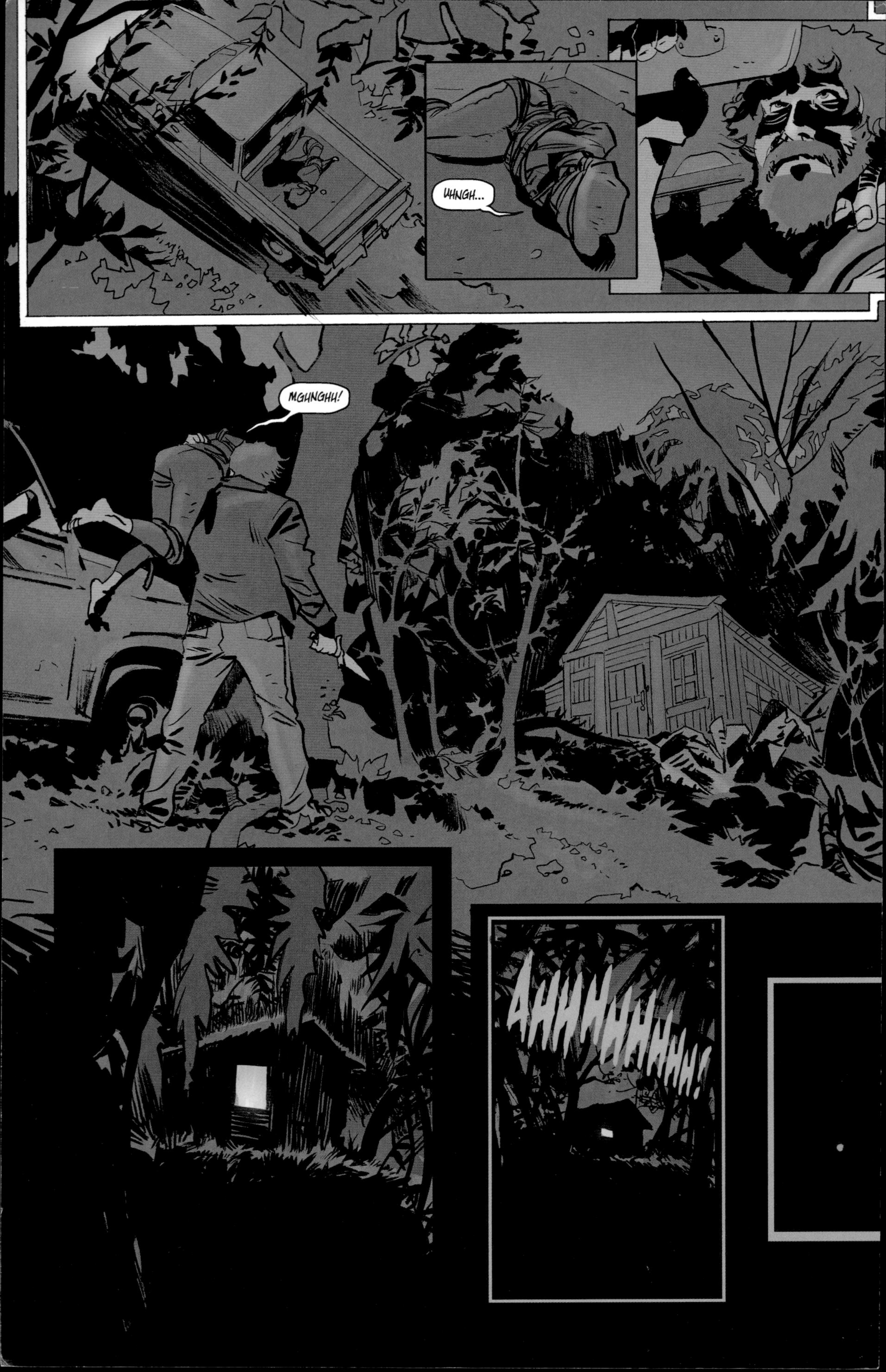
UHNGH...
MGHNGHH!
AHHHHHHHH!

BRIAN BUCCELLATO

&

J. YOUNG
STORY

MATIAS BERGARA
ART

B. BUCCELLATO
COLORS

TROY PETERI
LETTERS

ESTABLISHED
1986

A SOUTHERN ORIGINAL

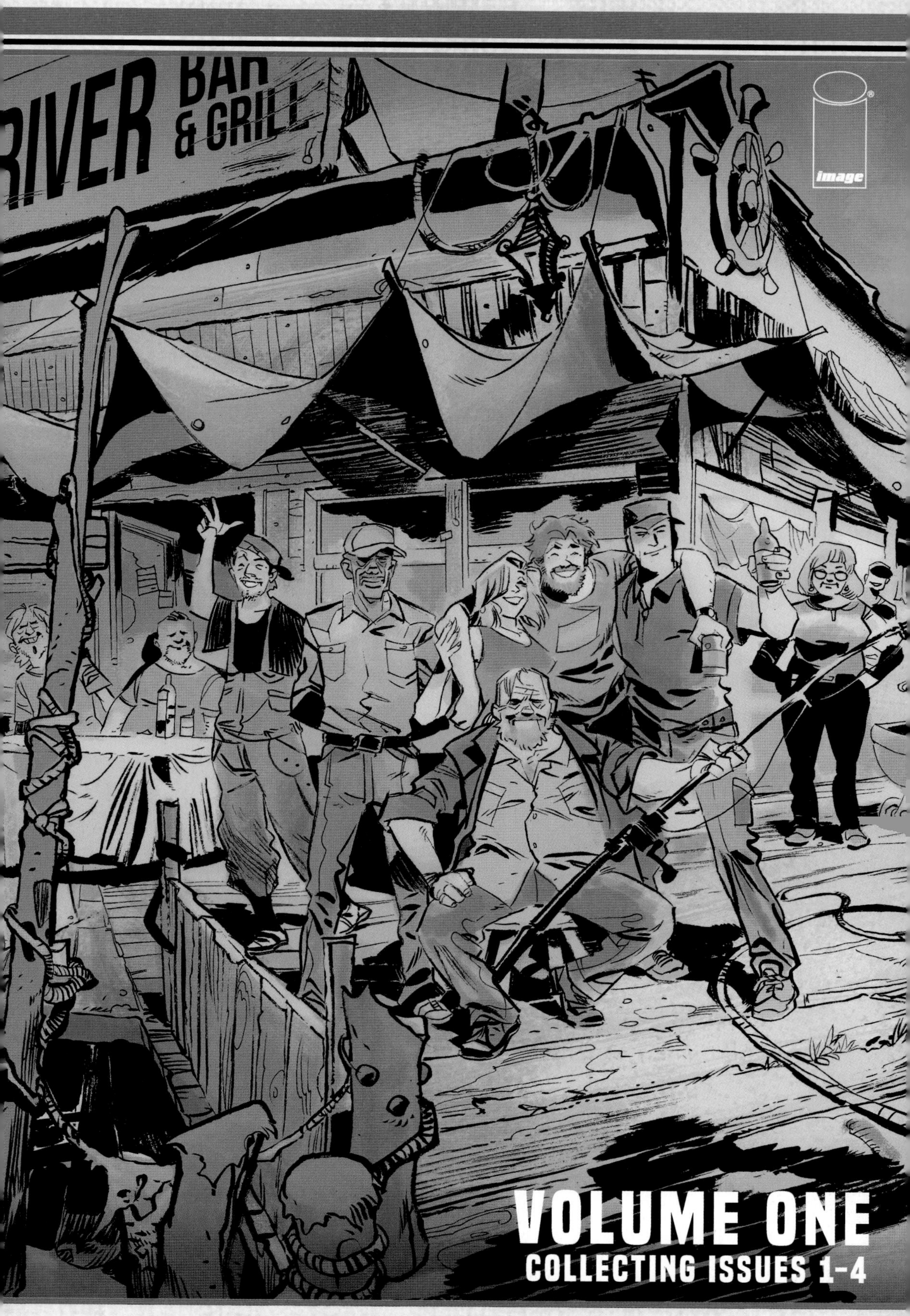
RIVER BAR & GRILL
image
VOLUME ONE
COLLECTING ISSUES 1-4

ALSO AVAILABLE

SONS OF THE DEVIL
BRIAN BUCCELLATO
TONI INFANTE
BOOK ONE

COLLECTS ISSUES 1–5

SONS OF THE DEVIL
BRIAN BUCCELLATO
TONI INFANTE
BOOK TWO

COLLECTS ISSUES 6–10

"Twisted, wild and gripping... horror comics in peak form."
—**Scott Snyder**

"A bold debut with equal parts style and sophistication... everything I love about comics—sharp writing, gorgeous art and intrigue on every page. Buccellato and Infante are my favorite new team in comics."
—**Kyle Higgins**

"Get on board with the SONS OF THE DEVIL, dummies. It'll kick your ass and be completely uninterested in taking your name."
—**Joshua Hale Fialkov**

"A visceral work, dynamically told, with the potential to head some decidedly sinister, disorienting places."
—***PASTE MAGAZINE***

IMAGECOMICS.COM

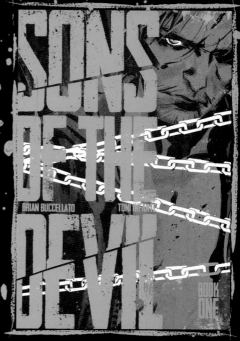

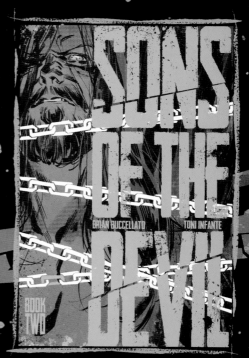